D1644475

CONTENTS

ACKNOWLEDGEMENTS

First and foremost, I thank The Lord for granting me the gift of the written word, which I have used to heal and find joy. True blessings have come in my life in the form of my wonderful family, Mum and sister, and my amazing Godmother and family, all of whom I love dearly and treasure.

A big thank you to all my friends, my work colleagues, my community choir group and my writing circles. You guys have given me bundles of love and support and I greatly appreciate it.

UrbanEdge – Skyy, Shae, Catherine, and the rest of the team, thank you for believing in me and for your hard work and dedication. God bless every single one of you!

SILENT PAIN

Lighting up. The flames of fury in their little oblong eyes flare up, and I get a hankering for the rich white powder, which lies beneath their shell. I reach for the bottle of pills, almost certain about what I'm going to do. My heart is beating fast, pounding, hammering in my chest. Then I hear mum's soothing voice wafting from the floor below, and I tear up. Slumping next to a lifeless body, my deadly arm returns to the ground. What the hell am I doing? This is not the solution to my problems. This is *never* the answer to any problem. If mum found me up here in this state, what would she do? How would she react? I close my eyes; my whole life flashes before me...

Agonisingly, I squeeze into a tight foetal ball, trying to stop the tears from flowing, trying to stop myself from falling into a black hole of no return. Rocking to and fro, to and fro, I can't help but think about my life. With everything that has happened, am I really living, or simply existing? "You have to face your fears and defeat them," both my mother and therapist often say. Try telling my hellish fears that same bull. See if they give a damn!

"Alena!" Mum shouts from downstairs, her voice charging, bellowing up the staircase, "It's almost time...

Come down, hunnie, and get your things together. We've got to go."

Mum continues speaking, babbling on about us not being late for the college registration morning. I hear her yell some more, her words racing up the stairs with tenacity, but I cover my ears, blocking out the sound, blocking out reality. I just want to wallow in my own self-pity. Can't mum shut up?

My head rises from the ground, slowly, wearily, and I peer up at the crimson vessel resting uneasily on my side cabinet, right next to my bed.

"Shall I take the lot? Save myself the grief of having to deal with the pain?"

There is no answer. Only silence. Only agony. Then suddenly, from nowhere, the words, 'No, don't do it!' reverberate in my head so loudly, that my ears pop.

Mustering all the courage and strength I can find in my fragile frame, I begin to fight this thing, and get up, holding back the tears, quelling those thoughts darkening my mind and essence. I scream out, releasing the ghosts of the past for a second, to stop my soul changing to a perilous shade of black. Determined to beat this dark mood storming within me, I dab the glistening tears forming in my eyes, and fully get up from the floor. Acting as if this major episode didn't really happen, I let out a huge sigh, plastering a phony half smile on my face. Yet my wobbly legs, slowly regaining their vigour, are showing the strain, and tell a different story, and so does my face, which is so pale and drained these days. This phizog I am staring at in the mirror, this girl who lives inside me, I hardly recognise.

Looking blankly in the mirror, gently combing down a head of flighty hair, I pretend to be okay. Pretend to be happy. This is the only way I know how to survive – how to weather such a terrible storm on a bright autumn morning.

Inwardly dejected, I chirp. "Almost ready. I'll be right

down mum."

More able to steady themselves and hold my weight, my limbs travel towards the edge of the bed, where two large bags of luggage are situated. A pair of shaking hands grab the travel cases, as I shake off the voice of doom ringing in my eardrums.

Minutes later, mum and I leave the house; I'm locking the door to my adolescent home, listening to the charming jangle of the keys, which are firmly in my grasp. It dawns on me that this moment is sacred, special; as this is the last time I will lock our front door for a while. College awaits. This will soon be a distant memory. Yet other memories, the painful ones, the ones I'm so desperate to let go, won't disappear so easily. Those ones never do.

"This is it then, mum," I say tearfully. "The day when I'm supposed to grow up – and find myself."

Mum smiles putting soothing hands around my shoulders. "No doubt I'm sad to see you go, Alena. But this journey will be good for you."

My dead eyes stray into the distance. "You think I can survive college, mum?" I bite my lip fretfully, pondering on the question.

"Honey," mum says, summoning a pair of roving pupils, "you've proved that you can survive anything. You're much stronger than you give yourself credit."

I beam, the sense of doubt reducing. "You think so?"

Her voice is resolute. "I know so."

"Well, I guess that should be reassuring."

Walking arm in arm to the car with my mother, the woman who's been my rock since forever, I plant a soft kiss on her cheek. She looks over at me, with a gentle glow in her eyes. I can tell that she believes in me. She always has. She's a wonderful and proud mother, filling with maternal tears.

Loading the boot full of my belongings, mum carefully packs my fragile teenage life away in the family car, saturating the vehicle with a billow of sprayed hope. There is a twinkle in her eyes. Her lips quiver as she opens the door, guiding me inside. I find myself restraining my tears, holding them in. I didn't think I'd be crying so much today. That's the funny thing about emotions; they can come on so quickly and take one completely by surprise.

Leisurely, mum gets in the car, and makes herself comfortable in the driving seat. We slam the doors shut in unison, and mum starts up. The vehicle purrs, humming beautifully, preparing itself for the 130 mile journey ahead.

I breathe heavily. "The University of Capendale – not sure about this whole college thing, mum. I'm getting cold feet. Can we go home?"

"You'll be just fine, honey," states mum decidedly. "Trust me. Besides, we cannot turn back now. Going to college is important. It's the best thing that has happened to you in two years."

"That, and therapy," I jibe.

"Alena?" Mum snaps.

"What?" I shout.

Twisting around to face me, mum subtly addresses my attitude. "A wise mother knows best. Baby, you are more than ready for this."

A grimace tremors my lips. "Yeah, perhaps. Nonetheless, time will tell if the voice of wisdom is wiser than the voice of youth." My tone is sarcastic, unintentionally.

Mum grunts. "Don't be so damn cheeky, okay?"

I feel a cold breeze swirl to the back of the car, a silent chill, which is designed to alert me to my improper behaviour.

"Sorry, didn't mean to offend," I say.

Uptight and full of ire, mum sighs deeply and puts the car in drive. We set off. The car glides along the street.

Rolling my finger down the closed window, which is building up perspiration at an alarming rate, I ignore mum's growing exasperation. I'm far more interested in watching the world I know and love, sail before my eyes. It's both sad and glorious to see.

"Goodbye, Surrey," I whisper, as a single tear runs down my left cheek. "Wish me luck!"

Hearing my new hopes and dreams thump and rattle in the cases in the rear of the car, I know it is time for me to accept change, and acknowledge that I have a future, in spite of the past, which is sticking to the base of my soul, a soul that is fragmented and working hard to heal its wounds.

THE COCKY GUY

Reluctantly, I vacate my college dorm room located in the beautiful botanical garden, and walk fifty yards to the playing field. My head pans around the copious space. I see nothing but swarms of people, an open arena of chaos. My quiet and lonely world has now met the eye of the tempest. This is the day I've been dreading for months – the first day of Freshers' Week. The first day of socialising hell. Focusing on the hectic scene, I notice that The Freshers' Fair is in full swing. There are stalls everywhere, students and college staff scattered all over the grounds. I can hear lots of chatting, laughing, and witness young people making connections. I'm feeling very anxious seeing all these overzealous first years at the fair.

Observing the actions taking place, I already know that I don't fit in. The overconfident jocks and other athletes are all flocking together; the snobby academics have formed a tight, enclosed ring; the air-headed cheerleaders huddle as one; and the science nerds, the loud nature activists, the pitch-perfect singers, and the performers have all found their position of authority on the land. And then there is me – the loner. I close my eyes for a second, count to ten, and then I re-open them. I'll have the confidence to stroll right up to one of the stalls in just one moment and sign up for something, anything. Quickly, I lose my nerve and scrunch up my face, hiding from the world. C'mon, Alena, approach someone, make your therapist proud and your mother even prouder.

Nine, ten – my lids spring open. Hello, interesting guy, three o'clock, by the drinks stand. Should I walk up to him and say hi? Should I befriend him? No, Alena, don't be foolish. He's a hip black boy. They don't mingle with Greek girls. Afro-Caribbean guys normally stick to their own. It's a cultural thing. Excuses, stop making excuses. The guy steals a look and our eyes meet properly. Oh, gosh, he has clocked me. What am I to do now?

Taking a deep breath, I venture over to the booth to get an ice-cold beverage and to check out the intriguing stranger. My heart is booming in my chest as I approach him, and I begin to chew my lip, nervous about what is going to go down here today. It is mid-September, a really warm day, and my throat is parched. That's what I'll tell him if he asks why I've gone over. Yeah, I am thirsty. Got it! Breathe, Alena. Breathe, and just talk to the man. What is the worst that could happen?

"Hey there," I say sweetly, greeting him.

"Yea, hi," he replies mechanically, his pupils boring into me.

I laugh nervously, sporting a fake grin. "Nice weather today, ha? Hope it doesn't rain."

Sharply, he raises his right brow and nips the edge of his sleek, black leather jacket. His expression is smug, condescending. "Are you for real, girl? You came all the way over here with that chirpy voice and that sugar-coated smile to converse about the weather? Original, ha!"

"Well, er," I mutter, not knowing what to say.

He scowls. "So, is that what you wanted to bore me with, girl? Or did you want something else?"

Oh crap, I'm speechless, lost for words. This guy is

gruff and super cocky, and he has so got the better of me. I throw my head to the ground, begging the muddy terrain to give me inspiration or suck me under. I wait. But nothing happens.

"Erm… Erm…" I mumble. "No, I just wanted a drink, actually."

Impishly, he taps me on the arm and chortles. "Your social skills suck, girly. They're verging on non-existent."

I double blink, stunned by his brazen response. "*My* social skills suck? Look in the mirror, boy. Talk about the pot calling the kettle."

"Ooh, defensive too," he sniggers. "Boyfriend trouble?"

A blistering fire is raging through me. "No! I don't have a boyfriend right now!"

"No surprises there," he taunts.

I'm crashing and burning here and all he can do is mock me. This is not working. It's time for me to leave with my tail between my legs. I'm so embarrassed. I need to go, now. Swiftly, I turn my back on him and prepare to leave whilst I still have a smidgen of humility intact.

"Where are you going?" he insists, his voice serene, yet commanding me to face him again.

I swivel around, surprised he still wants to talk to me. "I'm escaping, and going someplace else, okay?" I retort.

Frivolously, he giggles, amused by my woeful attempt to exit the scene. He looks at me, starkly. I stare right into his pupils. Our eyes suddenly connect; it feels weirdly magical. There is a sweet glow on his lips.

"Gees, I didn't mean to scare you off."

I shrug my shoulders, not knowing how to respond. Though eventually I say, "Didn't you?"

Keenly, his eyebrows rise in interest. "I was just playing, girl. I did not expect you to walk off and leave me."

"Playing, ha?" I assert boldly, kissing my teeth. "Na-uh! You were plain rude. Ya virtually drove me away."

8

My uncouth reply startles yet excites him. I am staring directly into his dark chocolate eyes. He is staring back at me, with a glint of intrigue. "If I was telling you to go, trust me, I wouldn't insinuate it. I'd say it straight out. I wouldn't hold back."

Childishly, my lips pout. "So, what's going on here, smart mouth boy? You want me to stick around or not?"

Gradually his face screws up, he is captivated by me. I firmly hold his attention for at least a minute. His stare is vampire intense.

"Yea, stay," he urges. "But stop talking about the weather, please. It's a really stale icebreaker."

"Okay, got it!" I titter. I'm finally getting his wry sense of humour. "So, what are you doing by the drinks stand all alone? Did a bunch of people walk off and leave, just like I almost did?"

"Wow! I guess I deserved that one."

"Yes," I state. "You certainly did."

He bursts into laughter. "So, Miss Weather Girl, what degree are you doing here?"

"English – and you?"

He grins. "Yeah, same."

"You studying English as a Single Honours degree?"

"Nah," he says as I feel his eyes travelling south, focusing on my breasts peaking in my dress. "I'm doing Joint Honours – English and Sports Science."

"Sports Science?" I ask, as I find myself admiring his pecs pressing through his white Adidas t-shirt.

"Yeah," he affirms. "I want to be a Sports Therapist. You want to be a journalist, right?"

"A journalist? No way." I let out a small flirtatious laugh as I play with my hair. "More like an elementary teacher. That's my thing. I want to be the best in my field."

"Cool," he asserts, smiling affably. "I like a girl with ambition."

Smirking boldly, he takes a sip of his cola and then

rests the can on the edge of the stand. Returning his eyes to meet my slim frame, his pupils do an enchanting dance. Slowly, he licks his lips, entranced by the thrilling sight before him.

I am wearing a loose red dress, clothes that are not accentuating my curves. But through it, I'm certain he can see the contours of my slender size 8 figure. White trainers, Reebok – the latest out – drag on my feet. He appreciates this sexy-casual look, I can tell. He is scanning me up and down, up and down, his eyes popping out of their sockets. They must be getting quite tired worshipping my body.

"Where you living? On campus?" he asks, grinning for England.

Completely hypnotised by my erotic curves, his mouth begins to drool, his pupils dilating. My hips are moving gently from side to side, rocking in and out of his eyesight. His light chocolate face illuminates, simmering in the atmosphere.

"Yea, I'm in Ridley House," I explain. "Ya' know the nice pad in the orchard. And you?"

Painfully, his face wrinkles. "Well, erm… I applied for halls really late. I haven't been assigned a room yet. Today, I had to come up to the fair by train. The Halls Manager said I'll have to come back tomorrow to see what he can do."

"Hope you get to live on campus. Ridley House and Rubert Hall are the best residence halls here. Fingers crossed you'll get a room in one of those places."

He bursts into a smile. "I pray I get a room in Ridley House, on the same floor as you. Then we could…"

"Then we could what?" I ask, staring into his naughty brown eyes.

"Then we could… get better acquainted in a quiet and private space." He laughs.

My pleasant expression changes, and I move away from him a little, feeling uncomfortable by his brassy approach.

"How old are you?" Cooling down his lascivious behaviour, he squints at me, interested to hear my response.

"I'm nineteen. How old are you?"

"Yea, nineteen," he confirms. "If you're already nineteen, you gotta be September born, like me."

"Yea, my birthday is September 4th."

Effervescently, he lights up. "Mine is September 5th."

I throw a couple of stunned hands over my mouth. "No way!"

"I know, it's crazy, right?"

"Our birthdays can't be right on top of each other!"

He leers. "Why can't we be right on top of each other?"

Addressing his candid remark, I wince, remembering. "That's a very forward comment, mister. We only just met. You're a bloody cheeky fella, aren't you?"

Seductively, he puckers his mouth, as if he is caressing my cheek from a distance. "Of course I am." He agrees. "It's fun to be a bit risky at times, don't ya think?"

"No, it ain't." I respond coldly.

Cocking his scandalous mouth to the side, he grins. In a slow throbbing heartbeat, his infantile jokes are forgiven.

"What ya doing later? Got any plans?"

His juicy lips roll into a pout. They are starting to look so damn cute. Oh my gosh, do I have the hots for this guy? Or am I simply dehydrated due to the freak autumn heat?

"Nah," I say timorously, toying with my long auburn locks, leaning my elbow on the side of the drinks stand. "Got nothing planned."

"Good." His face sparkles. "Wanna hang with me on campus, until it's almost dark? And then I can walk you back to the halls."

Fluttering my eyelashes at him, I give into his plea.

"Yea, sounds cool."

"Sweet!" Shamelessly, he moistens his lips, his eyes affixing to my large, rotund domes. "What's your name, babe? Should have asked this before now."

I tilt my head forward, which causes my lively brown tresses to fall onto my face. "That information is on a need to know basis."

Boldly, he takes one step closer, edging into my personal space, and gently, he lifts my head up to reach his dazzling brown orbs. His chestnut globes look so glorious when the sunlight hits them from a certain angle.

"Yea, and I need to know, right now."

"Why?" I tease.

"Because I think you're real cute. That's why." His smile broadens.

"Is that so?"

"Yeah."

"Hmm. Sweet."

Puckering my lips slightly, my mouth crinkles into a perfectly shaped cupcake case. My mouth then waters as his eyes descend to admire the red hot rims of passion that are waiting to be explored.

"Alena," I whisper, my voice whirling tenderly in his ear. "My name is Alena."

His breathing grows heavy, eyes expanding, heart wide open, lips rumpled, ready for action. "Phillip... I'm Phillip Gregson."

We are both fraught with emotion – the expectation of a hot, sexy kiss killing us both. I never thought I could ever feel this way about anyone, not so soon. The attraction between us is simply electric.

Just as things are going well, I sense a black cloud of doubt forming on his mien.

"What is it?" I ask, knowing he has something to say that I don't wish to hear.

"Before this goes any further, I need to confess."

"Confess what?"

"A secret."

I am alarmed but interested to hear it. "What kind of secret?"

"I used to be a bad boy," he professes.

Wanting to know more, I move a step closer, erecting a curious eyebrow. "How bad are we talking?"

"Stealing and joyriding, kinda bad."

"What?" I yell. "You stole and joyrode vehicles?"

"Yeah," he says feeling ashamed. "I boosted cars, motorbikes, mopeds. Anything I could get my hands on."

"OMG!" I blurt out. My jaw prises open in astonishment.

Hesitantly, he continues. "I also have a criminal record. I was in juvie for a while."

In mortal shock, I over blink. My eyelids work double time. "Did you ever harm or kill anyone?"

"God, no!" he shouts. "Never! It was just plain stupid stuff I did, messing about with my idiot friends. But I paid a heavy price. I went to juvie for 18 months."

"How long ago did this happen?"

"When I was sixteen, hanging with the wrong crowd. Now I'm nineteen, I'm responsible, sensible, grown up!"

"Are you sure about that?"

"Yes," he asserts. "That was the old me. I am not that person anymore."

I use my squinting eyes to assess his 'badness level' and decide he's just about passed the test. A radiated smile appears on my face.

"Seeing as you didn't kill anybody or harm anyone, and learned from your mistakes, I'd say this makes you even more brooding, and sexy, Mr. Phillip Gregson."

"Thank you," he avers.

Gleefully, I laugh. "You're quite a boy, aren't you, Phil?"

He flashes a licentious look in my scorching emerald eyes. "No, Alena. I'm not a boy. I am a man."

Little by little our bodies align, moving an inch closer

to one another's. My eyes beckon to his, my mouth pulsates; I call him with one zealous finger. Steadily, he comes closer. I clutch onto the ends of his jacket, my pupils embed into him. Our mouths dribble, a kiss is imminent. I don't feel scared. I want this. Hungrily, his lips touch and devour mine. Our tongues do a fast, energetic jive in each other's mouths. Gees, this is sensational. I enjoy every second. I feel alive; I feel free. Eventually, our lips part. Then my sight skews for a second, startled by a flicker of familiarity in his demeanour.

"I feel like we've met before, Phillip. You look… familiar."

Deeply, he peers into my visage. "Hmm, yeah, perhaps in a past life."

"I'm being serious," I confirm, inspecting his features with the keenness of my gaze.

Suddenly, he looks puzzled. "Where do we know each other from then?"

"Not sure," I say tentatively. "I'm certain that I've met you before, somewhere… Where d'ya live, Phil?"

"Brent Cross, North West London." A bemused expression remains on his countenance.

"Oh, shut up!" I exclaim. A look of surprise widens my small delicate nostrils. "I used to live in Brent Cross, too."

"Where, exactly?" He enquires.

"Near the tube station. I live in Surrey now."

"My house is right by the Shopping Centre," he replies.

"In high school, I spent most of my weekends in the mall with my friends, before…" I freeze in mid-sentence and gulp, clamming up, quelling the past by trapping it between my tightly pursed lips.

Phillip scrutinises me, his countenance filling with curiosity. "Before what?"

Crunching my bottom lip fretfully, I attempt to lie my

way out of this. "Oh, gees, I forgot what I wanted to say! I've got such a bad memory."

Letting out a burbled laugh, Phil knocks into me. "Better go buy a brand new memory card. This one is corrupt." He giggles and his eyes swim into my gaze.

Feeling a sense of relief, I chuckle.

"Alena, can I show you something exciting?" Phil asks energetically.

Hearing those ominous words unlocks a trauma from the past. These words rattle in the core of my mind, infecting my entire body. All of a sudden, that heavy feeling of tension returns, and I have the urge to wash. I feel unclean, all over again. Pressing down the creaky lid in my subconscious, the anxiety gradually settles.

"This something exciting – is it at all dangerous?"

Before I can get an answer, Phil has already taken my hand, leading me away from the safety of the enclosed field and onto the hustle and bustle of the main road.

When we venture outside the gates of the college, and the wind howls in my face, running fiendish fingers through my long rusty hair, is the devil himself. I panic, remembering. Those dark irrepressible memories still haunt me. God knows how I've tried to banish them, shake them off. Yet somehow, I still recall the sound of traffic whirring in the misty air, and the deep intonation of his voice, as he grew closer and closer. I ran at full speed. He was my shadow, running almost as fast as me.

Snapping back into reality, the loud vroom of a motorbike startles me. I look up, mesmerised by this shiny, dark object. This motorcycle is top of the range. Wow, I'm impressed! Hang on; I thought Phillip said he came up to the fair on the train? Perhaps I misheard him. Yeah, that must be it.

"This is what I wanted to show you, Alena. You like?" Straddling the bike, he beams. The wind races through his curly hair. He throws on the helmet.

"Yea, it's pretty cool, Phil," I reply, totally in awe of

the bike's resplendent beauty.

"There's space for two here – wanna jump on?"

I hesitate. Spontaneity is not my thing. Not anymore. I learned my lesson the last time I did something rash and paid a heavy price. "No," I shout, shaking my head. "I think I'll have to pass."

Tilting his head to one side, he begins to glow, his essence irradiating the dusky pebbles on the street. His lips curl, as he stares up at me, insinuating himself into my confidence. Calling me with a persuasive digit, he attempts to magnetise us. Feeling a strange yet compelling pull coming from the tip of Phillip's finger, I gravitate towards him. The wind, now calmer, gently strokes my forehead. I amble to the bike, and carefully, I get on. Not so sure if leaving the campus with a perfect stranger is a good idea. But it's done now. No turning back.

Casually, he hands me the spare helmet.

"Put it on, babe," he advises me.

A smile spreads across my face. I think this guy is actually *safe*. He seems nice enough. Sliding on the helmet, wrapping my arms around him, a warm feeling wells inside of me. This closeness is peculiarly nice. The sun slowly rests on my nose. I savour the sensation.

"You okay?" he asks, before setting off.

"Yea, I think so."

He larks. "That's good enough for me. Now hold on tight, babe. Okay?"

I nod. "Okay, I will. Promise."

Whizzing off down the road at fifty miles per hour, into the scorching ochre horizon, I am free, for just one moment.

It isn't just bikes that can take off fast, I soon discovered. Relationships can too. In only a few weeks, Phil and I grew closer, so close.

Never did I think that our relationship would get serious, so quickly. Never in a trillion years did I think that Phillip would be placed in Ridley House, the same halls of residence as me, on exactly the same floor – the third floor – where our relationship would blossom, hour by hour. Actually, I shouldn't have been surprised that Phil and I met and fell in love here, in this enchanting university, where the impossible dream can become a possible reality.

NO PARTIES, P-LEASE!

"Phillip! I told you, I don't do parties!" I bellow, glaring at him, and then slumping on the bed to release my anger. "I'm not ready for all that socialising yet. Why did you agree to us having one on our floor?"

Sighing softly, he sits beside me and blows a cool puff of air onto my cheek. His breath is meant to be soothing, reassuring. But it doesn't calm me very much. Turning sideways, I glint at him; he leans his body into mine. His lips almost touch my cheek.

"Honey, it's not a party, as such," he says, his voice whirring near my ear. "It's a social night, a small gathering. I waited four months before organising this, because I know how you feel."

I raise a sullen eyebrow in his direction. "And just exactly how do I *feel*, then, Phillip?"

My green eyes shoot right into his face, my lioness claws scoring the bed sheets.

"You over-panic, Alena," he blurts out, his dark, cold marbles rolling around the room to avoid my uncomfortable stare. Facing me again, ready to meet my ire, he adds, "Just calm down, baby, please. It will be fine."

Steadily, his manly arms descend onto either side of my shoulders.

Filling with frustrated anger, I turn away, my attention averts toward the door. I frown, refusing to give my boyfriend proper eye contact. "I don't socialise, Phil. I'm more than just super shy, remember? What I have is a recognised condition."

Freely, he laughs. "C'mon, baby. You can't be a social agoraphobic in our own dorm house. And it ain't no good, you're not meeting new people. Just embrace it. Besides, it is a small get-together, with just you, me, and a couple of my friends. It will be fun. Trust me."

"Fun? Trust you?" I bark, boring into him.

Feistily, I shrug his hands off my shoulders. There is no way he can convince me that he is in the right here. So he should quit pushing me into attending this 'get-together'. Regardless of how many people will be there, I don't want to go.

Unexpectedly, a warm mouth presses on my lips. Phil's deep, russet eyes soak into my soul. I shiver; I can't get enough of him, of his caress. I fall into him; his arms surround me and make me feel safe. What is this boy trying to do to me? Whatever it is, he has got me under his spell. Phil has a unique way of softening the sharpness in my eyes, making my problems melt under his hot, sexy affection. I don't know how he is able to do that. Boyfriend power, I guess.

I agree to go to the party. However, I don't trust Phil, not yet, not truly, and I don't get the impression that this is only a small get-together. I know what parties turn into – crazy places where teenagers get drunk, barf, pull, get laid, and get hangovers. Worst case scenario, unwanted pregnancies happen. And the thing that makes me really livid is that Phil has the nerve to invite his boneheaded friends –Ty and Donald – who make arsehole antics look like an Olympic sport! Great! I really don't want those two hoodlums coming over, watching my every move, expecting Phil and I to 'entertain' them by showering each other with kisses and partaking in stupid games, such as truth or dare. P-lease! I'm comfortable with Phil and I getting reasonably close in private, in our own rooms. But being put on display in the living room, making out in public to satisfy his friends' curiosity and make them believe we are having wild sex behind the scenes – that is definitely not my idea of an enjoyable evening. Clearly I'm not ready for this level of socialising. It's so wrong of Phil to thrust me into an environment full of horny adolescents. Well, perhaps it might do me some good. I've agreed to go, after all. I can't pull out now.

Six o'clock on the dot, Phil's friends show up. I peer at them from the lounge. They appear unkempt, like two guys my boyfriend has picked up off the sidewalk. Nevertheless, they are his friends, so I can't be too judgemental. Bowling to the door, Phil greets them with a bear hug. They are already behaving like a pair of untamed animals, making ridiculous hooting sounds. Still, I am keeping an open mind, for now.

Just as I'm starting to warm up to his street hooligans, I hear one of them ask, "Where is your bird, Phil? I hear she is a buff chick. She's coming, right?"

"Back off, Ty," Phil shouts, grabbing him by the collar. "That is my girlfriend you're talking about."

"I know who she is." He cackles. "Ever break up with her, and I'll be up that alley."

Phil loses it. "Cool down or get out, Ty. I'm warning you. Donald may have been stupid enough to let you steal his girl back in high school, but if you even so much as breathe near Alena, I'll kill you."

"Thanks for that, man," Donald says to Phil, his voice low and feeble.

Mischievously, Ty smirks. "I'd snatch that snowflake so fast, you wouldn't be able to stop me."

"D'ya want a snapped neck, Ty? 'Coz I can arrange that, right now."

Creating a fist of cemented wrath, Phil goes to punch Ty. Donald, although weedy, blocks the hit. He stands between them, stopping a full-blown war. Two macho characters growl at one another, their rage decreasing as their respective common sense takes over.

What kind of friends are these guys, Phil?

As silence and heavy breathing pollutes the air, I emerge from hiding, easing the tension in the hall. "Baby, are these your friends?"

"Yeah, these are my mates." Winking at me, Phil realises that I am intervening to reduce the masculine rancour. "We'll be down in a minute, hunnie," he adds.

Hearing their waxy voices travelling down the hall a few minutes later, Ty, Donald, and Phil saunter into the lounge.

"Hello," I say, staring at the two ripped-jeans-wearing streetwise guys, who are clearly not the type of friends Phil should have.

Donald nods in acknowledgement; Ty simply stares, his eyes carefully undressing me. I immediately feel uncomfortable. Instinctively, Phil stands in front of me, protecting me from Ty's inappropriate glare. We stay close to one another and sit on the couch together, holding hands. I notice Ty's jealousy; he is looking at the two of us as if it is a sickening sight.

Disinterested in the deadly three-way stare-down taking place behind him, Donald spreads a pair of beady eyes across the area, admiring his surroundings. Our dorm house is a new block the college had built two years earlier. It's clean and fresh, and every wall is painted in magnolia. The living room area is quite spacious. There are two sets of beige sofas arranged in a semi-circle, a stylish rug and coffee table in the middle of the room, and a huge TV screen on the far left. Even the long brown curtains fall elegantly, waving like a mermaid's mane. I can tell Donald is at home here.

"How long have you two been together?" Asks Ty

intrusively, his lips wavering, his pupils darting up and down my body.

Tyron seems to be fascinated by me, in a dark, unsavoury way. A flash of that fiendish face from the past burns in his pernicious eyes. Anxiety grows within me. Phil, too, is becoming restless and uneasy. As my apprehension subsides, I pat him on the knee, taming his inner beast. That is not enough to cool him down, so, strategically, Phil caresses the bottom of my black dress, fondling the ball of my knee.

"We've been an item for exactly four months," Phil confirms. "And we plan to be together for a very long time. Perhaps, forever."

Cutting his eye, Ty hisses. "Yeah, whatever, matey. Forever is six months tops for most guys our age. A long term relationship in the modern world is just a teenage girl's fantasy."

"My forever *means* forever. I'm not like most guys." Phil's solid resolve pierces through the blazing ambience.

Tittering to himself, Tyron claps, as if applauding a star performance.

Letting his friend know that this is his turf, his game, played by his rules, Phil kisses me, hard and passionately, his tongue dancing on the base of my lips. There is no doubt now, that I am his girl.

"Let's get a drink, baby," he says caressing my arm in a territorial manner. Carrying on with his manly show, he takes my hand, helping me up, and leads me to the drinks table.

"This was a *bad* idea," he admits, rustling a pair of frenzied hands through his short, dark curls. A dash of disappointment broadens his nose.

Affectionately, I rub his arm, as a way of consoling him. "It's okay, babe. It is not your fault that Ty is a total sleaze-ball. I will stick this out for you. We're partners."

Shaking his head defiantly, he completely disagrees with me. "No, Alena. It was wrong of me to do this.

You're not ready to deal with people like Ty, and I'm definitely not happy sitting there watching him ogle you."

"So, what d'ya want to do?" I ask, shrugging my shoulders.

"Let's go back to your room and have a party of our own. How about it?"

I guffaw, my hair tumbles beautifully over my face. "Yea, I'd like that."

Ardently, Phil pecks me on the mouth, tickling my senses. He takes my hand and guides me out of the living room.

"Sorry, guys," I hoot turning to his chums. "We're having an early night."

Loudly, Donald giggles. I wink at Ty as he scowls at the pair of us. One point to me!

Walking casually to my room, looking deeply into Phil's eyes, I recognise that I have found a really special guy.

Suddenly, there is a banging and crashing noise. There's a disturbance coming from the corridor. We both twist round, our eyes affixing to the entrance where the discordance is ascending. There at the door is a deep purple suitcase, an expensive one belonging to a spoiled little rich girl, perhaps. A twangy American accent wafts into the hallway, blonde hair, followed by soft, yet incandescent blue eyes, which appear out of nowhere, sail down the corridor. Long elegant legs, as if strutting on a catwalk, are in their element. Phil and I can't help but stare at the tall, gorgeous model girl making her Hollywood entrance. Her tight pink shorts, small cream tank top, designer high heels, and that supermodel poise, all scream *I'm a hip Cali girl with daddy's plastic*.

Our college seldom has painted doll, overly dressed teenage celebrities. So who is this new girl?

"Well, then," she wails, placing a pair of hands on her splendid, slender hips. "Am I going to get some help over here, or you guys gonna just gawk at me all night?"

"Who are you?" I manage to say.

Sassily, she glares at me, her fake eyelashes undermining her California girl attitude. "I am Becca Richardson-Smith, the resident of room 178…" Admiring Phil's muscles, she addresses him. "Help me carry that, please, Mr. Strong Arms." She points at the suitcase, which is propped up languidly by the door. "I'm not built to carry this case. Look at me! I'm a damsel in distress."

Phil and I try our hardest not to laugh. As asked, he assists Becca with her suitcase and takes it to room 178, which is exactly opposite my room, number 185.

I follow Phil and walk behind, with the American girl.

"I'm Alena." I introduce myself.

"Pleased to meet you, Alena."

"Likewise." I smile into her cold, motionless eyes.

Inquisitively, she looks at me from head to toe. "You're Greek, aren't you, Alena?"

Astonished by her accuracy, I gasp, covering my mouth for a moment. "Wow! No one has ever said that to me the first time they've met me. That's very perceptive."

"I'm Miss Know It All. The Queen of Perception." Her tone is pretentious.

"Well, I can see that," I concur, feeling belittled, yet adoring the charming kinks in her yellow tresses.

Becca's hard expression should have softened by now. She should be smiling at me. Instead, her eyes reduce into two small balls of confusion. There is a desperate need for her to seek clarification. "Is that guy with my bags your boyfriend?"

"Yep," I answer proudly, waiting to hear what she will say about Phillip. "That's Phillip, my boyfriend."

Artfully she grins, her sparkling white teeth making their debut. "Thank God for England!"

Hearing this audacious remark, Phil instantly reacts. "What the heck is that supposed to mean?"

"Oh, nothing!" Quickly, she is embarrassed, realising she's on the brink of speaking out of turn.

Feeling a burn of injustice, Phil won't let it go. "That wisecrack wasn't nothing! Don't you Californians understand British manners?"

Oh, crap! Is this a transatlantic war in the making? I cringe, feeling very anxious with the growing heat in the hallway.

Flicking her lavish watch into focus, Becca diverts the conversation. "OMG, is that the time?"

Being the new girl, she doesn't want to rock the boat so soon, so she puts her head down, rushes to her room and snatches her bag from Phil.

"Gees, it's late. I better go. See you in the morning, guys."

"See ya," I reply.

Under his breath, Phil grunts. "Bye."

Noisily, she slams the door, and then disappears inside.

Becca Richardson-Smith has entered the building. Ridley House had better brace itself.

BEST FRIEND

"Professor Sanford is a total moron," I holler, rolling my eyes up to heaven.

"Yeah, totes," agrees Becca. Her mouth opens exaggeratedly when she speaks, her lips moving animatedly, true Californian style. "I don't know why they employed this kook of a lecturer!"

"God only knows!" I hoot.

She laughs. "What normal person walks their dog at five in the morning, in the hope he might meet a mate for his deranged K9 who looks as demented as him in photos?"

"I know who does that?"

Clamorously, I giggle with my new halls of residence housemate. We are in stitches, standing with our backs against the doors of our dorm rooms, talking and joking, as if we'd known each other for years. In fact, I've only known Becca Richardson-Smith three weeks now. She is an international student from San Francisco, California, who's doing a study abroad year in the UK. The college she's studying at is UC Berkeley. Becca is on a prestigious scholarship programme, which allows her to complete three semesters of undergraduate study overseas.

Fortunately, she's studying English, the same subject as me – so we have had the opportunity to get to know each other really well and bond.

The two of us share everything, even underwear. Well, that was an accident. After using my en-suite bathroom last week, since her water was playing up, she tossed her panties in my laundry basket. I washed them and wore them, thinking they belonged to me. She owns exactly the same silky pink H&M knickers as I do, and we take the same size: small. The only slight difference is that her name is faded on the wash label. So it's easy to mix our underwear up. I could just about make out the 'B' for Becca inside her underwear yesterday, which is when I returned them to her. Clean, of course, and with no skid marks. But for some reason her knickers are somewhat bigger than mine, and far more comfortable. If I wasn't so weirded out by the fact that I was rubbing my lady parts in her prize pink panties, I would've kept really quiet and pretended the loose briefs were mine! Naughty, I know!

"And what about his teaching methods?" I ask Becca, smirking, thinking about parading around my room in her sexy, overstretched undies.

"Well," she begins, flicking her long blonde mane away from her eyes. "I think we'd learn more about social behaviour in the mall than we would from him. Don't ya think?"

"Oh, so true, sista!"

We burst into a fit of laughter and run in place, getting excited that we are agreeing with each other, yet again. It's like we are conjoined twins.

Skipping forward, she clumps me playfully on the arm. "Let's go make some dinner in five minutes, babe."

"Okay. I'll cook," I say. "Mac and cheese?"

She grins. "Yeah, sounds awesome!"

Simultaneously, we open our doors, slide into our boudoirs and exit the corridor. Two minutes later, we both emerge from our rooms. We run on the spot again, euphorically.

"Gees, we really are twins!" she yawps.

"Last one to the kitchen is a rotten egg!" I shout, racing down the hall at lightning speed. She's tall, lanky, and slow – strange but true. I beat her to the kitchen. Teasingly, I blow a raspberry and stick my bottom in her face. *Smack, smack, smack.* She thwacks my arse hard, like an African drum.

"Nice butt, sexy lady," she says bending forward and whispering in my ear.

We burst into hysterics.

At first, I got the impression that Becca was a lesbian. I now realise that's just her sense of humour. She's a real joker!

Ambling towards the low kitchen cupboard, I bend down, opening it brusquely, and begin to rummage around in search of a saucepan to start cooking my legendary mac and cheese. Becca makes herself comfortable at the table, sitting on the wooden chair nearest to the stove. As I yank out my famous pot located at the back of the dark, dense cupboard, I hear Becca entertaining herself behind me, like she always does when there is silence and she has nothing to say to fill the gap. There is a slight tap on the floor and then she generates a cacophony of sound, banging her unwieldy legs against the metal fastener at the base of the table, which holds everything together. Keeping still isn't an art she has learned yet. Her hands and feet need to be occupied; she's got fidgetitis. In other words, she enjoys a good fidget to pass the time.

I click on the electric cooker, and pour a litre of water in the saucepan. Carefully, I place the pan on the stove. The hob begins to hiss slightly, as it is obviously wet, since the last person who used it forgot to dry it off. Most likely Joanne Jackman, one of our floormates. She's a stuck-up cow, a messy individual with no manners and no consideration for others. The hissing stove begins to irritate me. I take in a deep breath, just as my therapist told me to whenever anxiety rises within me. But I can't stop the feeling of anxiousness. The violent fizzing gets to me even more, pushing deep down into my soul, into a dark, dangerous cavity suppressing the past. Stanley's perilous voice charges into my thoughts. I panic, breathing heavily, my cheeks reddening, burning, on fire. I knock into the pan, the water spilling over on the clean white cooker. My past waves into my reflection, polluting the present, and it starts to poison my consciousness. Stanley's wicked cackle penetrates my mind, my body, my world.

I scream.

"Get out of my head!"

"Alena!" Becca jumps up and rushes to me, wrapping her warm arms around my quivering shell. "It's okay, babe. I'm here."

"I saw him, Becca, he was laughing – and he wanted to hurt me again."

She holds me closer, her breasts pressing against my trembling spine. "Shh, it's okay. You're safe. He's gone, and he won't ever come back. He is in prison now, where he belongs. That evil asshole won't be coming out for at least another three years."

Turning my head gradually, I meet her kind face. "Yes, you're right. He's gone, out of my life forever."

"For good," she affirms. "Forever."

Ingesting Becca's benevolence, I smile at her. She smiles back, her kindness shining into my face. Our focused concentration beams into the centre of the kitchen, connecting and intertwining into one strong thread of consciousness. We are so connected, our thoughts on the same wavelength. At exactly the same time, we stamp our feet on the laminate flooring, and soon, we transform into Amazon women, which quickly becomes a sentience so deeply imbedded in our psyches. Hands on chests, we beat the drum of victory. Feet pounding into the ground, lips firmly and determinedly pursed, ready for war.

"Forever, forever, we are strong. Forever, forever, he is gone."

This is the chant Becca formed to help ward off my fear and anxiety about the past. It works, it really does. Becca knows my past; I've told her everything. That's why she can help me deal with my demons. Coupled with this fact is that she understands the mechanics of the human mind, as her Aunt Tilley is a leading psychologist in Ohio.

Softly, she kisses the top of my head, caressing my long wavy hair to pacify me. I now feel a lot better. Gently, I am rocked like a baby. She knows exactly how to calm me down right at the crucial point of 'an episode.' God, how lucky I am to have someone like her in my life.

Taking control of the situation, she guides me to the warm seat, the one in which she sat, and then continues to make dinner from where I left off. I bury my head in the table and take a deep breath. Slowly, I return to a state of serenity. I am calm. I feel normal, like myself again. I'm very safe in Becca's company.

An hour later, dinner has been devoured and the prospect of us scarfing dessert looks promising. We are in Becca's room, sitting on her bed, eating strawberries and vanilla ice cream. Mmm. Divine. My head pans round her bedroom. It is so cluttered. Books everywhere, clothes scattered on the floor. The only section of her digs that is clean and tidy is her marbled mahogany dresser. She loves to show off her ridiculously big and shiny beauty queen trophy and loves to admire herself in the mirror.

Becca is a total prima donna. She's a diva, a daydreaming movie star waiting for her big break. Hanging around her, I've kinda started to act a tiny bit the same, with a similar pouty, spoiled expression appearing on my face at times. I, like my bestie, comb my hair every day, my gorgeous, dark Mediterranean hair that sparkles meekly in the light. I also bring out my eyes with a thin layer of black eyeliner and metallic blue eye shadow, and I plaster my face with red lipstick and skin-tone-coloured foundation. Still, Becca's makeup is better than mine. She gets hers from the States. And God has granted her a beautiful model's body and luscious, kissable lips. Even with no makeup or lipstick on (which is only in the mornings and at night), she naturally looks prettier than me. Her ocean-blue eyes glisten in the sunlight; golden-blonde hair, so soft and gentle, falls elegantly off her shoulders like a shimmering waterfall. If she had wanted to, she could have easily pursued a modelling career, especially with those lovely long legs. I am relatively tall, 5' 8", but still three inches shorter than Becca (yes, she is a whopping 5' 11"). My legs are kinda knocked together, reedy and turned inward at the knee joint. Hers are elongated, sexy, catwalk-model type limbs. That's probably why she won Miss Teenage California two years prior and can get away with living in short, up-your-arse jeans and a tank top in mid-February. Maybe it's just a California girl thing. Who knows?

The former beauty queen pouts her lips at me as she scrapes the last drop of ice cream from the bowl and rests it by her overpoweringly stunning bronze legs. So many men have wanted to kill just to touch them.

"So tell me, Alena," she asks invasively, "why haven't you and Phillip had sex yet?"

I virtually choke on a strawberry. It was happily making its way down my gullet until she startled me, nearly causing my airway to block. I throw myself forward. She pats me hard on the back to dislodge the blockage in my throat. I splutter, and then, in a few moments, I'm able to breathe normally again.

"Are you okay, hun?"

"No," I answer, gaining back my strength. "No, I'm not okay. I can't believe Phillip told you that we're not *active*."

From day one, I've known that Phillip is a very

straight-talking guy. But telling Becca, a girl who's just moved onto our floor, about our private business, is way out of line. Perhaps he is having second thoughts about our relationship. Or maybe he's after Becca. She is blonde and a whole lot prettier than me after all. He wouldn't be a man if he didn't try to make a pass at her. Whatever the reason, there's no excuse for this level of betrayal. It's unforgivable.

My heart races; I feel upset, confused, angry, all at the same time. Internally, my emotions tussle in my mind, tangling into a dense, knot-like ball. *Raging* anxiety attack coming. Calm down, Alena. Relax. Take deep breaths. Think of cool ocean waves melting into the sea. Oh, fuck the ocean! I'm pissed off!

"Has Phillip attempted to kiss you, is that it? If I won't, then you will, is that it, Becca?"

Appearing bemused, she turns her palms face up, shrugging two neat, girlie shoulders. "No, not at all. I don't want him, Alena. Skinny guys are the type I go for. C'mon hun, it's a simple enough question. Why haven't ya' gone all the way with him?"

"I wanna know why he told you!"

"Because he's frustrated, Alena! He's a sexy guy and you are a pretty girl, yet he can't *get busy* with you. If I was your boyfriend, I'd be getting really impatient, too! It's been five months, Alena. The poor boy's balls must be crying out for sex!"

"Maybe in California it's cool to be forward like that, but I think less is more," I snap angrily.

Rolling her eyes, she sighs. "I forgot, you British are a bit prudish about s-e-x."

"Not as much as you might think," I reply coldly. "However, asking a friend you've known for twenty one days about her sex life is a little out of turn."

"For a Brit?"

"No. For me! These are my standards. I don't converse about *that*."

"Well, it must be a bit of a British thing, too," she says, getting annoyed. "My Californian friends have no problem with me asking them personal questions. C'mon, Alena. You and Phillip have been going steady for a while. Why haven't you gone down the road of humpy, hump, bump?"

"Humpy, hump, bump?"

"I invented that phrase," she says proudly.

"Ah ha. No kidding," I reply sarcastically. "Clearly, that's not in the dictionary."

Resting her hand on my thigh, she looks pitifully at me. "He's a hot nineteen-year-old guy, Alena. Waiting for one girl for so long to dispose of her baggage is like having a sex curse."

"Bec, please... You know my history."

"Yes," she says hesitantly. "But I also know Caribbean men."

"Please, Becca," I insist. "That's *so* inappropriate!"

"Alena, he's been sitting on the sidelines for ages. His eyes are lively; his heart is beating hard in his chest. He wants to start a game on the tennis court. He wants *you* to join him. Soon, if you don't play, then he may not stay, and might find another who grabs his interest. D'ya catch my drift?"

I scrunch up my face. "Yes, and no."

Leaning in closer, her blue eyes dive into my emerald blurs.

"Look, Alena, I know that you are troubled and afraid to go further with Phil, but he loves you. He won't hurt you. He'll take it slow, as slow as you need. But don't keep him waiting forever. Even the nicest of guys can't wait for eternity."

I stare into her eyes, yet disengage a little, pulling back, lessening the intensity of our connection. "Befriending the wrong person, back in high school, almost cost me my life, Becca. I can't trust again. I can't let anyone in, not completely."

"I know how difficult it's been for you, hun. But this is college, not high school," she advises me. "I believe Phillip is *the one*, the right man for you, and this is the right time. He's in love with you, Alena. That's why he's waiting patiently. Don't break his heart. He's tough, yet his heart is like glass. Once broken by his true love, it can never be whole again."

"That's deep, Becca."

Forlornly, she puts her head down. "I've broken a few hearts in my time, and had my heart broken twice as many times. Unfortunately, it's all part of life, love, and the pursuit of happiness."

"I really do want to experience *it* with Phil," I confess, biting my lip. "I'm just afraid of opening my heart to him fully. I am not ready to take things to the next level. Not yet."

"Just let go," she whispers, stroking my hair affectionately. "Allow him to touch you, love you, completely. Love is beautiful with the one you adore. Embrace it."

Painfully, I exhale. "If only things were that simple."

"It is simple, Alena." Rummaging in her pocket, she yanks out a condom. She places it in my lap. "This is in date. Keep it. You and Phil might be caught out one day."

I laugh coyly. "I doubt I will need it."

"When you let the emotions take you, trust me, you'll need it."

"Okay. Thanks, hun." I pop it in my denim skirt pocket. "Who knows what the future will hold."

"Yeah," she agrees. "But you and Phil are a sure thing."

"We'll see."

"Please don't tell Phillip off for opening up to me," she begs, summoning my gaze, appealing to my better nature.

I nod. "I promise not to tell."

"Thank you." She smiles. "Alena?"

"Yes, babe?"

"Can we be best friends?"

I grin. "Yes, sure. But I thought we were kinda besties already."

"Not officially," she says, still smiling. "But I'm glad we are now."

I beam. "Me too."

The two of us snuggle up together, enjoying the warmth of this special friendship. Becca turns the radio on low, and we drift off to sleep as the beautiful sound of a classical piano resonates sweetly into our ears.

THE ORCHARD

Ridley House has a splendid and serene parkland, which is situated just in front of the building. From my room, I can see the stunning botanical garden perfectly; this beautiful place, which blooms with life, especially now, at the beginning of April. Spring has arrived, and nature seems to burst with new colours, flowers, new life. In this quiet, private space, frogs and ducks have babies, and the young offspring learn how to swim and play in the pond. The trees appear more lustrous at this time of year, and showcase an almost effervescent glow. Mother Nature is in full swing now, completely in her element. She loves spring; she is a proud woman who relishes life, who adores this special garden. Her fingers are fruitful, creating brand new faunas, floras, and souls, so effortlessly, in this enrapturing province. If you look a little closer at the orchard, you will see, adjacent to the house, a quaint mere, which habitually smiles up at the tall, majestic Ridley House. The river is blue, rich, and gorgeous. Overlooking the clear water from a perfect right angle is a grove of small trees, fluorescent evergreens, which encircle the briny creek with glee.

I take a deep breath, cherishing this truly magical vista.

Daringly, I kick a small, sharp pebble onto the pathway that leads toward the pond. The little stone lands awkwardly on the shingled terrain and hits a nugget of gravel, and suddenly it flies up, shooting into the water. Gradually, the splash undulates and wells into a three-layer circle. Although buried in the subterranean part of the mini sea, the stone's dark essence can still be felt beneath the depths of the water. I can see the waves beginning to stir as the body of water tries to cope with this invasion. Handling its anger and complex emotions, the lake eventually returns to a state of equanimity, but never forgets its ordeal, much like a human heart that is fractured, and desperately trying to mend.

I'm sitting on a pale yellow weather-beaten bench that resides in the integral part of the peaceful common. Faithful Becca is beside me. From this view, we can see the swaying trees at the far end of the green, which are rocking gently in the afternoon zephyr, and the large pond, which is now shimmering, inviting, and tranquil. Grass of a pure green that is as soft as butter is spread across most of the grounds, and it tickles our bare feet, fondling our toes. The thin, silky blades move convivially with the natural drone of the whirling wind. In this enchanting place, nature is sublime, at its very best. It is still, pacifying. I have time to think, to ponder, feeling my heartbeat drumming in my chest.

My body is reposed; my face, now mirroring the calm surface of the water as it lowers in deep reflection. "Do ya think we will have everything our hearts desire, in say, five years' time?" I ask, turning to Becca.

She squints a little as the sun shines in her eyes. "Of course, we will be teachers, commanding an annual salary of 70,000 dollars, and we'll both be happily married, possibly with children, two kids, one girl and one boy each."

"D'ya really think that will happen, B?" I ask doubtfully.

Smiling with assured confidence she replies, "Yes, I do."

"And you think we'll both be living in America? You used dollars as the currency for our salaries."

Becca presses her arms into a fold and looks at me smugly. "You're moving to California when you graduate. Didn't I tell you?"

Impishly, I slide over on the bench and knock into her. "You will be in California for sure. But I'm not certain that I will be. I am rooted to England, couldn't live anywhere else."

"Okay," agrees Becca. "Right after I graduate, I will move to Surrey, with you, and we can stay in England until you're married. Then, Californ-i-a, here we come!"

Throwing her arms in the air like a playful monkey, she smiles in my face, staring into my meditative emerald eyes, which are skidding on the surface of the slow sinuous water.

"And to whom shall I be married?" I enquire, still mesmerised by the charm of the glistening water.

"Well, that's a no brainer. Phillip, obviously!"

I raise a sharp brow, and speedily, I meet her glance. "No one can predict *that*!"

"Yeah, I can," she says quietly, attempting to soften my countenance with a sweet smirk. "You and Phil are forever."

"That's if he doesn't break up with me before then," I state firmly. "Our expiration date is almost written in the cards."

Candidly, Becca laughs. "I can't see a break up *ever* being in the cards!"

I look into her eyes, confused, thinking that she must be delirious from the rush of the fresh air around us.

"This is not a Hollywood movie, Becca. Very few people find true love *and* have a perfect ending in the real world. This journey is called *life* – and life has a tendency to suck. Big time."

"C'est la vie, my friend! C'est la vie."

Listlessly, she shrugs her shoulders. The weight of the world pressing on her slim frame.

Then a dry laugh leaves her throat, and her eyes grow warmer. She seems to have thrown whatever had been burdening her, and allows my affection in once more.

"Yeah, such is life!" I concur.

Sharply, I exhale, kicking another stone into the pond. This time, the pebble hits the back of a duck's body. The duck quacks at me, angry that I have attacked it unnecessarily. Fuelled by aggression, the animal starts to come towards me. The creature's feet venture out of the water, touching dry land. Revenge is in the duck's eyes. Soon it gets distracted by its mate, who is quacking at her suggestively, begging her to come back into the aquatic haven to keep him company.

Becca bursts into hysterics. I do not. My expression is severe once more as my mind returns to my thoughts about the future with Phillip.

"With the hurdles we have to jump, we can't last, Becca. We *won't* last."

"Chill, babe," she reassures me, rubbing my shoulders soothingly. "Things will work themselves out soon. Trust me."

A cross expression pollutes my face. "When he is with another girl, a hot *it girl*, who can give him everything he desires, things will definitely work out for him, just fine!" I pout, folding my arms across my chest. Slouching on the bench, I press the weight of my problems into its weak wooden frame.

"Nuh- uh!" Becca insists. "You're the only woman he will ever have eyes for."

"Hmm," I mumble. "Maybe in a strange utopian society where a giant duck is president, men walk on four legs, and women are aliens with edible candy bars for toes."

Becca giggles and then says, "Ha-hmm," in a weak

attempt at a Donald Duck accent. I can tell she is enjoying larking about, and she comes right up in my face and continues speaking in her silly duck voice. "Maybe in a strange utopian society when ducks are presidents… Quack, quack," she twangs.

I look at her, giving her that 'you're a bloody weirdo' kinda expression.

Grinning at me puckishly, she carries on. "Right now," she shouts in her faux-duck tone, "I want to eat you. In my world, Duckytopia, we eat humans, and you look rather tasty, kiddo. Although, you're a bit on the bony side, I must say. I like plumper humans. Perhaps the blonde next to you might be a little juicier and have a bit more junk in the trunk! Quack, q-u-a-c-k!"

I pout childishly. I'm trying not to laugh. Defiantly, I hold it in. My lips, pursed, arms still crossed. Giggling, Becca glides into me, bumping my bottom playfully. I jolt. My mouth quivers and then we both burst into a fit of laughter, unable to keep it in any longer.

"Who do you see me with in five years' time, hun?" asks a curious Becca when we have recovered from our laughing fit.

"I see you with a very sexy man," I reply.

Mischievously, her eyes light up. "Taylor Lautner?"

I frown slightly. "No, sorry. He's taken."

"Well, I guess I'll find someone else, a special someone."

"You will. You're beautiful, babe."

"I know," she asserts, flicking her golden hair, and puckering up her perfectly-formed red lips. "So are you, Alena."

I raise a questioning brow, thinking her delirium is taking hold again. "Nah. Not so sure about that."

"It's true," she insists, her voice vibrating close to my ear. "You're flipping gorgeous, babe!"

"Says the dazzling beauty queen to the scrawny ugly duckling!" I sneer.

Becca punches me on the arm for making this snippy comment.

"No!" I shriek, undeterred by the flippant manner in which she reproached me. "I'm not that pretty. Just above average, of course. But not stunning. Not like you."

Now she is the one with the frown. "Let's not argue about this bestie, especially since I need to make a burning confession."

"Oh!" I am surprised. "What confession is this?"

Spiritedly she titters, averting a pair of guilty pupils to the ground. Her blue orbs dive vivaciously into the placating pond. "I am in love with Jason Derulo, too!"

I double blink in shock. "I thought you liked weedy men? What's the deal with that?"

"He is my second guilty pleasure!" She twitters, and leaps up, dancing around the bench in dizzy circles.

I watch her, amused. "What are you doing?"

Teasing her mobile phone out of her pocket, Becca eagerly taps a few buttons and Jason Derulo's "Talk Dirty" blares from her Nokia phone. She begins to shake her arse, rolling sexy, hot hips in deep, winding loops. Her long limbs tremor in perfect rhythm. Becca jumps back, grinding her bottom into my face. Impetuously, she calls out to me.

"Come join me, Alena!"

I quail, my heart pounding fast and strong in my chest. Quickly I tense up, feeling my fears overwhelm me. "I don't dance like that. Not anymore."

"Come on! It's liberating! Just try it!"

Repeatedly, I shake my head. "Nuh uh! I'm not coming!"

Flashing a grin at me, she continues to shake. "I'm going to Po Na Na tonight with Indigo Young and Keisha Wilson, two of the most popular sophomore students at this college. Come with us! Mingle with the in-crowd! We'll have a laugh, babe."

Like a kangaroo, I jump up and down on my seat. "I

wish I could go, but I can't. I'm scared Becca. You know I only really go off campus to go grocery and clothes shopping and to visit the bank. And on occasion to go and see my mum in Surrey. But that's it!"

Suddenly, Becca stops moving and turns off the music. She comes back to the bench and plonks herself next to me. Concentrating on me, her face is serious, her expression, pensive.

"No, Alena, that *is not* it! The college experience is not about hiding away. It's about finding yourself. Making friends here, making connections, is so very important. Don't ya want to be well-liked, and admired, like me? Don't you want to make your mark here? The students at this college need to know who you are!"

Burning tears scold me as Becca's words score my heart. "I want to be invisible here," I scream, "and I just need to get through college without losing the boyfriend, who might actually be my redeemer and the love of my life!"

Pain seeps into Becca's soul. She ripples with anguish. "If you want change, positive change, now is the time to be visible. Get out there, meet new people, find ways to heal the hurt, without expecting Phillip to be the saviour."

As the emotion clenches my gullet, I gulp. "The hurt is buried deep inside me, I cannot heal. I cannot mend. He is the only one who might be able to save me."

Resolutely, Becca shakes her head; her focus still remains on me. "No man has the power to do that. That's a fantasy. A woman has to save herself."

In complete disagreement, I ignore her statement and continue to speak my piece.

"I don't know how to find *me* again, not without him."

"You can, Alena. I believe in you. Two years ago popularity and confidence were your game. They can be again."

Firmly, I hold Becca's gaze, allowing her to see the storm raging in my eyes. "I don't want to be popular again. I know how dangerous popularity is and what it can do to a girl. It can desecrate a perfect life."

Becca glowers. Her tone is sarcastic. "C'mon, hunnie. That's melodramatic."

A little annoyed by my best friend's lack of empathy, I proceed. "No, it isn't, Becca. If popularity was a chemical, it would be highly corrosive."

Mordantly, she cackles, an acid laugh gurgling in her throat. "Being popular is every teenage girl's dream, Alena. There's nothing corrosive about it."

"It's every teenage girl's dream, is it?" I say tetchily, slightly upset by her attitude.

"Yes, it is." Validating my expression of disgust, she nods. "As crazy as it may be, every girl wants to be the best, even if it's only a secret hunger. We strive to be number one. We're just wired up that way."

"Like you, Becca, I *was* number one in high school. I lived *that dream* once. Everybody revered me. Everyone wanted to be my friend. In the end, living in a world where people worshipped me was a curse, a living nightmare. It got me noticed by the wrong people. And then, after *it* happened, *The Magpie Mob* turned the whole school against me practically overnight, and drove me out of town, within a matter of months. So, you see, being popular is not worth it. I won't *ever* go there again."

Becca's voice is resolute, yet it carries an equable air. Hands, so tender, rub my cheeks to soothe this growing anxiety.

"The past is the past, hun. Yes, it burns, it stings. Popularity is a bitch! However, we all have to learn how to move on, one way or another."

Tenaciously, I rebuff her advice. "I can't move on! You know that every day I am reminded of what happened. I will always be the girl that people judge or pity. That girl, who wound up in the headlines. That girl on the six o'clock London news."

"No, you are not that girl anymore. That girl is gone!

43

Let it go, Alena. It's time to change these destructive trends and start afresh."

"That girl is not gone, Becca. She sits right here – lost and broken. She's a fragile doll that has shattered into a thousand pieces and may never be restored to her shining glory."

A half smirk rolls onto her lips. Coltishly, she taps me on the leg. "You Brits are so damn theatrical sometimes, honestly."

"Shakespeare is our literary guide, so deal with it, California girl," I shout, slamming her leg twice as hard. "I'm pouring my heart out here, telling you how I am a broken dolly. You could at least try to care."

Dismissively, her two cyan orbs fly to heaven. "Broken dolly, metaphor overload, blah, blah, blah."

"That's cruel, Becca!"

"Nothing is broken, Alena! You are whole, all in one piece."

"Look at me! *I am* broken!"

"Alena, I care about you. Really, I do. However, I'm not doing this whole pity party thing. Not today. It's unhealthy for the soul." She refuses to acknowledge my fears anymore, and switches the song back on. Standing up and gyrating, feeling the base of the tune in her core, she beckons me to her. "Now come over here, Alena, and just try to dance with me! Let's get in the mood for tonight."

I look her in the eyes and signal 'no, I'm not coming' with one finger. Then, without warning, Becca grabs me. She has a tendency to be totally spontaneous at times, whereas I don't usually like anything that isn't safe and planned. These days, I hate random, I hate danger, and I shy away from new experiences – they bring on my anxiety.

"No, Becca!" I shout.

She doesn't listen; she hauls me up and stands behind me, throwing her hands on my pelvis and moving my hips robustly, forcing that creaky section of my anatomy to bump and grind under her watchful eye. Friskily, heatedly, Becca thrusts into me, and holds me close.

"Enjoy the vibrations, Alena. Let go."

No, I can't let go. I can't breathe. I can't breathe. I can't breathe. I find the strength to yelp.

Powerfully, I throw her off me, unable to take any more.

A look of concern finally appears on Becca's face. "What's wrong, Alena?"

I begin to cry, cupping my face in my hands. "The memories… You are bringing back the memories of *him*… It's just too much to deal with."

Mortified, she gasps. "I'm sorry, babe. I didn't understand how deeply he had affected you. I *so* shouldn't have done that!"

I stumble, distraught, away from her.

A different pair of feet step across the hard gravelly surface, approaching the scene.

"What are you doing, Becca?" I recognise this deep, powerful voice. It is Phillip.

"I didn't do anything!" she tries to assure him. "I was just playing."

Running to Phillip, I sink into the safety of his hardy physique.

"She is fragile," he reminds Becca. "You need to be careful."

"I'm sorry," she murmurs. "I didn't mean to…"

"It's okay," I mouth, the feeling in my legs beginning to return. For support, I still hold onto my man, letting his strong embrace keep me upright.

"We are going inside, now," orders Phillip.

Walking languidly along the pebbled pathway, the three of us head back into our dorm house. As soon as we reach home, I move past Becca and Phillip into my room and slam the door. I feel dizzy. My almost empty room, with only a bed, dresser, wardrobe, two chairs, and washroom, spins giddily in my panorama. There is nothing in this space that reminds me of the past, yet the demons still find a way to enter my core. I sit on the rocking chair in this large, uncluttered chamber, drawing the curtains closed, and shroud myself in total darkness. Curling up into a foetal ball in the shiny wooden chair beside the window and closing a pair of heavy lids, I sway, back and forth, back and forth; I feel safe in the dark. There is a gentle breeze circling and caressing my face. I shut my eyes tighter, allowing a modest piece of nature to caress my cheeks and touch the soft curvature of my thin upper lip. I lament, and eventually fall asleep in the sapping pool of my own sorrowful tears.

MIDNIGHT

A gentle, manly hand smooths over my rigid lines of anxiety, kneading them out of my back, legs, arms, stomach, and breasts. I am lying naked in bed with Phil, slowly surrendering to his every touch. A feeling of deep pleasure surges through my veins as his eyes light up, and he is exploring this rich new territory.

Phillip beams, a naughty expression elevating his cheeks. "This whole butt naked thing is so freaking awesome. Could get used to us doing this. Couldn't you?"

"Yea, perhaps," I murmur, getting a little overwhelmed by his feelings, as well as my own.

Instinctively, Phil grabs my hand, and escorts it to the head of his manhood. His flaccid member melts into my palm. Gees, this guy is trying to arouse me. He is on a mission. This boy means business.

"You like the feel of me, baby?" He says smugly.

"Oh, Jesus," I cry. "This is new!"

Internally, I begin to moisten. The joy is welling up inside. This feeling is overwhelmingly pleasing. My face reddens with embarrassment. I savour these new sensations as my fingers have a vacation in a brand new world.

Michelle Diana Lowe

"Love," he groans, "this is what it feels like. Feels good, don't it?"

Our bodies are tangled, pupils aligned; we are breathing at exactly the same time. It is beautiful to watch him, watching me.

"I love the idea of love, Phil. But letting love inside me, that is a different story."

Playfully, he chortles. "Put the past to bed, Alena. Or I'll have to tease it out of you."

He tickles me.

Responding to the tickle, my body recoils, and I titter. "You think it's possible for me to put the past to bed?"

His body draws closer. Every part of us is touching. A heat so strong, intense burns my cheeks.

"It is possible," he whispers, holding my small buttocks in the base of his hands. "I know it is possible."

Closing my eyes, I make a brave attempt to squeeze the fears of yesterday out of my mind. When I re-open them, Phil's lips have curled into a smirk, and he kisses me, rewarding my efforts. His hands remain moulded around my bottom.

"You just don't realise how gorgeous you are, do ya, baby?" he purrs, his scorching digits moving in a neat circle, touching me in the most private of places.

I shiver, my consciousness floats to heaven, yet it's being pulled back to earth by the sheer weight of my demons.

"I haven't had closeness with anyone since. Not sure if I'm – "

Stopping me in mid-sentence, Phil's lips graze mine.

"Closeness gives release," he says faintly, between kisses. "It can heal any pain."

"Can it really?" I ask, questioning his alpha male rationality.

"Yes, it can." His voice is defiant.

Touching me again in that magic place, Phil deepens his caresses. I can't help but whimper as the depth of his

48

love vibrates inside me. Who knew the power a zealous boyfriend possessed?

It is now midnight. There is silence. Phil climbs on top of me; his breathing is erratic, turning wild. He grinds into me. His length is excited, spanking the lips of my opening.

"Tonight, we should just relax and enjoy each other. Let's explore – find out what we like."

Disturbingly, my features wrinkle, shrivelling up. So does my confidence. "I don't know if I will enjoy it."

"Oh, you will, baby. Promise. I made these hands extra soft. Good for touching, for loving." He grins.

Phil's erotic frame presses firmly against me, his tongue gently licking the sensual hole in my inner ear.

Flippantly I roll my eyes, dismissing my boyfriend's unoriginal declaration. "A porcelain doll is hard to grab with supple hands, Phil. Some dolls are best left on the shelf, only to be admired from afar."

Striking the mattress with a jovial fist, he laughs loudly, as if mocking me. "No, Alena. Porcelain doesn't exist as an aesthetic object that can be admired from a distance, and left abandoned on a shelf. Men like to feel it, hold it. Every work of art needs to be touched, eventually."

Acrimoniously, a belch of laughter leaves my lips. I slice into his optimism. "Let's cut the bull, baby. We're not in Professor Sanford's English class right now."

Phil scowls. I can tell my words have wounded him.

"Alena, this ain't no bullshit talk. What I'm saying is true."

I glare up at him, not appreciating his conceited arrogance.

"Look, Phil, this whole set up is nice, sensual even. And I should be totally excited, being here with you, in my bedroom, talking sweet talk, with us ready to hump the night away. But I'm not excited. It's fear that pummels through my body."

Fervidly he kisses me, yet his lips are lethal, hazardous. "I love you so much, Alena," he cries, kissing me tantalisingly along my neck. "You're my sweetheart, the only woman I ever want to be with. Isn't that enough to appease you?"

I absorb his gaze, mesmerised by his potent affection. Yet my breathing is panicky, nervous and shaky. "No, it isn't enough, Phillip. I just need time."

"Let's just try. I won't go in too deep, promise." His eyes are gazing earnestly into mine now; he is so hungry, so very hungry, like a lion.

"Phil, I'm scared!" I tell him as my lungs restrict, and now I am shutting him off, my lady lips sealing shut under the pressure. "I can't do it! The past is crushing me."

Disquietingly, I begin to sob. He holds me, yet his arms are loose, unsure.

His glorious brown eyes lose their sparkle and his mouth quivers unnaturally. "You just need to relax, open up, let go." Tears are overwhelming him now, distorting his vision. "It's not that difficult."

"It's hard, Phil! So very hard!" I cry as I pull away.

"Yes, it is. But not for much longer."

I realise he meant that he is now also feeling the effects of my refusal, his arousal decreasing. That powerful member of his body soon turns limp and motionless.

"You don't seem to realise that I need it to survive. I need you, Alena. Don't shut me out forever."

Coming behind me, rubbing himself up against my figure, he groans passionately. I allow him to lick my ear as his comforting arms wrap around me. Our limbs intertwine beautifully; it is good to have this *safe* and comfortable level of closeness with my man. He summons my gaze, turning my head to meet his. A passionate spark flashes in his eyes. I blush, throwing my head down. My hair flops over my face. I soon raise my head up again to enjoy his scorching stare. Perspiring and shaky, my hand slides onto his, and slowly, our right hands, overlapping, heated, obsessive, travel to the door of my entrance. Lightly, his hand tickles the door of my lady garden. Totally blazing and breathless, Phillip then removes my hand from his, wanting to do all the amatory work himself. His warm fingers are delicious; they are touching and feeling me and melting into this delicate area, making me lubricious with his touch. This is dangerous, perilous, but I close my eyes, enjoying the sensation of Phil's long forefinger massaging me inside. I start to pant heavily. Though it is a deadly, dark, and boisterous pant that encourages me to widen my legs, and my opening, hot, wet, and excited, begins to flower like a tulip. Phil works deeper into me, his whole hand massaging my insides, and I whine with pleasure. He then sucks my neck, grabbing my breasts with his free, clammy hand. My whines turn into liberating screams. I feel Phillip's manhood beginning to grow again. I hear a bottomless grunting sound. Is it Phil? No, his voice is not reverberating in my ears. He is saying nothing, he's just enjoying me. If it's not Phil's voice and it isn't mine, then it must be a voice from the past – it must be *his* voice – Stanley Hawthorne's baleful groan blaring in my earlobes…

Despairingly, I whimper. My heart is beating fast. I'm really scared, and totally aroused at the same time. My mind becomes hazy, and suddenly I do not know where I am. Am I in my bedroom in the present time with Phillip, my boyfriend, who is arousing me, hoping for sex tonight? Or am I in the past, in Stanley's house, where he is taking advantage of my young vulnerability? Strongly, I wheeze, my eyes spinning in the middle of time and space. My indolent head is vacuous, whizzing between the past and the present, and as Phillip and Stanley's consciousnesses merge and I am not sure who is working through my body anymore, I begin to shed sad, sorrowful tears once more. Closing my eyes, I shield them from this world of incomprehension. My young nineteen-year-old heart is in the present, resting blissfully in my bed with the one I truly love, but my tainted seventeen-year-old body is dipping in and out of the past, dragging itself, like a weathered yo-yo, between a harrowing life of pain and a beatific realm of joy and everlasting love.

I lay supine, with my body melding with my man's on the mattress. My womanly flesh is throbbing, savouring every single salacious stroke and touch, and my sweet, compact treasure box is peppery hot, begging for twilight passion. It wants Phillip to enter the steamy shrine; however, it sees Stanley's length peering sinisterly at its dark, red opening. So it frowns, partly burning with desire, but also burning with agony. I moan, arching my back. Becoming completely awakened, my man meets my glorious movements with his frantic forward thrusts. The sensations are blowing my mind. I smile; happily afraid and treacherously awakened.

Love is drenching my red tulip. My breathing is carnal, precarious, and my legs spread further apart; I begin to groan louder. My whole body is moving in rhythm, and his increasing length slaps against my scarlet mouth. I scream with pleasure. I am on the brink. I am almost there…

"Oh yes!" Boorishly, I shout, licking my mouth, holding onto my man's firm buttocks, which move with my sweltering body.

"I think you are ready now," Phil purls, grinding into my taut bottom.

Ooh, the vibrations are divine, so sensational. He is my man, I need him, and I want him. I want him inside of me, now! This feels so right, it feels so very right. If Phil and I go all the way tonight, Stanley will get out of my mind forever, right?

My eyes are tightly closed. I can feel his breath over my mouth. His breathing is cavernous, voluptuous.

"You will never forget me, never forget this. I will make sure of that!"

Reaching for the thin sheath covering from the dresser, he rolls it on quickly. Phil fumbles back on top of me, his snake hissing at the door of my entrance. "Alena," he moans, sweating, kissing me vehemently, his manhood at the surface of my lady garden. "Let's do it tonight, baby. Let's make love."

"Who would've thought that one frivolous kiss would have led to a night like this," he rumbled.

"Get off me," I cried, as the weight of his frame pinned me to the floor. "I never asked for this!"

"It's far too late for tears, Alena," he growled in my ear. "So just relax, and keep quiet... I'm coming inside."

"No!" I hollered. "Stop!"

I felt myself fading as he took me hard. My body was not ready for this.

"Stop!" I bellowed, trying for the last time before I collapsed or died.

"When I'm done, bitch!" He groaned mercilessly.

"Get off me!" I wailed. "You're hurting me!"

I could feel myself slipping away. His potency was far too much for my small, powerless body to handle. Daddy flashed into my mind. He transported strength into my bones. I had to get out! I had to escape.

Phillip is on top of me; he is ready to take me...

"No!" I holler, shoving him off in a dirty cold sweat. "NO! GET OFF ME! PLEASE, I BEG YOU!"

"Baby!" His face is horrified. "What did I do? What is it?"

I cannot let him go any further; *he* is still in my head, in my body, creeping into my psyche, coming between our love. I cry. The tears are again rolling down my visage.

Swiftly, Phillip sweeps me into his arms. "Shh," he says, holding my shaking shell, pressing his lips gently to my cheek. "It's okay. I'm not going to hurt you, baby," he says softly, pulling off the sheath with one hand, and tossing it in the waste bin.

I am still trembling in his embrace. "It's not that I don't adore you, Phillip," I whisper, staring into his eyes. "It's just... I don't know when I'll be ready, absolutely ready, or when I'll be totally rid of *him*... I cannot get him out of my head."

Growling with rage and unequivocal hatred towards the malevolent man who is keeping us apart, Phillip grasps my face, pulling it to his, and with our eyes aligned, noses rubbing, lips grazing, he breaks down and cries, the pain pouring out of his soul. His tears fall wearily on the top of my pink nose and onto my curved eyelashes. For an hour we remain this way, face-to-face, heart-to-heart, lamenting my past and its damage on our relationship. We don't know what else to do. No words are sufficient. We are in too much pain to speak.

If I'm not ready by the time he asks me again, then maybe we are not meant to be together. Maybe then, we should consider calling it quits. Maybe I should allow him to move on and find a woman who can give him the physical love he craves. I can't bear to lose Phillip, but equally, I can't bear to see him suffering in this way. It is simply breaking my heart.

Gradually, he drifts off to sleep, his tear-stained face next to mine, his length floppy, his heart punctured. Silently, I continue to sob, trying to appear to be asleep. For a moment, I open one eye; I am curious. Lifting up the covers, I take a good look at his healthy equipment, his big, strong, and powerful manhood. I must be sick if I don't want Phil, my long-term boyfriend, to take me. Perhaps I should answer my therapist's calls and confirm I'm attending my therapy session tomorrow. But in truth, I want to solve this problem on my own.

Taking a shallow breath, my eyes begin to close and I start to fall asleep. I hear Phillip murmuring. I smile, thanking God that he is sticking by me, for now, and loving me, in spite of everything.

REFLECTIONS

I am on an East Midland train, the 10.59 a.m. express, a high-speed railway link between Leicester and London, St Pancras. My head is a ball of confusion, a thick mesh of knots. My consciousness is tangled in this dangerous web of complex thoughts. I release a puff of tense air, my eyes are glazed, teeth throbbing, heart beating rapidly in my chest. Leaning my head back onto the cushioned headrest, I try to fall asleep. The train bounces and hums irritatingly, the loud chatter hurting my tired ears. My head sinks further into the headrest. I yawn and begin to drift off to sleep.

After a few minutes, my eyes spring open, and impulsively, my neck rotates to the left, leisurely panning across that small section of the carriage. I am fascinated by the other train passengers and take pleasure in observing a fatigued-looking Indian man catching some winks, two older West Indian women engaging in idle, chatter, and a young, quintessentially English businessman in a sharp grey suit, probably on a 100,000-pound-a-year salary, who is pretending to be studious, scanning through The Leicester Gazette, but peering up from his paper intermittently to see who might be noticing his scholarliness. I smile broadly, admiring the joyous diversity of Leicester society, and then something else catches my eye. Across the way from me, in the adjoining seats in front, is a young attractive couple, no older than twenty-one years old, a similar age to Phillip and I, who are kissing and cuddling, displaying their affection openly in the train carriage. I don't know how I missed this lustful pair when I skimmed over the train a short while ago. Enchanted by this passionate expression of love, I smile sweetly.

Silently, I observe the twosome, trying to keep my gawking discreet. They see me looking at them, and the woman smirks, groaning in her man's ear deeply, which encourages me to ogle the couple even more. I'm interested; I can't help but stare. They are intriguing, and I am savouring the sound and sight of those deep sapping kisses. She breathes clumsily as he starts to explore her long, elegant neck, pecking and titillating her small chin. I cannot control the feeling of envy at seeing this couple so happy. Secretly, I wish that Phillip and I could be this way: sensual, liberated, enjoying each other in private as well as in public. I yearn for him to touch me until I simply melt into his arms, into his body. Right now, I can almost imagine the feeling. In reality though, we are crumbling, falling apart. We might never reach completion. Our deep emotions might always swirl aimlessly around a dark, flaming bedroom, and our desires may remain unsatisfied and unfulfilled. It's not him who is too scared to go down this road, it is me.

I'm a beautiful wreck, a young woman who refuses to accept professional intervention. My therapist, last time we spoke, almost a month ago, was comfortable labelling me as a social agoraphobe and a genophobe. Doctor Hannah is relaxed about using these terms whenever I go to therapy sessions. It's all well and good having medical terminology for such problems as mine, but I just can't listen to the doctor's recommendations and these limiting and boxed definitions of my issues. I am not her freakish study project, and I don't appreciate meaningless jargon, which seems to have been extracted from an old medical dictionary. If I listen to her and believe that I am what she tells me I am, then I am already doomed.

Unlike many people with these problems, I cannot be cured by a professional who simply wishes to strip bare my dense and complex layers in a safe and controlled environment, with four constricting walls and an ominous black chair. I do not appreciate the antidotes of a cynical and partially sardonic therapist, who charges fifty pounds per hour, and tells me acerbically how I can 'progress' my life. This used to work for me, but not anymore. I'm not a naïve seventeen-year-old who takes everything she is told as gospel; I am wiser now. I'm nineteen, and I am guarded, untrusting, and defensive. I have had enough of being somebody's patient, somebody's case study, somebody's analytical project, who is easy to mould and shape and manipulate. And yes, I already know that I am mentally screwed up. I feel as though I'm beyond help now. The only person who can really assist me now is God. And if He gives up on me, that's it. I should just make life easy for myself and become a nun or a hermit, and live in isolation, where I will not have to worry about the last time I attempted to sleep with my long-term boyfriend or how I felt when the voice of my high school attacker came rushing into my consciousness. Oh, give me a break! That shit is old! I can't count how many times Doctor Hannah has asked me these questions. She might as well make a broken record out of it!

From the very beginning, I was always Doctor Hannah's very unique client. I never did like my problems to be paraded around the therapy room, like an elephant in a tutu trying to dance ballet steps on a glass coffee table. In our most recent sessions, I gave her short, snappy answers where she had no scope to develop her questions or probe me any further. Age and experience has taught me how to outwit my therapist to some degree, which I take great pleasure in doing. I've wanted to get Doctor Hannah out of my hair for seven months now. I don't want her prying into my life anymore. I don't need her telling me how to live my life either. I'm a lone ranger, and I like dealing with my problems by myself. It is more liberating, rewarding, and less people judge you. I endeavour to wrap my hellacious predicament in cling film and roll it up inside a carpet, hiding it away, to help me return to some kind of normality. Then, I wish to kick it hard in the nuts, real hard, and curse at it, whilst it is in the hallway of Third Floor Ridley House. When I'm ready, I can eventually propel my issues out the door, and out of my life, forever. This is *my* unique approach of dealing with the past. Not the most effective strategy, some people might say, but this is the path I've chosen.

As my mind weaves in and out of the past, I glide my hand over the transparent window. The heat and perspiration from my palm makes the pane cloud slightly and steam with sensuous joy. There is a fading, shivering reflection in the glass, a faint ghost staring back at me. She looks just like me. Except it is not me. I am bemused; my face scrunches up into a thick blanket of bewilderment. I peer harder into the glass, the span of my hand pressing callously into the spectre's shadow.

Now, I can identify the unfamiliarly distinguishable profile; the semblance is clear. It is seventeen-year-old Alena trapped in the window, and she is crying, begging me to let her out of the treacherous looking glass. I can't allow her to be free in this world. She is meant for another place, another time. Squeezing my eyes shut, I take a huge breath, wishing her away, back into her own realm.

Disappearing into thin air, vanishing into the portal, which leads to home, seventeen-year-old Alena swirls back into the past. I blow a sweet kiss, bidding her farewell. I hope she will be gone forever so that I can finally move on with my life, and move things to the next natural stage with Phil.

A tap on the shoulder startles me. I jolt forward and look up at the stranger standing before me.

"Alena, is that you?"

I stare deep into the old man's grey eyes. He is unfamiliar. I do not recollect him.

"You don't remember me, do you?" He genuflects. His old, tired body and gleaming white beard roll toward me.

"Who are you?" My face is blank, empty, insipid.

"I'm Mr. Bernard, your former biology teacher. Remember me from Wentworthy High?"

As if my brain travels back two years, I recall his dead and weary expression, those eyes marked with crow's feet, and that crinkled forehead.

"Oh, yes, hi," I say cordially, greeting him casually like the average nineteen-year-old does, informally saluting an old acquaintance they'd previously forgotten.

"How are you, Alena?" he asks interested.

Insouciantly, I shrug my shoulders. "I'm doing okay," I say, telling a complete lie. "How are you, Mr. Bernard?"

His grey eyes gaze into my face. "I'm good," he says smiling. "Just get a spot of arthritis in my left knee every now and again. But apart from that, I'm well, all in one piece."

I frown. "Sorry to hear about the creaky bones, Sir."

He pats me on the shoulder. "Never mind. I'm still holding together."

Engagingly, his gaze rests firmly upon my pale countenance. I respectively give him all of my attention.

Mr. Bernard gives me a half smile. "Alena, are you at university now?"

I find myself becoming more comfortable in his presence. "Yes I am, Sir."

His face scrunches up as he thinks. "At which university do you study?"

"The University of Capendale," I tell him, replying with confidence.

"Interesting, hmm," he replies, a strange grin rising on his reddening visage. "Capendale University."

My expression is stark. I look him straight in the eye. "Yes… And I'm studying English there."

"English, hmm, intriguing," he says almost dubiously. "A surprising choice considering your history."

Soaking up his ambiguous statement, my green orbs expand. "What d'ya mean by that, Sir?"

He hesitates slightly before proceeding. "The experiences you had in high school should have put you off studying English."

Now my intelligence is insulted. My guard is back up. I grow suspicious of my old teacher, who I had thought was a pleasant character. He is not the same kind man I knew in high school. It is very clear to me that this man has a rotten interior, an evil agenda. When you scratch beneath the surface, one is likely to feel the true effects of his poisoned smiles, malevolent stares, and his dark, hollow and ostentatious *regard* for others.

"My experiences?" I say sternly. "To which do you refer?"

Uncouthly, he laughs. "Come now, Alena. Let's not play naïve. We are two adults talking."

I continue to play a game with him to tease his opinions of me out in the open.

"I had many experiences at high school. You will need to be far more direct and specific, Mr. Bernard."

His guise is showing cracks, his true nature seeping out. A more serious and sinister expression deflates his previously amused phizog.

"Your involvement with Stanley Hawthorne should have discouraged you from studying English. You clearly do not have the emotional depth or intelligence, Alena."

Venomously, I glare into his eyes. "You have no business judging me. You are a teacher, not a judge."

"If I were a judge," he says, snarling at me. "Stanley would not be behind bars, serving a five year jail sentence!"

I am absolutely astounded by the extent of his unprofessionalism and downright ignorance.

"Stanley harmed me. He earned his place in prison!"

A deep repulsion possesses his features. "The bottom line is you encouraged his flirtatious behaviour for months, right up until the day *it* happened…"

Lunging forward, I growl in his face. "I was an innocent child with a silly schoolgirl crush. I did not know he was *like that*. I did not realise *that* was his intention all along. And Maths tuition is what I went to his house for that evening, nothing else. He's pure evil – he is to blame for *everything!*"

"Oh, please! What a story!" He hisses.

Mr. Bernard's voice plummets into a whisper as a few passengers begin to stare at us, engaging their zealous ears in our heated conversation. "You must have known what he wanted, that's why you went to his house that evening in a short red skirt, Miss Pavlis."

Wrathfully, I slam my fist on the chair. "No, I didn't know what he wanted. He should never have wanted *that*. He was my teacher, a respected member of staff. We'd planned a study session. I went to his house straight from school, in my *red uniform* and with my satchel. It was meant to be a regular study session on a normal evening. I never knew he would do something like that."

He cackles viciously, throwing his head back. "Some seventeen year olds don't act like children, Alena, and so they find themselves in tricky situations."

I launch myself into his face. He flinches, a little taken aback by my brazen approach. "You disgust me!" I scream. "How did the likes of you ever become a teacher?"

Mr. Bernard squints, scanning my face with his poisonous eyes.

"Alena," he states firmly, directing my pupils, summoning my attention. "You followed Mr. Hawthorne around the classroom for months, and hounded him after school, until he acknowledged and admired you. What did you think this was going to lead to?"

Gathering myself together, I am determined not to let this fiend make me cry. I close my lids for a moment, thinking of Becca, reminding myself of how we transformed into strong Amazon women in the kitchen that evening in the midst of my ghastly panic attack.

Recalling that feeling of power surging through my core, I breathe slowly, in and out, in and out, growing more powerful with every exhalation. The Amazonian woman within my heart beats decidedly in my chest. I will be damned if I let this man defeat me. I'm formidable, indomitable. I *will not* have a panic attack here. Quickly, I go into a zone, surrounding myself with flames of courage. I know Mr Bernard is throwing insults at me, but I block out his voice until the fire inside my soul is bold, gutsy and unwavering. My eyes fly open; I am ready for him.

"You led him on. You've only got yourself to blame!"

Holding the tears back, I remain strong, steadfast, determined. I won't give this man the pleasure of seeing me break down. "Shut up," I bellow, stamping my feet on the ground in fury. "Stop this bullshit talk!"

Mr. Bernard laughs hysterically. Right at that moment, I could have killed him for laughing at me. In spite of my rage, I must stay centred. Must keep a poker face for as long as possible. I will not give him the satisfaction of knowing he has *almost* got the better of me. My eyes focus on him. I am dangerous, like a tiger.

A scornful smirk emerges on his mien. His sight is filling with demonic rage. "I can't believe the court bought your story, Alena. They should have seen the kiss that you and Stanley shared in the classroom earlier that day. That may have altered the verdict!"

Completely losing my temper, I boil over. Snarling, I slap Mr. Bernard across the face, hard. He winces, but endures the hit. Mr. Bernard knows he deserves it. Malignantly, he grinds his teeth, a glint of evil flashing in his eyes. I stay focused on him, my attention affixed to his iniquitous face. I speak no words. It is obvious that the irked fiend understands the universal language of belligerence.

"The liaison," he continues rubbing his sore cheek.

"Get it into your thick skull – there was no liaison. The kiss was a huge mistake, and I regret not reporting him to the head teacher. Right after we kissed, he invited me back to his house for extra tuition. I didn't think anything of it. That same night, I foolishly went to his place, thinking that he'd forgotten about the kiss. What I thought would be a maths tuition session, was not. He lured me there, and then attacked me. Stop pretending that you don't know what really happened," I say.

"The unfortunate encounter," he reluctantly corrects himself. "It implicated many people and nearly crippled the entire school! Social Services came down on us like a ton of bricks, for a 'catalogue of failures,' and then the press almost finished us off! Just a few weeks after you transferred to another school, they forced me out, ordered me to resign or face their wrath. I lost my job because of you, Alena!"

I weave into the depths of his animosity, trying to get to the core of his anger. "I didn't get you fired, Mr. Bernard. Why would they fire you over what happened?" I pause for a moment, thinking deeply, and then I continue. "Well, judging by the depraved opinions you have, I am not surprised they kicked your sorry arse out. The school needed to protect themselves from such a liability as your filth."

He is scared by my frankness. He can't challenge it; he knows I am right. Warily, he leans back in the seat to escape my watchful eyes, yet his ireful expression remains.

"Stanley was my best friend, still is. That's why they targeted me after the shit hit the fan!"

I laugh roguishly. "Everything you've said to defend him, and the degenerate views you have expressed, now make sense. No *normal person* would advocate the work of a brute!"

"Stanley is not a brute. You practically threw yourself at him! The man didn't stand a chance. Stupid, girl! You silly little girls never understand what your feminine wiles can do to a man!"

Heftily, he bangs his fist into the grey metal armrest on the left side of his body, the side furthest away from me. But still his behaviour is frightening, alarming. Nevertheless, I remain composed, staring at him full in the face. I will not be intimidated by this insolent and hateful man.

"Hmm. I was the innocent victim, yet you are blaming me for what happened. You see me as a harlot, don't you?" I shout aggressively. Inside I'm shaking, on the verge of giving in to a panic attack. "Say it then! Admit it, you pig."

"No comment!" he roars. "I'm not falling into that trap, oh no!"

I clasp my hands together, and say a little prayer out loud. "Thank you God, for putting that demon behind bars for five long years! That's where he belongs, in a cage, where he cannot hurt anybody else!"

Forcefully, his arms clamp down on either side of my slim shoulders. He shakes me. I tremble, afraid he might attempt to hit me. Stay composed, Alena. Stay composed. Do not have a panic attack. Breathe. *Do not* have a panic attack. Breathe...

"He did nothing terrible, not really!" The fiend replies after much delay, as if he is now questioning Mr. Hawthorne's innocence.

I find the strength to shake him off my body. His grip recedes.

"Irrespective of what you think, I know that justice is done!" I holler, my voice swirling around the carriage. "Justice is done!"

Mr. Bernard growls. His behaviour no longer has an effect on me. I have unflinching determination. I find the vigour to continue, growling back at him defiantly.

I feel the train tremor as it bumps and grinds into a station. Sharply, it stops. I look up and out of the window. We are at Bedford Rail Station. The demon's minion twitches and starts to rise from his seat. So, this is where the fiend lives? Interesting.

"Shall I give Stanley a message? I'm visiting him this evening," he says, getting up fully from the chair, his tall frame towering over me.

Evilly, I smile, seeing my chance for minimal revenge. "Yes, please do give him a message!"

"And what would you like me to say to him?" the beast asks, moving two paces forward, in the direction of the exit door.

Innocently, I look up at him, imagining a halo circling brightly aloft my head. "Tell him to go to hell!" I beam, the reflection of the sun radiates on my face. Chortling to myself, I feel a great sense of relief lifting my spirit. I am light, fluffy, weightless.

Mr. Bernard shakes his head in disgust and walks off.

As he is in mid-flow of exiting the train, surprisingly, he turns back, glaring into my eyes, and brazenly declares, "He loved you, Alena. Twisted as it was, he loved you. Now live with yourself, knowing that."

My triumph is short-lived. I judder, feeling a heavy impression on my shoulders and back, and I sob profoundly into my hands. I struggle to breathe and collapse, falling in a heap on the dual seat. The train whisks me away. Everything goes black, and I pass out. Suddenly, I hear an awful din, and I wake from my dark sleep. This is my stop, London, St Pancras. I let in air, my lungs filling up with clean fresh oxygen. Grabbing my bag from the floor, I leap off the train and run onto the platform, watching the express train disappear before my very eyes. Sprinting up the stairs, I dash to the next platform and catch the 12.14 p.m. railway link to Surrey.

Galloping up the stairs, I tap out my oyster train pass, and breeze through the exit door. Free at last. I soak in the refreshing air for a while, appreciating nature, appreciating God.

I continue my pursuit home. Taking off like a new rocket, I run down the road, cross the traffic lights, race through the park, dart out of the gates, speed past the lamp posts, bins, bus stops, people, houses… Then I'm home, at last!

Impatiently, I bang on the familiar green door. I wait for a few moments, and wait a few more. Then, as I expected, the door flies open.

"Mummy!"

Her embrace is warm, vivacious.

"Hello darling." She pecks the top of my forehead.

"Oh, mummy, I've missed you so much!" I tell her fervently, holding her close. Lovingly, she kisses me on the cheek.

I shed a tear.

"I missed you too, pumpkin. It's been seven months since I last saw you. Thank God you're finally home!"

"Yeah, I know! It's been a long time!"

"How is college?"

I nod. "It's totally different from high school, and being away from home is quite challenging. But it's alright, mum."

"Glad to hear that, hunnie." She looks me up and down. "You look thinner. Are you eating?"

I laugh. "Of course I am!"

"Maybe it's love that's keeping you thin." She winks. "How is Phillip?"

"He's okay. He is staying with his parents this week, over the Easter period."

"Why didn't you invite him over for Easter, Alena? I've been hearing about this Phillip Gregson for months. I am dying to meet your handsome fella." Her lips curl sweetly into a smile. "I haven't even seen what he looks like. Can I at least see a picture of him?"

"So many questions, mum, gosh, slow down. Please!" I bite my lip anxiously. "I want to take things one step at a time. Sometime in the future I will bring him over to meet you. Okay? For now, you will have to be satisfied with a photo."

"Well, then," mum smiles. "Let me see him!"

"Alright," I say slowly, in a way to calm her down. But she is not calm at all; she's jumping up and down on the spot, desperate to catch a glimpse of this man who is so important to me.

Whipping out my phone, I scroll through my picture gallery. Mum watches me as I skim through the photos. I can feel her breath on my fingertips. Impatiently, she is tapping her foot on the metal doorstep. I find a good one, before mum grabs my phone in eager anticipation. Selecting the best photo of all, where he has his top off, flexing his muscles, I show it to mum. Prizing the mobile out of my hand, staring into the display, she makes a funny sound.

Instantaneously, she blushes. "Oh, my word! Golly gosh!"

A look of alarm dashes across my face and my heart beats ferociously in my chest. I snatch my phone back from her, sliding it into my jean pocket. "Are you okay, mum?"

She nods, unable to speak.

"What's wrong? Do you not approve of him because he is...?"

Pressing her head into the door frame, mum chortles. "Of course I approve. He is cute, dark and muscly! I am just a little surprised that he is your boyfriend."

I chuck a pair of feisty hands on my hips. "Why is that

then?"

Mum hesitates, choosing her words carefully. "I just figured you'd go for a less virile looking guy, considering your obvious difficulties with…"

"Mother!" I exclaim.

She shrugs her shoulders. "What?"

"Phillip's not like that, he's cool."

"Is he really?" Mum replies, her tone dripping with sarcasm.

"Yes, he is," I bark.

Mum giggles raucously, cupping a curious hand under her chin. "For how long d'ya think he will be 'cool,' Alena?"

I am bemused. "What is that supposed to mean?"

Patting me on the arm, mum smirks. "All men are *like that* eventually, Alena. It's genetic!"

I roll my eyes to heaven. What the heck is she jabbering on about?

Firmly, mum holds me by the wrists. Her grip is hard, yet gentle. "Joking aside, I need you to understand that life is not a Hollywood movie."

I shrug my shoulders, completely perplexed.

"Put your cards on the table," mum advises me. "Tell Phillip the *real* truth about what happened, so he doesn't expect too much too soon. Be honest with him."

"Phillip is cool mum, but not that cool. It's best that I don't say anything about it. He'll probably judge me if I tell him who I really am." I feel the anxiety beginning to well up in my core as I speak.

"Honey, doing this is a step towards banishing the demons. You can't let your past trauma win. Phillip is a good guy. I can tell by his picture. I know it will take time before you are ready to go to the next stage with him, but in time you'll feel comfortable with taking things further. If he is the right guy, he'll be prepared to wait, and more importantly, he won't judge you. He will support you through this. Talk to Phil. Don't be ashamed or afraid of telling him who you really are."

My tears are overwhelming. Mum cradles me, making me feel so safe in her arms. "Mummy, I am really scared of telling him. And deep inside, I still feel so dirty. I don't believe I deserve happiness or for anything good to happen to me in life. What's more, Mr. Bernard thinks I'm a whore, he told me in the vilest of ways on the train."

Mum espies my eyes. Her gaze is tender, warm, deep. "That man is as malignant as Mr. Hawthorne. Since the trial, I despised him. I knew he was scum of the earth." Grabbing my cheeks, she pulls my face to hers. "Now listen, Alena, my baby. You are not a slut, or a whore, or anything else that ignorant people might say. It wasn't your fault; it was all his, all his. You're not to blame, baby. Please understand that. And you deserve to be happy, more than anybody I have ever known. I mean it. Happy endings aren't just on the big screen, baby. People like you can achieve happiness, too. True happiness."

"You really believe that, mummy?" I whisper.

"Yes," she says, commandingly. "I know it. I feel it. Now own that happiness. It is yours to take. Don't let anyone steal it away. It is God's gift to you. Hold it close, never lose sight of it. You hear me?"

"Yeah, mummy, I promise," I say, wailing. "I promise."

"Good. I hope ya gave him what for on the train. Did you?"

I nod my head, my eyelashes grazing hers. "Yes, mum. I cussed him out, gave him what for."

"That's my girl," she says in a hushed tone. "Don't let anyone define you, Alena. Nobody. We define ourselves. Understand?"

"Yes, mum," I say, gripping onto her beige cardigan for dear life.

Repeatedly, she kisses me on the forehead, and my expression lightens. I wipe away the tears, a smile forming on my mien.

Mum lets go of me, leaving me to stand upright on the porch. A wave of humour streams through the atmosphere, and I let it seep into my soul.

"Are you going to invite me in, or shall I stay out here on the porch for the whole week?"

Dabbing her tears, mum chuckles. "Of course not, this is still your home, baby."

I give mum a wink. "Thanks mum, for being there for me and for… being you."

"Of course, honey." She smiles broadly, reaching forward to stroke my hair. "I will always be here for you, Alena. You're my daughter, and I love you."

My eyes well up again. "I love you too, mummy."

Quickly, she takes hold of my bag and guides me inside, and together, we shut out the world, savouring the joyousness and specialness of this heavenly mother and daughter relationship. This is, by far, the best relationship in the history of the universe, and the least complicated – at least for me.

THE BAR

I enter Red Raven, the on campus bar. Immediately the late afternoon sun fades, and darkness descends, swooping upon the tavern like a crow. The breeze, grim, crestfallen, engulfs my form. The smell of deadly liquor impales my nostrils; a feeling of nausea spasms my throat. Then a devilish chill penetrates the depths of my soul. The riotous sound of students conversing, shouting, and a roaring wave of noise pierces my eardrums. The vicious sound of a glass smashing into the ground, and the stomping of persistent feet increases my heart rate and stifles my breathing. My palms are sweating, head thumping. I start to feel woozy. Spinning in circles – the bar begins to revolve. Seats, students, and goblets appear distorted, blurred and fuzzy. The large bar reduces in size. People are drawing nearer and nearer to me; the tavern is birling out of control. Undergraduates are whirling around me, spiralling dizzily in, and out, of focus.

"Want a drink, darling?" An eerie voice croaks, crawling into my ears.

"No," I holler, my eyes circling muzzily around the room.

My head begins to reel, and I'm unable to locate the

individual who just spoke. Oh gosh, I feel awful, and so frightfully disoriented.

All of a sudden, the bar feels crowded and claustrophobic. Everyone seems to be merging into one another. The sight of so many people is horrifying, and causing deep anxiety to well inside me; a fear that rises from my toes all the way up to my brain. My airways are closing; I feel lightheaded, as if I'm going to pass out. I don't know why I came to the college bar this afternoon, by myself, to get a beer. What was I thinking? It is clear that I am not yet ready to venture out in public places without someone accompanying me. I am prone to anxiety attacks where large numbers of people assemble. This is the reason why Phil and I rarely go out socialising, and seldom go off campus together: to restaurants, bars, and clubs. We only go grocery shopping together once a week and the odd occasional clothes shopping trip. I can't handle people surrounding me, closing me in. It is horrible not being able to enjoy normal life, going out, making lots of friends, and it can be so isolating and lonely sometimes in my problematic world. Thank God I have Phil and Becca, otherwise I would be miserable.

Just as I'm wheezing hard, losing the sense of gravity, and on the verge of a frightening blackout, warm, sturdy arms envelope my body, keeping my feet firmly on the ground, making me feel incredibly safe and secure. I know these hands; these hands have touched me before, bolstered me before. And I know that smell, that charming whiff of Bleu De Chanel. It is divine.

Slowly, I turn my head to the side, to confirm my hunch. From the corner of my eye, I see a powerful, dark figure staring pensively at my face. His gaze is intense, and assuring. I burst into an elated smile as Phillip's masculine frame presses against my body, holding me tight. Turning around fully, I resume our closeness from a different angle, an angle that allows me to feel his manhood gently prodding my crotch. This I can handle. I relish him teasing me in this natural, involuntary fashion. As I bind my arms around his solid, square shoulders, he pulls me closer, holding me steadfast around the waist.

Kissing me soothingly, he massages my lips with the fullness of his potency.

"You sneaked out and came to the bar without me," he says, surprised.

"Yeah, I did," I reply, biting my bottom lip, accepting that he ought to scold me for going out of my comfort zone.

"I am so proud of you, baby, for taking this giant step. This is real progress."

I'm stunned and joyous at the same time, because he did not wish to reprimand me, but to instead congratulate me on being brave and taking this courageous step in the right direction. Yet there is a dangerous smirk on his face – a look that speaks a thousand words. Going to the bar alone is one thing; being intimate with him is completely another. Though I can tell by the concentration of his stare that he is making these two separate things into the same, when they both should be seen in isolation.

I inhale deeply, pushing my treacherous anxieties into the subterranean chamber of my soul. I want to enjoy this small victory for a few moments without the voice of fear wounding this special feeling of marginal triumph.

***

Standing outside the bar in a flimsy blouse, I find myself shivering. Phil encompasses me, wanting to warm up my core. His warmth, however, is not enough to stop me from trembling. In spite of the cold, a pair of zealous green eyes, full of pure glassy adoration, glide into their attractive target. Seeing the growing concern in his countenance, I feel a shred of guilt. No longer can I keep lying to my boyfriend. It's time I fessed up. Phillip Gregson needs to know the truth, about me, about who I am.

I had gone to Mr. Hawthorne's house for extra Maths tuition that evening. Without thinking, I did not tell my mother where I was going, and I didn't inform Emma, my best friend, or any of my other schoolmates as to my whereabouts. Of course, I had a crush on Mr. Hawthorne. Most girls did. However, that wasn't the reason I went to his house. I was falling behind, and my maths grades were suffering, due to a personal family tragedy that I rarely talked about. Naturally, I thought I would have been safe at his house. After all, I knew him well, he was my teacher, and I was the most popular girl in school – admired by everyone. No one would harm the most popular girl in school. C'mon I was the queen bee, untouchable.

A frivolous kiss that Mr. Hawthorne and I shared during class, earlier that day, had already been forgotten. By me, anyhow.

Sauntering to his front door, I pressed the buzzer. Strangely enough, the door was unlocked. I ventured inside.

"Sir," I said, "Are you here? Remember, we have that session today."

From nowhere he appeared, coming up from behind me, not acting anything like he did in class. He was acting really weird and the potent smell of his aftershave poisoned my nostrils.

He hugged me, his breath creeping up the side of my neck.

"I've been waiting for you, Alena," he whispered. "Waiting patiently for us to start our session."

"Okay, Sir." I was rather perplexed by his peculiar behaviour. "Let's get started."

"Before we do, can I show you something exciting, Alena?"

"What is it?" I asked hesitantly.

A drum so loud, a noise alarming me to danger, banged in my head. Quickly, I made for the door. Anticipating my move, he grabbed me by the arm, ushering me to the living room.

Like a bird of prey, his eyes descended on my body.

"I know how you feel about me, Alena, and it's okay, 'cos I feel the same way."

"How I feel about you?" I yelled, shaking my head. "Clearly, we're not on the same page, Sir."

"Yes," he groaned, "we are."

Fiddling with his trouser belt buckle, he looked me straight in the eye.

"Oh, shit! You're crazy!" I screamed. "I'm getting out of here!"

Speedily, with my heart beating frenetically in my chest, I ran towards the exit, desperate to escape this nightmare.

Completely shelling his 'teacher' façade, Mr. Hawthorne turned into a behemoth, running after me and pulling me back into his clutches. As he hurled my schoolbag across the room, and he wrestled me to the ground like a wild cheetah, my whole life flashed before me.

After my ordeal, a white towel swaddled around my battered body, as if attempting to restore a fragment of my dignity. Lying flat on the carpet, shaking and crying, I did not know if I would survive.

A flicker of evil flashed in his eyes one last time. He had every intention of finishing me off. With the final grain of strength I had, I kicked him in the face, and escaped, only by a whisker. Running to the main road, running for my life, with the monster trailing behind me, I staggered as far as the tube station, trying to reach home. Dressed in nothing more than a bath towel, blood spurting from every orifice, I collapsed on the pavement. That moment, I thought would be my final one. Then a voice, and the soothing hands of Jermaine Gregson, stopped me from perishing.

I remember his name, and the expression of horror that polluted his face.

"What did he do to you?" He had asked, exasperatedly.

"Just call my mum, the ambulance, and the police, please," I begged.

My eyes leap into Phillip's, stabbing his sight with determined persistence. I see Jermaine reflecting in his eyes. They have the same black hair, the same expression, a similar nose, that distinct West Indian twang. Jermaine is tall, dark, and elegant, just like Phillip. They could pass as twins.

"Phil, I haven't been completely honest with you."

His nose twiddles, arching with intrigue. "About what?"

"A North London schoolgirl was attacked by her teacher two years ago, and found by a passerby near Brent Cross Station," I say, struggling to get out the words.

Befuddled by my sudden outburst, Phil's eyes squeeze into two small lemons. "Yes, I heard about that. It was terrible. But why is this relevant, Alena?"

"I can tell you the date it happened. It was February 12th, 5.15 pm, precisely. That day was chilly, freezing, around 5 degrees. The sound of traffic bustled and whistled in the road, the screams of a young girl cutting through the air…"

Involuntarily, his body jolts forward. "How do you know all this? Only my cousin and the girl he found that night could possibly know all of those details."

Shaking my head, I quiver and begin to cry. My tears are ferocious, angry, weathered. "I know all those details, Phillip, because I am that girl. I'm the young woman Jermaine saved that evening near the station," Breathing haphazardly, the pain ruptures the glass in my dark green gems.

Gripped by total disbelief, he laughs in shock. A quivering hand swathes his open mouth. Phillip ambles toward me, pulling me into his chest. "No, Alena. It couldn't have been you. A random stranger attacked you in the bushes on the way home from school that night. Remember?"

My face turns to stone. I fly into his eyes, almost smashing his sight with my resolve. "I lied, Phillip. The circumstances of the attack I changed, to hide the truth from you."

"No!" he says, shaking his head profusely. "You're confused! Your attacker that evening, on February 12th at 5.15 pm, couldn't have been Mr. Stanley Hawthorne, the notorious teacher that everyone in the North London area was talking about. No, another vile bastard hurt you."

"Phillip," I say breathlessly, "It *was* him! I thought you would've worked it out by now. My face was on the London news and in all the papers."

A look of sheer agony crinkles his forehead. "I was in juvie at that time. I didn't watch the news or read the newspaper headlines. Jermaine happened to tell me the story when I got out. The story of a girl named Alena, who he saved from a terrible ordeal. The other girl had the same first name as you, that is all. Your attackers were two totally different people. It's purely coincidental that both incidents happened on exactly the same night."

"No, it isn't a coincidence, Phil! Me and that girl are the same person!"

My breathing is laboured and heavy. His breathing is profound, cavernous, and gravelly. As he pulls me close to him, my breasts press into his sturdy frame. Tears are flowing from his visage. Finally, he realises that I'm telling the truth.

"Oh, Jesus! Oh, God! I can't believe that *you* are the girl who went through that agony."

Our noses caress, our pupils are parallel. His gaze is soft, tender, yet potent.

"I was left in a bad way. I didn't think I was going to make it," I say, whispering into his jaw.

"Thank God Jermaine found you when he did," he murmurs.

Woefully, I cry into my hands. "If it wasn't for Jermaine, I wouldn't be alive!"

"I know!" he cries.

Moving in to kiss me, opening my quavering palms, his breathing is carnal and clumsy. "Why didn't you tell me the truth, Alena? Why didn't you tell me who you really were?"

Looking up at him, I welcome the softness of his squidgy red lips. Trembling, I answer his question.

"I did not want you judging, or pitying me," I say, susurrating between kisses. "Most people do both, and it infuriates me."

Kneading his lips into my cheek, rubbing himself into the crux of my smarting pain, he laments. "I would never judge or pity you, Alena, I'm not that kind of guy. You know me." A spark of jealousy ignites in his deep chocolate irises. "Does Becca know the truth?"

"Yes." I nod. "She does. But she doesn't know that I kept it from you."

Phil is upset. He holds his anger in. "At least now I truly understand why your fears are so deep-rooted. We can work through this, as a team, as partners. I'm gonna support you, okay?"

Chewing on the nervous anxiety, at the base of my bottom lip, I sigh. Phil smiles falteringly, stroking the ridge of my mouth.

"Thanks for having my back, baby."

"I will always have your back. You're my girl."

"Good to know." I burst into a smile. "I love you, Phil."

His lips tremor. "I love you too, Alena."

The moment I confessed my secret, I thought that Phillip would end it with me. I was wrong. I totally misjudged him. He's not like most guys. He doesn't wish to condemn me or treat me like 'damaged goods'. All he wants to do is kiss me, hold me, be there for me.

Forgetting about the frosty sting of the whirling wind, the heavy crunching of leaves as they scrape across the ground, and the commotion coming from the bar, we focus on each other, intently. No chance is there for the darkness swirling around the tavern to enter our hearts. Only love is able to penetrate through us. Our lips lock, we caress, moaning passionately under our breath. Letting the emotion take him, Phil holds me closer, kissing me deeply, patting my hair. His warm breath soothes the anguish, which is beginning to rise inside of me. In his embrace, I am safe and secure. I don't ever want him to let me go.

KEEPING CONFIDENCE

Provoked by curiosity, I run my index finger over the luminous poster, which is hanging lopsided on the wall adjacent to my lecture hall, Room T3. Something about the design, the bright colours and snappy title, 'Could this be you?' twinkles my eyes with excitement. Closer, I peer at the eye-catching advertisement, whilst waiting for the fashionably late Phillip, and the ridiculously tardy Becca, to meet me for class. When I read what the poster says, it soon dawns on me that God has thrown me a lifeline:

COOLETTE SINGERS! THE BIG AUDITION!

If you're a sassy songstress in the Freshers' year, and think you can sing, come and try out for the new on campus singing group. We want you! Sing a famous song or some of your own material. It's up to you. The best singer on the night will secure lead vocals in all the summer term's shows.

Date of audition: Tuesday May 16th.
Time: 5pm sharp! Don't be late!
Location: Elderflower Building,
Room: E30

A singing audition, in five weeks' time – aah, music to my ears. I used to love singing so much back in high school, and was a member of High Note Harmony – Wentworthy's renowned all girl choir. Before my life got complicated, I often performed solos in practice sessions and in school shows. We were even entered into regional singing competitions in the South East of England, and national contests throughout the United Kingdom. Some of which we won, when I sung lead vocals. In High Note Harmony, we belted out pop, jazz, soul, and reggae songs. Emma, my best friend from high school, knew how talented a singer I was. So did the rest of the school.

"Pure as a songbird that voice. I could listen to your singing all day long, Alena," Miss Dundridge, our music teacher would often say.

Expressing myself in this beautiful and natural way is so liberating. I almost forgot how being part of a choir made me feel. Could singing be my escapism, my answer to therapy? Perhaps.

All of a sudden, a shadow eclipses the poster, darkening the incandescence of its radiant form.

"What ya looking at?" Rocketing behind me like a thunderbolt, Phillip causes my blood to curdle with fright. I scream.

Abruptly, I revolve to face him. "God, you scared me, Phil."

"Sorry baby. Didn't mean to frighten you," he says apologetically.

Excusing his senselessness, my cheeks curl into a smile. "Okay. You're forgiven."

More intently, he focuses on my face. His pupils shrink with concern. "Feeling any better after sharing *those details* with me yesterday?"

"Heaps better." I sport a lavish grin. "I'm so relieved I finally told you the truth."

He beams. "Glad you trusted me enough to tell me."

"Yea, I do trust you now," I whisper, my eyes floating into his.

"Good," he states. His tone is solid, affirmative.

Twisting me around, pulling back my hair, his lips trail across my neck.

"That's nice," I hum, welcoming Phil's closeness when no one is around. It is just us here. We can be free and ourselves for a moment.

Soon, the combination of Phil's hands and lips massaging the knots of tension out of my shoulders invigorates me.

"Babe, what do you think about me getting a Saturday job?" he asks me suddenly.

My eyes roll, curving into his eyeline. "A job? Don't you have enough money or something?"

"Yeah, I have money. My student loan is covering most of my expenses. I just want some extra cash and the experience of working. Maybe as a checkout assistant in a local supermarket."

"Oh, I see," I reply dubiously. "Mum would never expect *me* to get a job. I'm only here to study. Mum pays for everything out of her own pocket – my tuition fees, board, etcetera. Becca's dad does the same for her... Working and studying is not a good combination. It can seriously impact on your grades."

"Well, you two can afford not to work whilst studying. Both your families are in a *different bracket*," he says boldly. "The silver spoon bracket!"

"No, Phil, it's called working your arse off!" I shout, pivoting to face him. "It took my mother five years to become a successful restaurant manager. It didn't happen overnight."

Disdainfully, he laughs. "My parents have worked in retail for ten years. They are clerks not managers. In over a decade, they've never been offered a raise or promotion. So I had to get a loan to pay for my education."

"Don't get a job, Phil! I'll give you money if things get

tight."

Pulling away from me, blowing out a puff of icy air, he flings a pair of restless hands in his hair. "Boy, she was so right."

"Who was so right?" I enquire with a puzzled expression.

"Joanne!"

"What, Joanne Jackman, the slob on our floor?" I snap scathingly. "What has she got to do with anything?"

"She ain't a slob, Alena!"

"The girl doesn't even know how to clean a hob after she's dirtied it! She's bloody nasty," I shout.

Phil glowers. "She's clean and smart and funny, actually."

"Excuse me?" I bellow, throwing two boiling hands on my hips.

"Yes, she is," he growls. "Joanne said you'd be opposed to me getting a job. Clearly, the girl is perceptive, too."

A bitter taste sits in my mouth. I can tell this is the onset of jealousy. "Why are you defending her, Phil? And since when did you two become chummy?"

"We're not friends. I'm defending her, because you are on the attack!"

"Why are you talking to this girl, Phillip?" I snarl, my finger pointing viciously at him. "Why are you taking advice from her?"

I am seething and I want to scream again. Not sure that this is a good idea now that most of the students from our class have arrived and are huddled behind us.

"She gets me, Alena," he admits, chomping his bottom lip. "Ya' know, she's a Willesden girl. We are on the same level."

"I get you too, Phil," I say wrathfully, "and I'm originally from North West London. Remember?"

"Yea, but now you live in *Surrey*." He says this sardonically, as if ridiculing me for moving uptown.

"Phillip," I say empathically, surprised by his change in attitude. "What's come over you?"

"That poster," he says, diverting the conversation. "What was that poster you were looking at before I got here?"

Slapping a clumsy platypus palm over the flyer, I respond. "It's nothing, nothing at all."

After his outburst, I want more than ever to keep something to myself. Something that is special, and only me. To heal and find me again, I need one thing that is mine, and completely separate from my relationship with Phil.

As Becca struts down the corridor supermodel style, turning her head up like a supercilious movie star, a few guys begin to ogle at her, admiring her profile. Grinning and wiggling a taut nineteen-year-old backside at the growing audience of droolers, she approaches us. Iggy A's latest tune is blasting in her ears. Casually, she hooks off the headset.

"Ready for our first of two weekly torturous English lectures with Professor Sanford?"

"As ready as I'll ever be." I chuckle. My bestie is so funny. She always knows how to cheer me up.

Phil's shoulders jerk back. "Chill, Becca. Don't sweat it. Just concentrate on acing this module. Forget about Sanford. Besides, he ain't that bad."

Tossing a cold stare in Phil's direction, Becca admonishes him. "Say what?" Agitated and pissed off, she lets out a low grunt. "What planet are you on, boy? This man is a fricking arsehole!"

Pushing past him, rolling her eyes to heaven, she seeks me out to restore her serenity. Inwardly, I sigh. These two really need to learn how to get along. If not for themselves, then for *my* sanity. No girl wants to see her boyfriend and best friend at loggerheads.

Letting Phil know how much she loathes him, Becca grimaces. Then she tosses a kinky wink in my range.

"Come, Miss Alena P, my twin sista from another mother. Let's head inside."

Belittling Phil, she signals him like a dog, ordering him to walk behind us. Brimming over with vexation, he reluctantly complies. A glint of flaming hostility is burning in his eyes.

"Keep calm, for me," I mouth to him. "You owe me."

A hissing pair of teeth proves that my words have no affect at all.

Just leave it, I say to myself, not wanting to aggravate the situation anymore.

Making a mental note of the vital information from the poster, I walk arm in arm into class with Becca. One eye is on her, the other on my angered boyfriend.

"If you were to ringlet that long wavy hair, Alena, it would look *so* freaking adorable. Can I do it for you at the weekend?"

"Alright, B." I nod. "If you wanna."

"Swell," she chirps, banging into me blithely. "I'm so pumped about this."

Cheerily she grins, guiding me to the table. Phillip has already decided to sit next to Russell, one of our outspoken classmates. Sitting near Becca would either drive him insane or make him want to hurl. For a moment I feel distant from him, like we are slowly drifting apart. More and more obstacles are dividing us. Hastily, I shrug off that thought. I have happier things to fill my mind with.

Throughout the lecture, the growing feud between my boyfriend and bestie and my relationship issues with Phil, are a distant memory. Swirling delightfully in the centre of my brain is singing. Nothing except singing. My heart is urging me to audition for the Coolette Singers group. Yet my head is telling me that Phil is the only viable solution to my deep-rooted problems.

I gulp, as the thoughts in my head and the feelings in my heart tussle chaotically, fighting for supremacy, in the dark chamber inside my consciousness.

THE FALL

Professor Sanford is prattling on as usual, delivering a two hour lecture on Shakespeare and Renaissance Drama. I am sitting at the back of Room T4, not soaking in any information and not really feeling like my normal self. On the whole, I enjoy this module, and at times, I contribute, sharing my wisdom with the class, and knowledge that I've obtained through research and study. Phillip and Becca are naturally smart. Neither of them has to study as hard as I do to achieve excellent grades, and they offer wonderful and comprehensive input to class. In seminars, though, the three of us work together as a team. We're on fire in every session. We bounce off each other's opinions and ideas like rubber balls, an act which leaves the whole class stunned and decidedly in the dark. Well, we did all get straight As in our high school exams, so we are a clever bunch of college students. It's not that the others are dumb. It's just that they are not on our heightened, and in sync, wavelength. We are simply amazing at this course. We're a small cluster of eggheads.

The wacky professor, a sagacious man of English and Scottish descent, is a slender gentleman who dresses garishly sometimes, much like a mad hatter. Despite his appearance and varying states of sanity, he knows when he sees perfection in his star pupils. Professor Sanford often admires us, the mighty trio, from behind the interactive board when we commence a vivacious three-way debate.

From the corner of my eye, I can always see that broad smile. He totally gets what we are saying, and nods bountifully, asking us probing questions to tease further knowledge out of our minds. Knowing his three stellar protégés are so brainy and putting the rest of the English students to shame is a real victory for him. He's never had students do really well in all areas, so he's happy that the three of us are acing his class. We are consistently achieving First Class Honours in every aspect of this core module, which runs over two semesters. Most people despise the professor for his kooky theories and bizarre demeanour, and the three of us don't particularly like him either, but at least the wacko does encourage us, which, I suppose, is a good thing. And the Head of Department is singing his praises for the first time in five years. Nevertheless, deep down, the professor discerns that Becca, Phillip, and I are almost smarter than him, which must be, at some level, unnerving.

Nevertheless, today is not a regular day where I shine akin to a bright star. This is the red hot day of my cycle, and I am on my period – first day of hell. Sometimes I feel so ill when it comes on, and it seems to get a little bit worse each month. I hate being a woman at these times. My head swirls, my stomach complaining. I am burning up, and it feels like I'm about to burst into flames. An inferno that soars all the way up from my toes to my head is starting to cripple my small body. Sanford continues to babble on about the seventh century, and Desdemona, and the patriarchal Venetian society, and all manner of things that I stopped caring about five minutes into the lecture. My eyes are drooping, and I am fading fast. I slope forward in my chair, and I am falling, falling to the ground. With my last bit of strength, I lean over and tap Phillip on the leg, who is sitting next to me. I have no energy to speak. Phil's eyes catch me falling, and there is a flicker of concern on his countenance as he registers that I am obviously not well.

As I plummet towards the hard blue floor, he reaches for me just in time and grabs my arm, preventing me from falling to the ground. These reassuring arms clutch onto me.

Steadily, my eyes begin to close. I feel the warmth of his breath spritzing my nose.

"Alena," he whispers distressfully, trying to gain as little attention as possible from the surrounding class. "What's wrong?" He thumps Becca, who is sitting in front of us. "Bec! Help me!"

I hear a gasp. That must be Becca. "Oh, gees, Alena!"

I know she is stroking my hair. I feel her soft hands running over my forehead and hairline. She is checking the pulse on my wrist.

The whole room is quiet, suddenly. I hear nothing except my heartbeat, Phil's erratic breathing and Becca's concerned voice.

"What's happened?" I hear Professor Sanford say in a deep, troubled tone.

"She's faint, and on the verge of passing out, Professor!" Bec confirms.

"I'm calling an ambulance!" Phil says quickly, his voice trembling.

"No, Mr. Gregson... You stay with Miss Pavlis... Let Miss Richardson-Smith call the ambulance. She can explain things better to the paramedics, since this might be related to, er, a woman problem..."

He is right. I do have a woman problem, which I feel pumping out of my body and onto the floor, as I realise that my pad is drenched, my turquoise skirt soaked right through. Oh, shit, everybody in class knows I've got my period, even Professor Sanford. But I can't open my eyes, can't move, I can't cry. The whole weight of my head is now burdened in my man's sturdy arms. My legs are dangling on the floor, my torso held caringly by Becca, who is stunned and in total shock.

"Miss Richardson-Smith," Professor Sanford says hurriedly and full of panic. "What are you waiting for? Call the ambulance, *now*."

I perceive scuffling and inaudible chatter. Phillip is still holding me. He is speaking, saying something, but I cannot identify any of his words. It just sounds like unintelligible jammering. My head hammers; I am giddy, so giddy.

Everything grows darker, dimmer, and then everything turns black.

***

I'm lying in my bed. I don't know how I got here. Last time I was awake, I remember being in the lecture room... Oh yes, I passed out, didn't I? Someone must have brought me here.

Little by little, my sore eyes open. A circular brown blob and a milky oblong smudge are floating in my hazy gaze. Am I in heaven? No, I don't think I am; I can feel my heart murmuring in my chest. My focus fully returns, and I see that these shapes are Phil and Becca's faces, both of which carry a look of grave concern.

"Oh, thank God, you're awake," Becca exclaims.

"Thank you, Jesus," Phil says relieved. "I was so worried."

"Me too," Becca says edgily.

"You were in the hospital for hours. God, I was beside myself! Becca had to calm me down!"

"Well, it sounds to me, like more than one of us should've seen a doctor," I joke, trying to lighten the tone.

Heartily Phil laughs. I see the deep and indisputable love in his eyes. Returning his affection, I stare lovingly at him until he bends forward to give me a series of tender kisses. His lips are sugary and delicious. I deserve a nice treat after my ordeal.

"Thank you for looking after me, Phil." I summon his eyes and then Becca's. "Thanks, bestie."

"Anytime!" they say simultaneously. It seems as though they're competing to see who can shout over the other's voice.

Is this another transatlantic battle brewing between the two rivals?

Moving forward slightly, Becca steps into dangerous terrain. Her hand is reaching out, ready to touch mine. Deftly, Phil issues a stern side glance as if warning her not to come closer. He is becoming territorial, claiming me as his. I do not have the energy to challenge him. It's bad enough coping with a bad period. I'm not adding a panic attack to the equation.

Respectfully, Becca retreats, defusing a potentially explosive situation. She is really upset, but says nothing. Keeping herself occupied, and out of trouble, she sits on my rocking chair and plays a game on her mobile phone.

Slanting his body, coming in closer, Phil explains what happened in the hospital. "They gave you Tranexamic acid pills to slow down the bleeding and an iron supplement prescription. The ward nurses wanted to clean you up after that, but I fought them off, insisting that I bathed you. I could tell that the hospital staff wanted to wring my neck!"

Lifting up my sore arm, I place it just behind his head, so my warmth envelopes his crown. "I don't remember you bathing me, Phil. Are you for real?"

"A-ha!"

"Was I nude when you bathed me?" I ask curiously.

Shamelessly, he snickers, a cheeky grin spreading across his phiz. "Not long after that whole drama," he says, avoiding my question, "the doctor performed an ultrasound. The results came up normal. So, the doc said it was just a bad month and that you'd be fine with medication and plenty of rest. I called your mother to tell her all of this. She was worried, but I convinced her that I'd take good care of you."

"That's great Phil!" I state dismissively. "Thanks for sharing that. I still want to know… was I naked when you washed me?"

Deeply, he chuckles. "How many people do you know who wash with their clothes on, Alena?"

As I peer at him, my eyes narrow. "Phillip Gregson – that was a yes or no question!"

"Yes, okay," he whirrs, "you were butt naked, and I enjoyed washing you." A jovial grin erects on his face.

Secretly, it made me feel a little turned on to hear that my boyfriend bathed me naked and enjoyed doing it. Having this thought is unusually sexual for me. My therapist would be stunned, if I actually went to sessions and shared this with her.

"Aren't guys normally squeamish when it comes to *women's stuff?*"

He laughs loudly, his lips descending on my nose. "Not this guy. I grab squeamish by the balls!"

"By the balls," I repeat, giggling. Developing a deeper expression, my cheeks turn pink.

"Yeah, gotta grasp the balls real hard. The big round balls!" Phil japes, drawing attention to my flushed face, which is growing ever brighter, illuminating with embarrassment.

Becca looks up; she's blushing. She knows exactly what we are talking about, what we are joking about, and I think she feels out of place here. We all know that three is a crowd, so it is time for her to leave.

"Becca, I appreciate your support today."

I try to make the situation less uncomfortable. By her face, though, I can tell that she feels like an abandoned puppy, left out in the rain.

"No probs," she mutters.

Exiting my room and slamming the door, Becca displays her anger and frustration at being left on the other side of it. However hurt she feels, she must understand. She is my bestie, and Phillip is my boyfriend. At this moment in time, he is the only person who can nurse me back to health. She cannot be that individual. She's not my partner. And whether she likes it or not, she will always come marginally in second place after Phillip. Becca will have to get used to that. Besides, I met Phillip way before I met her. Oh, this is ridiculous. I refuse to defend myself about something like this. I am just going to take pleasure in kissing and snuggling up to my man, and I'm going to concentrate on building up my strength again.

"I got you soup, baby. Tomato and basil. Eat up."

"Thank you, honey." This is some serious stuff. I love this soup, and I hope that I can keep it down. My stomach seems to like the warm, rich sensation of this delicious combination of tomato and basil.

Phil positions himself behind me on the bed, cocooning me with his soft and soothing adoration.

"You look so cute and helpless when you are sick."

Charmingly, I smile. "That's nice to know."

"You're even cuter naked." He smirks.

"Is that so?" I enquire, whilst grinning.

"Hell, yea." He tweets.

As I continue to slurp the soup with a smirk on my face, Phil plays with my ear.

A steely expression alters his countenance. "Boosting cars and hustling was my game before I met you," he professes. "Life, back then, seemed good, thrilling, addictive. Can't lie. That life was dangerous though, and had no future. Everything lead to one place – the slammer." His stare becomes solid and focused. "Love, however, is different. It gives me a better buzz. It's my new craze."

Soaking in his sincerity, I'm glad he is finally opening

up to me. "I never knew anything about love, either, before I met you, Phil. In fact, I didn't even know what being in a relationship meant."

Waggishly, he chortles. "Well, one of these days I will show you the true benefits of having a boyfriend."

"Yeah, one day, when I'm ready," I say, nervously twiddling my fingers, getting redder by the second.

He nods coolly. "Trust me, we'll produce fireworks on that special night."

Gawkily, my pupils dash and scuttle, colliding with his naughty smirk. "You sure it's only loving me that you're crazy about, and nothing else?"

"There is something else I'm crazy about, too," he confesses.

"What's that?" I enquire, focusing on him, totally interested in how he will respond.

"Being with you forever," he says. His mouth flowers into a pucker. "I've never wanted anyone or anything so much before."

Grabbing onto my man with both arms, I twist my body towards him, balancing the cold soup on my lap. "Aren't you the mawkish one tonight!" I exclaim breathlessly.

He grins. "Are you crazy about me too, babe?"

"Yes," I say in a whisper. "I've never felt this way about anyone."

"That's good. We can be crazy in love together."

Relishing his words, my receptive nostrils meet his. "Can we work through our issues, Phil? Will we be *okay*?"

"Yea," he says his teeth gritting determinedly. "I guess we'll have to try."

My face is flushed, my eyes streaming. "I hope we can make it, Phil, because I can't lose you. If I lose you now, then that's it; I know that the demons of the past will take me, suck me under. I don't ever want that to happen."

"You'll never have to worry about that," he implores. "We will never break up."

I squirm a little, praying his assertion is right.

LOVE MEETS CONFUSION

Rocking me from side to side, Phillip cradles me in the warmth of his embrace. His breath is tickling the back of my neck, and I hum as I enjoy the stellar scent blowing on this sensitive area.

"How's my baby today?" He looks earnestly into my shimmering green eyes and cocks a half smile.

I smile back at him, treasuring this warm, delectable cuddle.

"Much better, thanks."

"Good." Zealously he pecks my chin, like a love bird. "Yesterday was an insane day. Wasn't it?"

Snuggling closer to him, I appreciate his concern. "Yeah, it was the worst day ever!"

"Has that hemorrhage thing happened before?"

"Once before."

"Gees," he yells. "That's bloody awful."

"Welcome to my world!" I shout.

Grotesquely, he gurns. "Yowza!"

"You haven't seen nothing yet, Phil. Watching a baby being born is far more gruesome. I saw a live birth on TV once. I almost passed out."

"No kidding!" He laughs uneasily. "The joys to come."

Gurgling loudly, losing control of my laughing fit, I throw my head into his pecs. "Yes, the disgusting miracles of life. But all worth it."

"I guess so," he says, cringing.

Candidly, I howl with laughter. "You couldn't last a day as a woman. Could you?"

"Ya damn right about that, babe." He hoots.

In unison, Phil and I snort, our merry voices swirl in sync around the room.

We are relaxing in Phil's *amazing* room, where everything is pristine and clean. His bed, which we are reclining on, is spread very neatly, with not a single crease visible on the duvet. All of his clothes are folded in an orderly fashion and have been hung up in his wardrobe or placed in a clear container at the foot of his bed. Nothing is on the floor. Books are tidily and meticulously stacked in a perfect pile on his desk, which is situated next to the closet. A small red box of trinkets is filled with his vintage car collection, playing cards and some rumpled old belts, all of which huddle together in the confined space. Even his en-suite bathroom is immaculate. Not a single scum mark or piece of hair can be found in his bathtub or sink. Phil has always had a squeaky clean apartment. He takes pride in his personal space. It's quite extraordinary for a man to be this clean. Unlike most teenage guys living in halls, my boyfriend's boudoir has a beautiful bouquet. His room doesn't have a distinguishable 'bloke's smell' or a musty, decrepit odour, usually caused by unwashed and overly loved socks. He, and his room, smell of Bleu De Chanel, his favourite aftershave. I've met very few men who are this hygienic and take sanitation seriously. I have only known one other man like him. This man was my father.

Dad always revelled in tidiness. His whole world was abundant in order, sense and reason. He was a stickler for cleanliness. I remember that growing up, dad kept the entire house spotless all the time. Not a crumb was left on the floor in any room. The dishes were always done, ironing completed, vacuuming ticked off the to-do list every day. He did everything, except the cooking. That's all mum had to do. As a wife, that is a dream come true.

Ambrose Pavlis was the perfect husband and the perfect caring, loving father, who incessantly offered sound advice, helped me with homework and took me and mum out to dinner on family nights. During the summer, he whisked mum off to romantic holidays and let his sister, Aunty Reah, look after me on these occasions. Mum and dad would always return with a very healthy glow and wide grins on their faces. And he had the best laugh in the world, a rich wholesome laugh, much like my Phillip's.

However, dad's flawless record dropped one day, when he dropped his pants for his secretary of two years, the far too young and pretty Jasmine Daniels. One stupid mistake, one impetuous moment, created a lifetime of heartache and pain. Why he did it, I don't know. He and mum were happy, so happy. Maybe he was bored of his ideal life and wanted a bit of danger. Maybe he was never that perfect after all, and never that in love with mum. Who knows? But what I do know is that this moment of madness, which he confessed to mum one evening after dinner, destroyed their marriage. Mum went ballistic! I peeped through the banisters, watching her hurl cushions and vases and cups at him as he tried to duck and dodge her fury. Hours after he confessed his terrible transgression, mum packed his bags and ordered him out of the house.

For days, I sobbed with mum, as we wilted into the ground, dying from the agony of this cruel betrayal. Dad lamented on the telephone, saying sorry to mum, to me, a thousand times, begging for forgiveness. Mum wasn't having any of it. Furious and bursting with rage, she called up our family solicitor, asking how to file for divorce. She rebuffed reconciliation. What was there to reconcile? He had destroyed our whole family with his stupid actions. He had made the decision to spurn us.

In the weeks that followed, dad tried, but failed, to get me on his side. He wanted me to choose between him and mum. I stayed firm; there was no choice. At the time I was only sixteen, but like my mother, I was headstrong and determined. I insisted I would stay with mum, by her side, forever.

I rejected dad. He made me sick. I grew repulsed by him. After the divorce, things were difficult. Mum was an emotional wreck. She couldn't deal with her own issues, let alone mine. I stayed with my loving and caring yet broken mother, doing the best I could to support her through this terrible transition. Since I was young, and still a child, I couldn't be as strong for her as I would have liked. In her own way, she acted like a mother, worrying about me, making sure I was safe, fed, clothed, loved, and provided for. It was hard for her to support us financially and emotionally. We coped though, and we survived.

A few months later, Ambrose's health declined, and he got diagnosed with testicular cancer. I cried as I saw my father deteriorate slowly, day by day. Despite our differences, he was still my father, my flesh and blood. When dad passed away just four months later, I fell apart. Mum hid her pain behind closed doors to protect me. She pretended that she was fine.

Eventually, mum admitted that she couldn't cope and went to counselling. I refused to go with her. I'd allow no professional to unveil my deepest emotions. I wanted to keep them enshrouded. Those pent up emotions though, were destroying me, and that's when the infamous Mr. Stanley Hawthorne entered my world. After he almost ended my life, everything snowballed out of control, and I tumbled into a terrible state of regression. For a while, things got a little better. Then soon enough I lapsed, slipping backwards into a black hole of consuming darkness. That's when Phil emerged, and the warmth of

God's love came back into my life.

Gradually, my eyes meet his. I am so grateful he is the man God selected for me. I am so blessed to have found such a caring and understanding guy to help me heal from such traumatic childhood experiences.

Reaching over, pressing the bulbous red button on the radio, Phil clicks it on. Demi Lovato is warbling through the wireless.

"I love this song," I purr, relishing the sweet music, swaying from left to right.

"Hmm, it's alright, I suppose," responds Phil, his face scrunching up. "Hip hop is more my vibe."

"Why is that?" I probe, interested to hear his reasoning.

"It's got that thumping beat," he says, bobbing his head from side to side. "Penetrates straight through me."

Flippantly, I laugh. "Pop ballads have far more depth. You need that music for the soul."

"Hip hop is for the soul too. Those tunes are real bad arse."

I grimace. "The lyrics in some of those songs make reference to arses, for sure. Not quite my cup of tea."

Lightening the tone, building a bridge between our differences, Phil rejoinders. "At least you can say you've got an urban bad boy. That's hip hop enough for me."

He chortles boisterously.

"I have a totally reformed and rehabilitated urban bad boy," I reply, revising his statement.

"Reformed?" he mumbles. A somber expression flattens the base of his nose. "That is a matter of opinion. I will never really escape my past."

Calculating his level of melancholy, my eyes narrow. I attempt to banish this looming shadow of doom hanging over his head. "There are a lot worse things you could've done than stealing vehicles. So let the memories go, Phil. It's ancient news."

"I can't let it go," he says, his voice slightly hoarse.

"Stealing and joyriding is real bad. It's so bad; it's a criminal offence. Yes, I did my time in juvie, but that doesn't excuse the crime or make it disappear."

"C'mon, Phil, it's not like you committed murder. There's no need to feel guilty for old mistakes."

Tears form in his eyes. He forces them back. "I feel guilt, even now, despite me trying my hardest to shake it. For years, my mum and dad drummed into my brain that the Lord's wrath would be great, and eternal, and that He would never release me from the shame of being a youth offender!"

"Why would your parents say such damaging and demeaning stuff?" I ask, furious at the people who brought him into this world.

Profoundly, he swallows. He's finding it difficult to speak. "It's culture, Alena. Some traditional Caribbean families take this view when their children get out of line. I dishonoured the family. That's why they behave this way towards me. This is just the way it is. I have to live with it."

Incensed and enraged, I scowl. "No you don't, Phil. Confront them about it."

"Alena, they will disown me. You just don't understand how my family operates."

Robustly, I shake my head refuting his misguided statement. "This is not civilised behaviour, Phil. No parent should ever berate their offspring in a way that demoralises them. It's so wrong. To me, *that* is a crime!"

Like a dangerous missile that's reached its prime target, Phil explodes. The radio is slammed off and flung to the far edge of the side cabinet. "You've said quite enough, Alena. Now leave it!"

Refusing to put out the flaming rage in my heart, I glare at him. I cannot abide by such ignorance and unworldliness in others.

"No!" I holler. "I'm only just warming up!"

Taking a deep breath, he's about to speak his piece.

Deadly venom is shooting from his mouth. "You know nothing about my parents, my culture or my people. So just butt out, okay?"

Immediately, I am both hurt and baffled. "Where is this hateful anger coming from, Phil? I am not your enemy."

Ashamed, he puts his head down. "She reckons that you are the enemy – the foe, the troublemaker dressed up in a smart white wrapper."

"Who's she? Which girl said all that crap?" I elevate his heavy head with one skillful finger. "Is this Joanne Jackman you're referring to, yet again?"

Audaciously, he pouts. "Let's face it, Alena, we are not the same. We may be a couple; we might have both been born and raised in Brent Cross. Nonetheless, we are miles apart, come from two totally different worlds, two different cultures. For this reason, you'll never truly understand me or my family." His mouth is trembling, and it's clear that history is dangling precariously over his head. "She is my people, Alena. She understands me, inside and out."

"Such a coward!" I scream, my voice bouncing from wall to wall. "Letting someone else tell you who to be and who to be with."

"I'm no coward!" He shouts fearlessly.

"Yes, you are…"

"No, I'm simply speaking from the heart, like she told me to."

"And if she told you to jump off a cliff, Phil, would you do that?" I shout sarcastically.

"Just shut up, Alena!" he screams. "Shut the hell up!"

"No!" I bellow, hitting him on the arm. He dare not even try to hit me back. "If ya want that cheap ghetto bitch so much," I screech, "then go bang her! See if I care!"

Crinkling up his face like a burned potato chip left unattended in the oven, he lets out a peculiar shriek. "I don't want to do anything with her, Alena. I'm just not sure about anything anymore or who to trust. God, I'm so confused."

"Confused?" I say mockingly.

"Yes, confused," He affirms.

"Confused about what, Phil? Her prejudice tendencies? Or are you confused because you don't quite understand how ya fell for a white girl?" I holler, speaking outside of my comfort zone.

Phil double blinks, shocked that these forthright words have escaped from my lips. "My friends – Donald, Ty, Russell, and now Joanne, are all calling me a sellout. I can't handle the jibes for much longer. It's burning my soul."

"This is our relationship, Phil, not theirs," I say, a dark cluster of indignation surging through me. "If they choose to be ignorant, let them be. And just shake it off. The taunting phase will pass."

"It's not as simple as that."

"Yea, it is."

"No, it ain't!" He thunders.

"You just want to bed Joanne Jackman! That's what this is all about, isn't it?" Gritting my teeth, I restrain a billow of fire, which is ready to blow out full force and char Phil's heart. "You just wanna get from her what you can't get from me!"

"No, that's not true!" He shakes his head boldly. "You are the only person I want to be doing anything with."

"I don't know what to believe anymore, Phil." I grunt, slamming my fist into the bed, staring fiercely at him.

"I love you, baby. Honestly, I do. It's just, culture is weighing me down. History is dictating my thoughts, my feelings, my actions."

"Oh, gees, that's super dramatic. And I thought I was the messed up drama queen!"

"That's harsh, Alena. Real damn harsh."

Cupping his chin in one persuasive hand, I implore.

"Stop listening to them, Phillip. They are just haters. Small-minded knuckleheads."

"Are they *just haters*?" He is distressed, bewildered.

"Yes," I whisper, as I incline, crying into the bridge of his nose, my tears soaking into the crux of his silky skin. "They are stupid arseholes! Don't absorb their insults."

Fearfully, he nips the edge of his mouth, pondering on my words. The soft pucker of his lips meet my tenacious pout. Slowly, we kiss.

"We love each other. We've got differences for sure, but we're meant to be together. Stop being uncertain about us. They are the ones who you ought to be uncertain about. Love don't see colour, Phil. Humans do. Remember that."

He nods in agreement. However his focus slips away from me, it's now on the floor, and his mind looks like it is taking an agonising tour of the past.

"Yes, I shall keep reminding myself," he insists. His words come out slow, slurred and unconvincing.

"Has this issue been bothering you for a while?"

"Longer than *a while*," he whines. His lip quirks, and his face screws up, appearing wounded, like an injured animal.

"I thought so." Tenderly, I kiss the top of his forehead. "Don't be the person they expect, Phillip. Be the person you are meant to be. That's the great guy I fell for. What we have is good. We shouldn't let anyone spoil it. Okay?"

"Okay." Breathing a sigh of relief, his exhalation is jagged, unsure. "I'm so glad Becca is in her own room this evening, and has been for the past few days. It's given us a chance to *really* talk."

"Yea, true," I admit. "But how is Becca a threat to you?"

"She's clingy. She has a way of hogging you."

"Nonsense!" I snicker, rolling my eyes up to the skies. "She is my best friend. Of course she wants to spend time with me."

His face is straight, severe, and uncompromising. "And I am your man. I take precedence. Right? And this is the second time in two weeks we have eaten dinner together. Not good."

"Yea, it's not good," I retort, realising I have no leg to stand on. After all, he is right about Becca. She is dependent on me, at times.

"Every time Becca releases you from her dungeon, I am relieved that you haven't devolved, turning into a carbon copy of her," he says petulantly.

Suppressing his pungent, lime-green jealousy, I smother his remark with sarcastic wit. "Honestly, babe, that's super childish."

"No, it's not." He states firmly. "I barely get to eat with you or spend time with you. So I am allowed to be upset." Intensely, he kisses me, reminding me how damn possessive he can be sometimes.

"It's just food, Phil. Don't get worked up about it."

"It's intimacy," he says seductively. "Eating together solidifies the bond a man has with his woman."

I can't disagree. "Yeah, I suppose."

He beams. "I like cooking with you, too. It's fun and so romantic."

My eyes illuminate and sparkle under his gaze. "Yeah, it is really good for us to connect in this way."

"I can do the eating bit well. My culinary skills need a little work, though." He laughs.

Tapping him on the nose, I smile. I love it when he's a teeny weeny bit helpless and needs my encouragement. It's so adorable.

"You did good tonight, Phil. You didn't overcook the spaghetti, and the meatballs, and peas were divine. Nothing burned."

My words invigorate him setting his eyes on fire. Tantalisingly, he moistens the nape of my neck with his tongue. Oh, gees, that feels freaking awesome. I sigh contentedly as the deep sensation vibrates in the core of my body.

Licking his lips suggestively, he explores behind my ear. His hands press on my breasts. Yowza, that's sensational; that is dope. "Hmm," I murmur as he travels around the circumference of my neck more vigorously with the tip of his blazing oral weapon.

"Sexy," he purrs, pecking the base of my chin. "So sexy, you are."

I giggle, enjoying his touch. "Am I really?" I grin, loving his hearty confession.

There is a twinkle in his eyes. Then his face bursts with passion. "Yes, you're my Greek goddess," he whispers, rubbing my nipples through my tight white t-shirt. The friction, his delectable fingers, his warm touch, sends me to heaven and back. I rock, relishing him intimately fondling me.

Showering him with beautiful kisses, I simper. My hands venture down to his butt. I feel up his butt cheeks, savouring his hard, firm backside. He is indeed the man of steel.

"Next time I'll teach you how to cook Moussaka, my favourite dish from the Mediterranean."

His strong brown eyes enrapture me. "Sweet. Looking forward to cooking and tasting it."

Gently, Phil takes my hand, resting it comfortably on his heated lap. "You and me," he begins softly, beckoning my green eyes with his own. "We're like white pasta and brown meat. We look great together, taste good, and complement each other well."

I have a bemused expression on my face. I'm completely mystified by his random comment. "Us, like pasta and meat? How exactly?"

"We are two races, two cultures, fusing together..."

"Yeah, we are," I say, confused as to why this is back on the agenda. Colour should not be an issue in our relationship, for either of us. I really can't understand why he is bringing this up again.

A contemplative frown alters his attractive features. "I know we shouldn't need to keep on talking about it –"

"What's bothering you?" I am staring at his cocoa irises, struggling to keep up with them as they dart like rockets around the room. I try to ease his agitation, but to no avail. It concerns me that he is disconcerted about something else.

Finally, he reveals the source of his trepidation. "Do you think your mother will *like me*?" His concentration is immense. It hurtles around the room, blasting into the centre of the bed. The mattress judders as his perilous thoughts wreak havoc in his turbulent world. "Will she accept me? Is she *okay* that I am...?"

Hearing his potent words, I stop him in mid-sentence. I don't wish to racialise our relationship anymore. It's making me feel rather sad.

"Phil, you're going on as if my mum doesn't know about you. My mum has no issue whatsoever. She adores you, and she loves the look of you, actually."

Boyishly, he mopes. "If that were true, why doesn't she wish to meet me? You never invited me to your mother's house for Easter. It's been seven months already, babe. Why?"

Reassuringly, I stroke his cheeks. His gloomy eyes do not seem to receive my affection well.

Outstaring my boyfriend, I display a deep degree of discontentment. "You were staying with your family over Easter. So what's the big fuss?"

"You should've invited me to your mum's place, Alena," he says, sulking. "Or am I not good enough to meet your mother, is that it?"

I take umbrage at his remarks. My face crinkles with vexation, and I lose my cool. "Well, where was my invite, Phil? Did it get lost in the mail? I could take that same stance that I'm not welcome at your home. Have your parents got a problem with *me*, then?"

Whizzing about the room, his anchor is uprooted, homeless. There is a nervous embarrassment circling around his crown. "I wouldn't say they don't like you. They are just stuck in their ways, that's all."

"In what sense are they *stuck in their ways*?" I ask rigidly.

"Erm, well... They like you as a person... The idea of interracial relationships just kinda scares them. They are..."

"Ignorant people like your boneheaded friends!" I am blunt, and my words are acerbic.

"No, not ignorant. More like unworldly, locked in a time warp. In their heads, the year is still 1950. My mum and dad are a pair of ghosts that live on Windrush. They remain in the time of the British Empire, in their minds."

Acrimoniously, I unleash a cockerel's crow. "They are warped, Phil. Behind the times."

"Hey, these are my parents you are talking about. A little respect, please."

"Respect has to be earned." My lips are pursed. I am furious at him for tolerating and making excuses for his parents' insensate attitude.

Patting my hand graciously, in a way to say sorry for the views of his folks, he attempts to pacify me. "My father, especially, is very steadfast in his beliefs and in his dogmatic approach to life. I pity him sometimes. Bet your dad was never like that, even after the divorce, was he?"

"No, he wasn't. Ambrose was a kind yet foolish man, who completely lost his direction. And then he died before he had a chance to mend the error of his ways." Already, I begin to feel the tears come on. I am on the verge of a panic attack.

"Shh," Phil whispers consoling me, holding me close. "It's okay, baby. I'm here. Sorry, I didn't mean to unsettle you."

"Mum has been asking to meet you," I say once relaxed and back to my normal self. "I told her it wasn't the right time." My eyes are still red and puffy. I try to give my man an earnest expression.

"Why, Alena? Why is it not the right time?" He asks sedately. "Why would you deny me the right to meet your mother?"

"I am not denying you of the right," I correct him, staring innocently into his eyes. "I simply want our relationship to be perfect when we meet my mum together, as a couple. That's all." I nibble my lower lip, knowing that I have failed to sell my reasoning to him. "Of course I wish for you to meet my mother eventually, babe."

Pushing me away from him, as if we have demagnetised, he moves to the far corner of the bed, nearest the wall. The light around his face darkens. "When we're *perfect* I can meet your mother? That sounds like emotional blackmail, Alena," A glower blazes on his face. He squeezes into a tight foetal ball. It's both sad and distressing to see.

"Baby, please," I beg.

Getting up from the bed, staring intently at him, I am rather disturbed by his state of disillusionment.

Elevating his head akin to a prince that is powerless in his sovereignty, he attempts to reclaim his kingdom, punching a hole, a pair of lethal stalagmites, straight through my heart. "Why is it you calling all the shots round here?" he yells. "Who made you queen?"

"I do things when I am ready, Phil. That's how it works. No man tells me what to do!"

"I've noticed that," he says bitterly. "Well, this is what I get for being inquisitive, and picking the green apple in the other field."

"What the hell is that supposed to mean?" I holler, demanding an explanation.

"Nevermind, it's street language. Middle class folk wouldn't get that."

"I get it!" I scream, pointing an acrid finger at his pathetic attempt to assert a Neanderthal mentality. "You think I ain't on your level. And you believe I moved to 'poshville' by choice. I gave into the nasty gang of girls after I got attacked, and *chose* to relocate to Surrey. Did I, Phil?"

"I never said that."

"You didn't have to. I understood perfectly."

"Well, there's hope for you yet, then." His tone is irreverent.

"You and Joanne deserve each other. You're both on the same *level*."

Phil's expression turns spiteful. "Don't push me, Alena, or I might just go ahead and screw her one of these days."

"Hump away, Phil," I yell, mashing my livid feet into the ground. "I'd never chase you if you left me. I'm worth more than that."

Slamming the door hard, I exit in style. As I stumble down the corridor and back to my room, I'm shaking, nonetheless. I try to block out my hurt. I'm determined not to have an anxiety attack over this huge argument. At nineteen, I am a big woman. I need to handle this another way. By sleeping it off and waking up refreshed.

The next day Phil talks about the spat jestingly, acting as if it was a misunderstanding. But the quarrel sticks to the walls of my memory. I can't let the distress go.

In the pit of my stomach, I have a feeling that this is another obstacle driving a wedge between us, a wedge Phil claims does not even exist. Yet we both know differently. I discern how serious the fight was and I get a terrible ache in the base of my belly, which tells me this fighting could ultimately lead to our demise. No woman can dismiss her female intuition forever. No woman can completely disregard her natural God-given instincts. As much as we would like to, we can't. It is innate, inbuilt, part of our systems.

IS THIS REALLY LOVE?

Flicking my long copper ringlets, which were styled and highlighted by the voguish Becca, I watch them arc, and fall elegantly, onto either side of my shoulders. Quietly, humming a classic Mariah Carey tune in the centre of the library, I feel buoyant, with a renewed sense of freedom. Skipping down the book isles, familiarising myself with the smell of a thousand stories, in this fruitful forest of knowledge, I suddenly have the inspiration to open a blank page in my consciousness, and rewrite the story of my life. The melodious sound of music that vibrates on my lips is beginning to sew me up from the inside, helping me to repair, to mend. Helping me to reshape my future.

Phillip Gregson never was that magic prince from an untold fairy tale, that schoolgirl happily ever after fantasy, as I once imagined him to be. He, as I have discovered, is a real man, flawed, and fallible. A rugged, street-smart twenty first century guy, who's so far away from being the perfect gentlemen, it hurts. Hence, my story, my life, must start and end with me. Phillip is not my saviour. Nor is he my chivalrous knight in a gleaming silver coat of armour, galloping to save me on his faithful white steed. He never was that dreamlike person.

As I float out of the storybook and come back to reality, I select my research material and find the workstation reserved for me in the library's study room. Approaching my desk, I feel a fiery pair of eyes descend on me, burning a hole into my pallid skin. Pulling out the chair, I sit down, and set the mountain of literature on the desk. Curious to identify my enemy, I swivel round at a 90 degree angle. Boring into my flesh from the adjacent workstation, is none other than Joanne Jackman, who is sitting with two of her girl friends. Strategically, she twirls her lengthy black weave, and pouts, asserting a silent pre-eminence. Her dark ebony skin and sable eyes shimmer in the light, and she pulls a regal face, as if she is royal, majestic, some sort of *Princess*. Unleashing a phony laugh, my opponent looks at me austerely, contorting her features, carefully sizing up the competition. Joanne hates my guts and she wants to steal my man. She thinks she's superior, better than me. The envy blazing in her dusky eyes is the birth of hatred. Diluting her poisoned stare, I welcome this animosity with a wide open grin. Not knowing how to respond, Joanne's pupils dart, returning their full attention to the friends who are smirking at her defeat.

My vindictive dorm house rival, who lives exactly opposite my boyfriend, and is doing a Sports Science degree just like him, may think it's easy to claim a man who belongs to another woman. What she fails to recognise, is that a vice so simple to perform, comes with a price affixed to its acerbic tail.

Entering the study room all of a sudden, Phil appears flummoxed. He scans me, and then glances over at Joanne. His allegiance is split. So are his loyalties.

As if claiming a prize, Joanne signals Phil to come over to her table. I glint at him, waiting for his legs to move in her direction, waiting for him to choose her over me. If he does, he knows we are finished. Done. I won't be any man's second choice. It's all or nothing, Phil. All or nothing. Take your pick.

Profoundly, the dark, tainted knight inhales, deciding upon his state of play on the chess board.

As he ambles towards me, I blow a huge sigh of relief. Joanne's snarling anger swirls in the air. I bat away her disappointment and embrace the sound of triumph, which is trumpeting in my ears. My gaze is fixed firmly on my man.

Faithfully, Phil sits down on his chair. He places his books and bag on the flat mahogany surface. His eyes dive into mine from across the desk.

"It's *you* that I want, Alena," he reassures me. "*You* are my sweetheart."

Reclining into the seat, folding a pair of military arms across my chest, I carry a stern comportment. "I am your sweetheart?" I say condescendingly. "That wasn't the hymn book you were singing from the other night, *hunnie*."

"We all say things we regret in the heat of the moment," he mutters, rubbing my leg friskily under the table with a smooth, frolicsome limb. "Today, I wanna generate a different kind of heat."

"Oh, really?" I quip.

Audaciously, he winks. His lips curl into a smirk. "Yes, really."

Inwardly, I smile, not letting him know how his leg massage is getting me all hot and bothered under my purple and white dress. One more touch and I'll simply lose my capacity to do any more work. I issue him a playful warning look, indicating for him to stop. He gets the hint and orders his feet to behave themselves and return back to their position on the ground.

There is silence for a while as we begin our assignment on Shakespeare, gathering our thoughts, examining manuals and cumbersome textbooks, and then putting our ideas and findings down on paper. With every assertion we make, it has to be supported by evidence and must be cited and referenced in our essays, which is tedious work. We continue working in absolute silence for twenty minutes. The quietness starts to kill me; I am bursting to speak.

"I hate assignments," I grumble, as I attempt to write another five hundred words of the 8,000 word essay we have to complete on *The Art of Deception in Othello*.

"This module is heavy duty!" I add, releasing a large puff of air from my anxious lungs. My shoulders slump and I lean back in the hard wooden chair. I am completely overwhelmed by the amount of time, research, and concentration this task requires. I'm also dreading the thought of having to spend more time and effort typing up all of my detailed notes on the PC later on, to produce my first draft of the essay. "Oh my gosh, I'm feeling *so* agitated and *so* stressed out right now!"

"It's not too bad, babe," he says. "I'm quite enjoying it. We are doing so well in this class; be happy about that. If we work really hard, we can achieve a First Class Honours Grade in this module."

Mechanically, my eyes spin. I moan. "I know. That is something great to work towards. But I just feel a little overwhelmed right now, and this essay is *so* tedious. I wish this wasn't a core module, and then I could've opted for an alternative module. This would've been a good way to get out of this boring paper."

Phil reaches for my hand and caresses it gently. "You want to be an elementary teacher, baby, the top in your field. That's why you're studying English," he reminds me. "Think of all the children and teenagers you'll help in the future."

Edging forward, careening over the table, I plant a kiss on his mouth. "Thank you, Phil, for reminding me why I bothered to even come to college in the first place."

"You're welcome." He cocks a cute half smile. "And besides, being at college may help you figure out your own issues," he adds frankly.

I squint, twitching slightly. "What issues, exactly?"

Wryly he laughs and perches rather awkwardly on his seat. He knows he has hit a sore spot and crossed the safe conversation line. My lips are tightly pressed together in an angry line. I'm boiling inside.

"Are you bringing up the other night again, Phil? I thought you had accepted my decision about us delaying meeting my mother as a couple."

"Well," he says, choosing his words cautiously. "I haven't accepted it. I've swallowed the decision, but the pain has not yet digested in my stomach. It's still hurtful to me that we can't go visit your mother, especially since she has expressed an interest to meet me. And furthermore, the other issues you have, that have not yet been resolved, are starting to affect our relationship."

I raise a shaking palm up straight in front of his face, stopping him in mid-sentence. He can see I am visibly upset; he's seriously crossed the perimeter of inappropriate discourse.

Still trembling, I lean forward, tumbling into his disenchanted eyes. "I have a traumatic past. I'm broken, Phil, and I'm sorry that I can't be the perfect, flawless girlfriend you want me to be. But you've always known that, from the start."

"Alena," he says forcefully. "I'm not asking you to be flawless. That wouldn't be feasible. I just think that you need to go back to therapy. I go sometimes, and it's really helpful. My therapist listens and gives great advice. She is brilliant at what she does."

Vigorously, I deny his statement, shaking my head, my auburn tresses bouncing from side to side. "Therapy can't stop Joanne Jackman poisoning your mind, as she slowly infiltrates, stealing you from my grasp!"

"This is why you need therapy, Alena," he says curtly. "You're insecure and a little paranoid."

"I am neither of those things, Phil, and I don't rebuff the talents of a therapist. I'm handling this, handling everything by myself! I'm fine! Just fine."

"You're definitely not okay, baby," he disagrees, banging his flat palm on the desk. "You need *support*. Perhaps I should call a young person's helpline to get some advice for you."

"No, just leave it alone, okay?" Flinging my books aside, taking in a deep lungful of air, I let rip on my boyfriend. "I've had enough of this crap. Can we take a break now?"

"What kind of break are you referring to, Alena?" he says angrily, a dragon's fire burning in his irises.

I throw my head down on the desk, frustrated about everything. "Are you bored of me, Phil?" I ask him tearfully, mortified by his obvious anxieties and dissatisfaction about our relationship.

"Bored?" he asks, raising his eyebrow, as if confused by the enquiry.

Raising my head up, gaining a small degree of strength from the adrenaline in my veins, I decide to lay my cards on the table. "I know that you spoke to a certain unnamed individual about our excuse for a love life. I *know* you are unhappy," I say softly, staring into his forlorn face.

I speak in a hushed voice, so not to bring any more unwanted attention to the table. There are two other workstations in the study room. The table on our immediate right is Joanne's table. Talking noisily about such intimate matters would be a great soap opera to excite my rival and distract all the students from studying, allowing them to gossip liberally about us.

"She told you?" he says, covering his mouth, completely in shock. "I told her not to share this with anyone, especially not you."

"Becca is my best friend, Phil. We share everything!" I say honestly. "Besides, I could feel your sadness on the night we almost –. I can feel that you're hurting, regardless of whether or not you say it."

He puffs, filling with agitation. "It's just that I'm

frustrated, Alena. We don't go on dates, or see the city – you're too scared to go off campus unless it's for grocery shopping or to see your mother – and we can't have the relationship we want. We're trapped, Alena. Imprisoned, because you can't let go of your past and allow us to move forward."

"I know, and I'm sorry, Phil." I recoil, reverting back into a shell. "I'm sorry, okay."

Resting my head on the table, my hair flops on the surface. I now look and feel like a wreck. Peering at me dolefully, he, too, slumps his head on the table top.

"I must say, it's starting to kill me, having a girlfriend whose heart is made of glass and is so breakable."

"Please, be patient," I beg, breathless and filled with heartache.

"I'm trying, Alena," he groans deeply. "God knows how I'm trying."

My head remains motionless on the smooth veneer upholstery, and then soon enough, I feel alive again, revivified, and an array of thoughts fly like birds in the core of my brain. I sport a smile. A partial solution to our relationship problem has just sailed into my noggin. This could be ingenious! Eager to share my fresh ideas, I sit up.

"What if I cook us a special dinner tonight? We can have a romantic date with candles, music, and slow dancing. How about that?" I say timorously, hoping he will be in agreement.

Brightening up almost immediately, he grins. "I would like that. It's a start. A step in the right direction for us."

"Good!" I clasp my hands together; a feeling of mirth colours my cheeks. "I have a lot to prepare."

He wets his lips and then gives me a deliciously sugary kiss. I throb with desire.

"I'm looking forward to it, Alena!" He tells me warmly. "I really am."

"I'm glad to hear it!" I beam.

Heavy footfalls upset the ambience. It is Becca, and

she has just slapped her books on the desk.

"Can I join you guys?" she asks brashly, pulling the spare chair out at the centre of the table, and she sits down before we respond to her request.

Phillip and I sneak a quick glance and chuckle. This is so Becca, killing a passionate moment between me and my man. I guess it's okay. We have already finished our private conversation.

Out of the blue, Becca's radar picks up the vibration of our heated emotions.

"Am I interrupting something?" she asks, her big blue eyes staring blankly at the pair of us.

Animatedly, I shake my head, so as not to make her feel unwanted or uncomfortable. "No, B, it's cool, stay. We could do with some help."

Phil frowns. I kick him under the table, hard.

Stridently, I clear my throat, hoping he will catch on quick and follow my lead. "We could do with some help, couldn't we Phil?"

"Yes, yes," he agrees, finally getting with it. "You've come just at the right time Becca."

Looking at us both from the centre of the table, she giggles, elated that we have made her feel welcome.

I give my man a nip of a kiss as she opens her textbook and begins to read one of the relevant acts of *Othello* with her big overexaggerated facial movements. Phillip savours Becca's company, even though he never likes to admit it, and I love her, despite her unbridled flamboyance.

TOUCH

Spinning into focus, his deep brown eyes gaze into my virescent ones. They are glistening in the incandescent light, which is coming from the late afternoon sun pouring through my open bedroom window. Phillip presses his soft palm into my chest, into the neat bridge just above my breasts. I savour this degree of closeness with my man. It's comfortable, enjoyable.

"This is the best romantic night we have ever had, baby," he purrs, kissing me seductively on the mouth. "I'm really happy we did this. The food was great, and the whole candlelight thing with the slow dancing was *so* sensual."

I lick my lips, slowly, excitedly, as I touch his broad, square, chocolate shoulders that are simply to die for. Caressing those big guns he has for arms and his Herculean torso is enough to send me to heaven. "The night hasn't finished yet. Your massage is still on my list."

He stretches, grinning broadly. "Yes, I know. I'm looking forward to that."

I chew my bottom lip. "So am I!"

Playfully, I arch my brow into a tunnel shape and throw a lewd half smile into his cushioned mouth. He beams, his eyes unable to look away from mine, our gazes meshing together as one. Snatching a few quick breaths, I find myself mesmerised by his body. We breathe in sync, our bodies and minds acting as one person, one consciousness. Phillip embeds his hand into my cleavage deeper, and starts to wiggle his sweaty span into the crux of my breast bone, in the centre of my bosoms. Then, he begins to feel up the bulk of my breasts, and his eyes burst into lustful flames. Unfastening the buttons on his shirt and pulling it clean off, I smile, watching it tumble to the floor. I rub his bare naked six-pack, admiring how smooth it is and how gorgeous it is to the touch. Suggestively, he begins to moan.

"Alena, this feeling's so freaking good. Keep going."

Shooting north, his eyes rise to the skies.

"Don't worry, I won't stop," I whisper into his ear.

Creating fiction, I move up and down his trunk. His moaning increases, tenfold. He rocks from side to side.

"Sit down on my bed. It's time."

"Do you have the baby oil?" he murmurs, his eyes glazed, his mouth slightly puckered.

"Yes," I answer vehemently. "Now sit and enjoy!"

Loosening up his body, he relaxes on the bed, and I sit behind his muscular frame, wrapping my legs around his lower body. This level of intimacy is rapturous yet overpowering. I soak in my fears, letting go a little, and I reach for the baby oil, which is on my dresser beside my bed. Massaging a drop of sweet liquid on his cocoa skin, I begin to knead his shoulders and back, fondling every line, every muscle, in that part of his body. Swaying gently, groaning joyously, he enjoys this heated session. I avert my attention to his pectorals, so divine and so wonderfully shaped. Grabbing the mass of his large muscles and nipples in my hands, I massage them, until he growls heftily like a wild animal. Gradually, his head reclines into my breasts. He trembles, his face squashing, teeth chattering, nose wrinkling. I move more vigorously over his back and chest, with deep powerful, movements. Quickly, his eyes light with passion.

"Beautiful!" he shouts at the top of his lungs. "This is beautiful."

Soon, his body convulses and he licks his lips over and over again. I have a sense of satisfaction knowing that I am the woman making him feel this way.

When the massage is done, he gazes at me, thankful for this passionate concession.

"That was amazing, baby. Thank you."

"You're welcome, honey," I answer sweetly, smiling for England.

"Let me give you one now," he insists, his face lighting up. He removes the oil from my hands. "C'mon, it's your turn."

My face changes. The anxiety begins to well in my heart. "No, I can't."

He is bemused. "Why not? Doesn't it feel good to be massaged by your amour?"

"I can't have those kinds of sensations. It might lead to sex, and I wouldn't be able to handle that."

Getting up from the bed, he grumbles. He's got his shirt in his hands; he is about to put it back on and leave.

I am stunned. "Where are you going, baby? It's only nine o'clock. We can watch a film together. How about a romance?"

He moues. He's upset. "I am concerned about *our* romance, Alena…"

I am confused. "I don't understand, Phil, we are having an amazing night. Why are you getting annoyed?"

He grumbles once more, but louder this time. "You don't get it, do you, Alena?"

Scrunching up my face in confusion, I move to the edge of the bed, closer to him. But I sense that we are further apart than ever. "No! What am I missing?"

"Your future, and our future!" he snaps.

I still don't get what he's trying to say. "Are you

insane? Of course I have a future. Of course we have a future."

Defiantly, he shakes his head. "No, things are hanging precariously on the brink, because you keep blowing hot and cold on me, and it's making me angry and frustrated. If you don't let go of the past, then you won't have a future, and *we* won't have a future. Is that what you want?"

I am aghast. "Please, Phil, just stay."

He is perturbed. "The fact you can't answer my question speaks volumes, Alena. Goodnight."

"Goodnight?" I scream. "Phillip, stop this nonsense!"

"Only you can, Alena. This is out of my hands. I can only support you if you let me. But as far as you're concerned, everything is fine. So what am I supposed to do? Tell me, please."

The past is polluting my thoughts again. Stanley Hawthorne's malignant cackle swirls in my mind, preventing me from speaking. I open my mouth, but nothing comes out.

Phil mumbles a few profanities, opens the door and marches out. Forcefully, he slams it shut. His fury reverberates through the hall as he stomps down the corridor.

I am numb; I cannot feel anything, not even pain. I'm beyond feelings, emotions. My spirit is an empty vessel, a dead fossil, washed up on a deserted beach.

THE THERAPIST

It's been four weeks, six days and fourteen hours since I last visited my therapist, Doctor Hannah Radcliffe, whose swanky office is situated on the slip road beside the main town centre of Sutton, in Surrey. I first went to see the gregarious yet perceptive Hannah two years ago, following a string of unsuccessful first appointments with a bunch of nasty, patronising therapists, all based in the Sutton area. Surrey, on the outskirts of London, is a beautiful scenic place full of beautiful landmarks, country manors, and idyllic views. It reminds me of Leicestershire, in some respects. My mother now lives in this glorious part of the country, in England's south east corner. We did live in the busy, hectic town of Brent Cross in North West London, two and a half years ago, prior to the news of the attack hitting the press, the Magpie Mob targeting me at school and neighbours talking about us, saying how I brought the whole situation upon myself, due to my *careless actions*! My mother strongly felt, with all these negative influences, that she couldn't protect me in a secure maternal bubble anymore.

People's cruel and senseless comments in the local community were seriously damaging my self-esteem. Mum was right; the name calling at school and the neighbourhood's impervious remarks were beginning to depress me. And as a result of this relentless bullying and ostracisation, I began to develop phobias and became very introverted. Mum saw the pain in my eyes every day, the deep disturbing lamentation; she had to do something to ease my pain. So, she listened to the advice of a local victim support charity, taking matters into her own hands, and decided we should relocate to Sutton. At first I didn't agree with her decision. I wanted to stick it out in North London and not be forced out of my home. After time, I realised that moving on was the best decision. Staying in Brent Cross only reminded me of what happened, and since I had already started to hear Stanley's voice in my head, to the point where I had serious behavioural problems and mood swings, it wasn't healthy for me to live there anymore.

A few months after we moved out to Sutton, I started to feel a little better – the air was cleaner, the people seemed friendlier, and the neighbours were kind and hospitable. I continued my schooling in a local Sutton school, where I must admit, I was a lot happier and healthier, mentally and physically. Of course I missed my best friend Emma so much, but having a fresh start in a new and different region of England, with a new class of people, did me a world of good. It wasn't until I was about to head off for college that I had a funny turn...

My therapist, Doctor Hannah Radcliffe, who, with my mother, convinced me to go to college, has been kneading those painful memories out of my mind for years. For a while, it looked like she would be able to succeed in curing me and help me get rid of the past for good. I visited Doctor Radcliffe twice weekly from the first day Stanley was formally charged. That arrangement continued up until a month ago, when I suddenly stopped seeing her altogether. Hannah does not know why I stopped attending sessions. I never admitted the reason why. Doctor Hannah has called me every week for four weeks straight to find out the answer, but I won't answer my mobile phone when she rings me. I've been avoiding her as I could not address any of her probing questions. Only last night, I realised why I have been behaving in this strange way. It's because of my relationship with Phillip.

When I first met Phillip by the drinks stand, last summer, during the Freshers' Fair, I thought he was my quick fix, who could release me completely from the pain. So I got my therapy from his deep, heated kisses and passionate caresses. He stroked my hair, and I felt better; he whispered sweet nothings in my ear and I felt the buzz. But that wasn't enough to sort out my problems that were lingering beneath my skin, lying in wait to devour me from the inside out.

As our relationship progressed, I realised I had overestimated Phillip's ability to fix me. I had been far too optimistic. I'd made the wrong choice, by choosing him to heal me rather than therapy. Though once I'd made my choice, I felt I couldn't go back. I didn't wish to admit that I had made a mistake, not to Hannah, not to my mother, and certainly not to myself. That's when pride got the better of me, and I decided to face my demons without seeking any further professional help. Going back to Doctor Hannah with my tail between my legs wasn't an option. I am not one who likes to admit that I am at fault, not on this big of an issue, anyway. I will not go back to Hannah to see that kind yet triumphant smirk of her face, the smirk that says, "I told you so."

Putting aside the grossly overpriced sessions and her obsession with reflective sarcasm, Hannah is quite a good therapist. In fact, she is the best therapist is Surrey, and I can tell you this with confidence because I have been to most of them in that area. Deep down, I know I should have gone back to see her. However, I won't. What's done is done. I've made my choice. What else can I say?

Just when I think Doctor Hannah has quit her pursuit

of me, my mobile buzzes, at 7 o'clock in the morning. Phil and I are in bed together, doing nothing except sleeping.

I wake up to that buzzing sound, and I see a text from Doctor Hannah Radcliffe:

Hello Alena, hope you are well. This is a reminder that you have a therapy appointment today at 5pm, with me, Doctor Hannah Radcliffe. Room 4. I look forward to seeing you.

Immediately, I delete the text. I have no intention of going. My mind is made up. Two minutes later, my mobile phone rings. The number is withheld. I answer it.

"Hello," I croak. "This is Alena Pavlis speaking."

"Well, well, isn't this a surprise," the voice chirps. "I didn't think you still existed, Miss Alena Pavlis!"

"Hannah!" I am stunned that she is calling me right after I discarded her SMS. Darn it, I should never have answered a withheld number call. Note to self: ignore all calls where the caller hides their telephone number.

"Yes, Alena. This is Hannah."

"What can I do for you, Doctor Hannah?"

"So, I've gone from Hannah, to Doctor Hannah, in less than a minute. Bad time?"

I decide to play her game. "Yes, I'm bonking my boyfriend if you must know. It's a really *really* bad time."

She laughs wryly. "Are you referring to the boyfriend who is snoring next to you?"

Phillip is in a deep sleep. She obviously heard him snorting in the background. Darn it!

"So," she continues. "Are you still with Phillip Gregson?" She asks this mechanically. I can tell she is reading from her notes.

"Uh-huh," I answer in affirmation.

"Is he the man who you are with right now?"

"Yes, it is Phillip lying next to me."

"Are you both naked?"

"Excuse me?" I ask, rather shocked.

"Well, then?"

I decide to comply. "Yes, we are naked."

"Fully naked?"

"Yes, Doctor Hannah. We are fully naked."

She is curious. "Do you like the sensation of him being naked next to you?"

I hesitate. "It's okay."

"How far have you two gotten in your relationship? You've been together nearly eight months now."

That crosses the line. "I'm not answering that question! That's way out of order, Hannah!"

"Is it?"

"Yes!"

"I guess it is, when I'm speaking to a genophobic and a social agoraphobe."

"Hey!" I yell. "Only I can call myself those things!"

"Why is that?" she asks directly.

"Because you're a professional."

"And?" she goads.

I halt deliberately. "And you diagnosed me, so it's weird."

"Alena, that doesn't make sense," she says cogently. "How did you really wish to respond to my remark?"

"No comment!" I snap.

"Alena?"

"Okay," I wail.

I pause.

"Yes?" She prompts me commandingly.

"Hearing you say it, out loud, makes me feel like a freak."

"You are not a freak, Alena."

"Yes, I am!" I cry.

"No!" she confirms forcefully. "You are not a freak."

I am furious; I feel as though she is mocking me. "Don't patronise me, Doctor. I don't appreciate it."

"I am not in the business of insulting people," she

replies sharply. "I direct, guide and dispel patients' misconceptions and negative thoughts and opinions of themselves."

My voice is harsh. "I am not a patient, Hannah! Not anymore. Please do not refer to me in this manner."

Through the receiver, I can almost see her smirking. "I notice you removed the 'Doctor' before 'Hannah' when you addressed me, and confirmed that 'you are not a patient.' But you are, Alena. There is no shame in needing guidance and support from a professional such as myself."

"Isn't there?"

"No." Her voice is soft, warm, kind. "There isn't!"

"Alright then. If you say so," I reply dismissively.

"You weren't really *bonking* Phillip this morning, were you Alena?"

"No," I answer honestly. "I wasn't."

"Alena, have you had intimate relations with Phillip in the past month, since you stopped coming to sessions? Have you two gone off campus on dinner dates, romantic walks, etcetera? Are you doing any hobbies or activities to help relieve your anxiety?"

"Erm..."

"Well?" she prompts. "Please clearly verbalise your response."

"Am I paying for this telephone session?" I ask, avoiding the question.

"No!" she sighs, obviously a little exasperated. "I won't apply a charge."

"Thank you."

"Alena?"

"Yes, Doctor?"

"I would like answers to my questions."

I am sharp with her. "No to all three questions! Are you happy?"

"I don't think *you* are happy, are you, Alena?" She asks, throwing a reflective question at me down the receiver.

Suddenly, I start to panic, and I feel my airways begin

to close.

"Breathe, Alena. Breathe." She is concerned.

"I brought everything on myself, Doctor… It was my fault he attacked me… I'm to blame for it all!" I murmur, as the tears fall from my face and I feel myself drowning in my sorrow and all-consuming guilt. "That's why I'm being punished for my sins!"

Quickly, Hannah snaps me back to a rational state.

"You are not to blame, and I won't allow you to define yourself as the perpetrator."

"Why not?" I ask candidly.

"Stanley was a manipulative predator. You are not to blame. The child is never to blame. He is the one to blame. That's why he is in prison, Alena, serving a five year sentence." She catches her breath, feeling the weight and gravity of her powerful words.

"That may be the case, Hannah, but I am living in my own prison, my own hell. I am trapped by the past. I cannot move forward."

"Yes you can, Alena. You can get through this. Come back to sessions. I can't promise an easy fix, but together, we can battle those demons."

"Those demons are mine. I have to get rid of them on my own."

"Why?"

"Because…"

"Why are you holding onto your demons, Alena? Let them go."

Rudely, I snort. "What's it to you? I'm just another patient. Take me off your books, Doctor Radcliffe. Save us both the trouble of exploring these issues!"

"Wouldn't that just give you the easy way out?" she says serenely. "Why should I give you this option, Alena?"

"Because this is my request," I snap.

"Why aren't you having an intimate relationship with Phillip Gregson? Why don't you two go on dates? Why don't you have any pastimes? Why have you created a prison for yourself on campus? What is holding you back?"

"My demons!" I confess.

"Exactly! So you need to dispose of them. Start enjoying life, and you need to improve your relationship with Phillip Gregson too. He is knocking at the door of your heart, Alena. Don't lock him out forever."

"Hannah," I say sighing gravely. "I shall never be fixed. I'm doomed. And I will always have a glass heart that locks people out, particularly Phillip. You need to understand this. Phillip will leave me and move on soon enough, and go off with some sweet piece of arse that doesn't have my baggage! That's how this story will end. Okay?"

"If that were true about Phil, Alena, then why is he sleeping in bed with you right now, completely naked?"

Pausing for a moment, I think deeply about her question. "Erm... He said he was cold and needed warmth."

"He could have got warmth from a dressing gown, don't you think? But he wanted *your* warmth, Alena. Why do you think that is?"

Sluggishly, I shrug my shoulders. "I don't know, maybe he loves me."

She chirps victoriously. "Yes, I think he *really does* love you, that's why he yearned to lay beside you with no clothes on. He needed your warmth last night, even though he knew his desires would not be met."

"I guess," I reply reluctantly.

"That's why he hasn't left you for some 'sweet piece of arse', Alena."

"Suppose that's true," I state aversely.

"I see you've made a little progress in the confidence department. Last time we spoke you and Phillip hadn't even considered laying together in a bed. Making that decision is a big step for you. Progress will happen slowly, day by day. However, healing from the past is achievable.

It will just take time."

I am thankful for her advice, yet still bemused. "Are you going to force me to come back to sessions, Doctor?"

"I can't force you to do anything. I am not a tyrant, Alena. I am a therapist."

Triumphantly, I smirk. "You said 'I am a therapist,' not 'I am *your* therapist.' Does that mean you are finally letting me go my own way?"

"Hmm. Your English degree is really starting to pay off."

"So you thought I wasn't good at it before? It's only *starting to pay off!*" I jest.

"I will remove you from my books, Alena. Is that what you want?"

"Yes. Thank you, Doctor."

"One word of advice."

"I'm listening!"

"Let go of your past, live life, and invite Phillip into your world completely. Respect, commitment, and trust are two-way things. Both the man and the woman need to develop these qualities if they want the partnership to survive."

I raise a curious brow. "Are you judging me, Doctor Hannah?"

"No," she says compassionately. "I am guiding you."

"Okay, thanks Hannah... Goodbye."

"Goodbye, Alena, and I wish you all the best with everything. I hope you and Phillip work out in the end."

"Thank you, Doctor." I smile. "I really mean that."

"You're most welcome... and Alena?"

"Yes, Hannah?"

"I read in the press some time ago that Hawthorne has the best lawyer money can buy. So, if he demonstrates 'good behaviour' in prison, they might go ahead and release him early. You must prepare yourself for this eventuality, and ensure the college steps up campus security if this should ever become a reality."

All of a sudden I feel my airways beginning to tighten again, but I stay strong, refusing to let the mention of him cut off my air supply. "I will prepare myself, Doctor."

"You may also have strange conflicting emotions at the time of his release. What I would say to you is this: don't attempt to have any contact with him before, or after, he is discharged. This will take you right back to square one. I don't want to see you fall into a dangerous state of regression. You have come too far to go back now."

I am touched by her concern. "Thank you for your bolstering words, Hannah. I can safely say I shall *never wish* to see that man again. Never!"

"That is very good to hear." Her voice sounds relieved.

Content, I smile to myself.

"Remember, Alena, the door is always open if you need to talk. We keep old patients' details on our system for five years. Before the end of the day, I will ask my personal assistant, Daphne, to mail you out a list of useful contacts – helplines, charities and organisations, which offer urgent help and support, if you ever need it."

"That's great. Much appreciated... Goodbye Hannah."

"Goodbye, Alena Pavlis."

Clicking the end call button on my phone, I hang up, exhaling deeply. That went better than I thought it would. I'm surprised; I actually feel good having spoken to Hannah at length. She has given me a glimmer of hope that Phillip and I might actually be all right in the long term. With any relationship, especially with ours, there will always be bumps on the way. It is just life.

Placing my phone back on the dresser, I lay a slow, drooping head on the pillow, holding onto my man. As two sleepy eyes begin to close, I make up a little prayer, and murmur it aloud, begging God to let us stay together forever. Hopefully, I'll be able to hold onto Phillip. Deep within my heart, I believe that we could be very happy together forever, if it is written in the stars, that we are meant to last.

EMOTIONS

Phillip and I have parked in a small, secluded lane opposite the college. We are sitting in his rented car, quietly, listening to the tuneful shrill of the Merlin bird, who is happily resting on the fringe of the rouge bonnet, proudly fluffing the feathers of its solid two-tone body. He looks at us, almost peering into the automobile, before flying off into the sky, finding another place to call home. You could cut the silence the bird left with a knife. There is nobody else around. No other forms of life are prevalent in this abnormally remote region. There are no buildings, houses or shops in this section of the road, only a dense population of evergreen trees, which beautify the glorious hideout, making it the perfect place for reflection, romance, or both.

We are alone, all alone, in this beautiful yet isolated part of town. All I can hear is Phillip's heartbeat, and our heavy breath, which swirls slowly and intensely inside the hot sweltering vehicle. Gradually, our ponderous puffs of air intermingle, and I imagine that they compose near transparent lines, thin, long, and serrated, and kiss as Phillip and I share a pensive stare. This deep expression of love permeates my soul. I see my whole life in his heavenly gaze, my whole world storming passionately in his sexy chestnut ogles. He is also the one who can break my heart, and end our future together, by speaking three murderous words that have been quivering the ridge of his mouth for two long days – the lethal triage of romantic discourse: "Let's break up!"

I have seen these words forming on his lips for days. But he won't utter them. I don't know why. Maybe he loves me more than life itself and is prepared to wait an unforeseeable length of time for when I'm ready to shed the scales of the past.

Even though he loves me, why should he stay in a relationship that has no chance of progressing? Phil doesn't deserve to be held back, he deserves someone who can give him the life and future he desires. I may never be able to grant him this. Might never be able to let Phillip into my heart completely.

I can tell by his short, sharp breaths that he is now looking for a fix to my problems before he feels as though he will burst into flames. He knows as well as I do that we are fated to be together. We did not find each other by chance. We're written in the stars, meant to be. Except I don't notice that energy, that excitement, in his eyes anymore that substantiates this. We are falling, slipping; our beautiful partnership dying and withering away, day by day. And mending us, is beyond Phil's capabilities now.

"I can't believe I passed my test," he says, rummaging his hands through his hair, looking at me guiltily as if these are not the true words he wished to express. "After two long years, I've finally done it!"

"Well done, baby," I say jubilantly, though a hoarse feeling is starting to cut the back of my throat, the sensation that reminds me I am avoiding the obvious problems in our cracking relationship. The issues we have are rising behind the car like a dangerous tidal wave, waiting to completely wipe out the happiness and joy we've built up over the past eight months.

"Thank you," he replies, his voice now terse, his lips trembling violently. "I'm glad the university let me rent this car so I can drive us around. It's nice to be able to take us for a spin in this cool, vibrant city."

"Yea, it's really nice." I smile, gazing into his chocolate eyes. He is about to let me in, allowing my emerald orbs to dive into his irises, but suddenly, I am stunned as I feel shut out by glassiness that creates a barrier in his eyes. I am hurt, isolated, closed off from his world. A tear of melancholy escapes from my eyes.

"But I hardly see the point of us driving around in dizzy circles, Alena. It's rather pointless, don't you think?" His face wrinkles painfully, and he is looking at me with a vacant, glazed expression. I feel the glass in my heart tighten, and I form a tough, impenetrable wall around it, making it impossible for his eyes to read my emotions. Now he is sad that we are distant; I can see it in his eyes. In his reflections, he's regretting his decision to cut me out of his world.

"I'm tired of moving nowhere, Alena. It's breaking my heart."

He is no longer talking about the car. He's talking about us and our excuse for a relationship, which has reached a crossroads. I turn away from his excruciating stare, averting my sore eyes to the floor of the vehicle. Burning tears rush down my ashen cheeks.

"What do you mean by that?" I say sternly, begging him to be straight and honest with me, telling me exactly what is in his heart.

"I've tried, Alena!" he shouts, his cold glance piercing my perturbed expression. "God knows I have tried to help you get over the past. But it hasn't worked. What else do you want me to do? I'm dying here!" Banging his fist repeatedly onto the steering wheel, he yells in frustration. Descrying his sorrowful and despondent face is torturing me. I can't handle seeing him like this. It's heart wrenching. Crying into my palms, I break down.

"I don't know!" I wail, my voice muffled in my hands. "I no longer have the answers, Phillip!"

Distraught and fearful about our future, I gingerly look up, lifting my blurry vision. Seeking out the object of its desire, my green glassy globes hover waveringly over Phil's noggin.

Uneasily, his head is resting on the wheel. His eyes turned away from me. "No, I can't accept that!" he howls fervently. "You need to tell me what I am supposed to do, Alena!" Breathless and exasperated, his head welts into the wheel. "Please, tell me baby! I need to know."

Steadily, his head rises up, and our glances meet across the space of the automobile. He observes the black eye shadow and mascara running from my cheeks. My mouth is trembling with trepidation, and soon I scream to release the agony. I feel as though I'm wilting, unable to breathe, from the pain of the very plausible possibility of losing Phillip. Yet, I know, that I can't do this anymore. I can't do this to him anymore. I'm not even sure if fighting to keep Phil is worth it, either. In order for me to fight for our love, he has to want me as much as I want him, but I don't think he adores me enough. My greatest fear is that he will stray into Joanne's arms. I'm fearful that I'll lose him for good, forever.

"Maybe," I cry. "Maybe it's time to call it a day, and go our separate ways! I hate the idea, but it looks to me as though that's where we are headed anyway. Let's face it."

Pushing his pate into the dark steering wheel once again, he peers at me sideways. He is enchanted, mesmerised, by the very lips which spoke those words. His body draws nearer to mine, and gravitating towards me, his forehead presses to my chest instead of the steering wheel.

"I can't break up with you, Alena. I just can't!"

"Why not?" I bawl as my tears drench my face and fall into his thick black curls.

"I've met some rubbish in my time. You are the best.

The best I've ever had. You are *the one*."

"I can't still be *the one*, Phil," I whisper, as I elevate his head to meet mine and clutch onto his face desperately.

"You are," he affirms. "Even after I confessed about my record, on the day we met, you stood by me. Most girls would have run a mile. And so many times, I've doubted our love, listening to what my friends, to what Joanne, is saying about our relationship. You've been so loyal and faithful throughout. So how can I abandon you now, when you need me more than ever?"

Unable to handle the unbearable hurt crushing my heart, I close my lids. "Phil, just leave me... I don't deserve you, anyway."

"I'm the one who doesn't deserve you, Alena," he says, crying, moving his hands to hold onto the soft circumference of my waist. "I am the one who made mistakes, who's still making mistakes."

I kiss his temple, loving the feeling of his velvety skin beneath my lips. "I forgive you, for everything. Please stop feeling guilty, baby."

He looks up; his coffee-coloured eyes are full of feeling. "I am allowed to feel ashamed, at the very least. I am not your perfect boyfriend, so I shouldn't expect you to be my perfect girlfriend."

I absorb his deep and earnest affection. "No one is flawless, baby, especially not me. I am the one who has wronged. Stanley Hawthorne kissed me in the classroom earlier that day, and I allowed him to do it. I didn't report him. Hours later, I naively went to his house. What happened that night was all my fault."

His hands tremor, his eyes fill with an unfathomably chilling distress. "Alena, that's screwed up talk. You didn't do wrong; he did. He abused his position of trust and harmed a vulnerable girl who'd just buried her father."

"But I willingly went to his house, Phil. I was so stupid," I say, falling into him, my body flagging.

Softly, he kisses my hair, stroking the back of my head.

His hand uses slow circular movements to soothe me. He tries his best to console me, too.

"This evil man manipulated and duped you. Jermaine, and the evidence he gave in court, helped you put him away for five long years. Now, you have to move on from it, create new experiences, new memories, with me." His lips move to my ears, kissing them sensually. "You and me are real, Alena, no pretences. I can show you what real love is, without the guilt or pain or sorrow. I can show you what proper love feels like."

I pour my adoration into my lover's chocolate eyes. "I don't deserve such love, Phil. I am tainted."

"No!" he shouts avidly. "You're not!"

I am now glaring at him, my sharp emeralds cutting into his face. "Mr. Hawthorne has contaminated me, spoiled me for you."

"Well, let me wash you clean with my love."

"You can't!"

"Why not?"

"Because my body is dirty. My whole being is infected."

"I can cleanse you with my love, Alena. Let me in. For God sake, let me in."

His voice is desperate, pleading.

"Phil, I'm scared," I say, my voice weak and wavering. "I'm afraid to let you in. What if I have an episode and freak out and think of *him* again?"

Incongruously, he laughs. "I am not someone you need to fear. I'd never hurt you like that. Never!"

"I know!" I yelp, banging my bonce on the headrest, feeling my frustration and his anxiety heading for a crash collision in the centre of the car. "I know! It's just... I'm so mentally tangled up."

I can read the agony in his countenance as our eyes meet, curving into one another's peripheral vision. We both sense that this partnership is precariously balanced, in danger of imminent death.

"So this is now an obligation, you staying with me?" I ask, fascinated by his thick, erotic lips, which I am so desperate to suck and kiss.

"No, this is respect, trust, loyalty. Love," he corrects me, equally enraptured by my pink kissable mouth. "You looked past my flaws; I have to look past yours too! Though, in truth, I'm not sure how much longer I can do this." He breathes deeply, "Let's take one step at a time. Maybe tomorrow we can go for a long romantic walk *outside*, off of campus and not in the botanical garden. Let's start there."

Shaking my head profusely, I inhale a tired breath. "If there are lots of people around, and I'm in any enclosed spaces, I will panic. I can't do it, Phil."

His face droops into a frown. "How do you know if you don't try?"

"I already know my limitations. There's no point trying. Just dump me, Phil. Release yourself from my hell. Find yourself a normal girlfriend who can do all those *normal* things with you."

"I can't," he insists, "because I have already found her."

"You've found a girl with deep-rooted phobias, that's what you've found."

Determinedly, he drags my troublesome eyes into focus. "I have my princess right here. She just needs to believe she is one."

Phillip's words render me speechless. The words from the man I love resonate in my ears. Hearing his speech, and his attempt to fight for me, to fight for our love, makes me melt into a puddle of tears. I beckon his lips with mine, and grab him close, kissing him, sticking my tongue into his mouth and relishing the feeling of his tongue greeting mine. We are barely breathing, just kissing, touching; him mounting me, and we are dry humping. This is confusing. I thought we were meant to be breaking up?

Piercingly, he glares into my pupils. "I can't live without you, Alena. I love you so much."

"Phil," I say peering down at him, enjoying every second of this unexpected session. "I can't promise that I'll be unbroken soon, so why wait for me?"

"Because I will surely die without you. I won't be able to survive."

"Sometimes," I reply breathlessly, as I feel him rubbing hard against my aroused lips. "Sometimes, love isn't enough."

Blowing into my chest he is fuming, angry as hell. "Gees, Alena, you do know how to kill a special moment."

"Everything around me dies," I mumble pessimistically, stopping him from licking my tender lips, which are still searching for his.

Phil grunts loudly, a forlorn expression forming on his wounded visage. "My friends say I'm crazy for staying in this relationship, especially since we haven't brought it to completion," he mutters. "Am I crazy for wanting to fight for us, Alena?"

My face crinkles in anger. I erupt. "You told your friends about our sexual problems? How dare you, Phil!"

"Erm... only two of them. My college friends, Donald and Ty..."

"You told Donald and Ty, the two biggest shits in college?" I holler. "Did you tell Joanne, too?"

He falls silent.

"I asked, did you tell Joanne too?" I repeat, my voice roaring into the atmosphere.

Timidly, he nods in confirmation.

With all my strength, I push him off of me. Like a falling star, he tumbles onto the window, hitting his head on the solid inflexible glass.

"Alena, I had to tell someone," he cries, nursing his sore head.

"You already told Becca. That's where it should have

ended. By telling all those people, Phillip, you've humiliated me!"

"Alena, I…"

Quickly, I unlock the car and push open the door. I attempt to escape. Without delay, he yanks me back by the arm. I slap him hard across the face.

"Piss off, Phillip! I hate you. I HATE YOU! You're a bastard!"

"Well that's good then!" he screams, hurling his fist into the dashboard, his stare like a knife stabbing me. "'Cos it's Friday night, and I'm gonna go to Po Na Na with my mates – and I'm going to get myself plastered and laid tonight!"

"Fine then!" I shriek. The words almost spit out of my mouth. "I hope you catch something vile tonight, Phillip Gregson!"

Abruptly, I get out the vehicle and slam the car door shut.

Opening the door aggressively, Phillip screams. "I'm glad to be free of your shit! You're far too complicated for me. I should have left, cutting my losses a long time ago!"

Pointing my finger in his face, I snarl at him. "So, the gentleman has flown! This is the real you. I thought you were different, Phillip. I was wrong. You're just like the rest. How did I ever put my trust in you? Just take your new rented piece of metal and get lost. We are done Phillip, over!"

"We all make mistakes and I'm gonna get away from mine right now, in my *borrowed* car!" He shouts, his palms slapping on the leather seat.

"The car was rented from the college, you idiot," I snap, correcting him.

Roguishly, Phillip sneers. "God you're so naïve, Alena. What university rents cars to students? How many nineteen year olds do you know who own a new top of the range bike? C'mon, girl, get real! If ya thought for a second that I'd completely changed, you are a fool. Bad boys don't change. We can never be reformed. We're hustlers, streetwise, and we do what we need to do to survive in this crazy world!"

I run off, crying. Phillip starts up the automobile and drives away.

In the corner of my eye, I see a car following me for fifty yards, until I arrive back to Corefield Road, where the main campus is based. My trail of tears pollutes my vision as I sprint for a couple of minutes. Reaching King Street, I lose the person shadowing me. My hands flop onto my knees. I am puffing, completely out of breath. Finally, I am safe. I've escaped his asphyxiating tenacity.

As fast as a rocket, I race all the way home, to my first safe house – the wonderful Botanical Garden overlooking Ridley House. My breath is short and jagged, my hair plastered across my face. My mind is everywhere, but nowhere. Two distressed eyes dart into space and then plummet back to earth. They bump on the vivid, shiny grass and slide along the blades of warm green turf, rolling about on their glorious homeland. There is a sense of calm and tranquillity around me. My long, charming white dress sails like a boat in the wind and flies loosely around my slender figure. I shut my eyes and take one big breath in and out, inhaling this sweet degree of peace.

Upon opening my eyes, the breeze's scent, once magnificent, turns cold, impassive, harsh. I now discern that I have not escaped anything by coming to the Botanical Garden. In the garden itself I am free, yet trapped inside a sealed box, which is positioned in the integral part of the orchard. The coppice is magical. It can relieve my sorrow, for a moment, helping to lighten my burdens for a short time. However, it can't take me out of the dark, horrid boxed confinements in which I reside. Only I can do that with the power of the mind, and the sore truth, *my sore truth* still remains, fluttering like an injured bird in the nucleus of the garden. I can run anywhere I want, even to the ends of the earth, but I cannot run from myself. No matter where I travel, where I go, the past shall be stuck to the bottom of my shoes, pressed against the sides of my cheeks, and might wish to follow me like an oppressive shadow as I go about my daily life. And soon enough, I will have to face all of my problems, head-on, and overcome them, with or without Phillip.

Facing my past is a fearful prospect, but an inevitable reality.

SOMEONE TO COUNT ON

My sweaty hands desperately clasp onto the fridge in the kitchen, scratching its white superficial surface. Beneath it resides a black, ominous coating, lingering hazardously below. The blackness crawls into my nostrils, seeping into my delicate system, entering my blood stream. I try to breathe naturally. It doesn't come easy. Welling up with tears, I am rasping, choking, dying. The darkness gradually leaks into my chest, and engulfs my weak chattering ribcage. My breathing is erratic, painful; my lungs find it difficult to suck in clean air. Ferociously, my heartbeat plummets as the shadows of the past crash into my core, attempting to destroy me. Gutturally, I scream in pain. I feel the violent waves of poisonous mist cracking my heart in two. I'm beyond fragile, beyond breakable, crippled by perilous anguish.

It soon dawns on me that this pain is an intense feeling of sorrow, because Phillip Gregson and I are over forever. Our love has decayed, and it's entrails have fallen into the abyss that stole my happiness two years ago.

With my hands shaking crazily, I fumble in my skirt pocket and take out my phone. There is only one person on this earth who might just be able to realign my thoughts and stop me sinking into a state of regression. I need to speak to this person, now.

Frantically, I dial the number. My breathing is serrated, irregular.

The phone rings and connects.

"Mum," I wail, my lips pouting, tears rolling down my face. I plonk on a seat at the kitchen table, endeavouring to maintain a degree of composure. "Mum!"

Her voice is kind, warm yet alarmed. "Hunny, baby, what's wrong? It's two in the morning!"

"Mummy, sorry I had to call this early. I'm so upset. Phillip and I are finished, and tonight, he's gone to Po Na Na's with his friends. You know the type of girls he'll pick up – girls like Joanne. Skimpy, scantily dressed sluts, just looking for sex! He wants to get laid by one of *those* girls tonight, mum!"

"Slow breaths, Alena," she encourages. "In, out, in, out."

"Mummy, he's gonna screw some bird tonight!"

"No, Alena. He won't."

"How can you be so sure?" I ask, as tears rain from my visage.

Her voice is firm, yet loving. "Phillip loves you, he has since day one."

"No," I holler, disagreeing. "He never loved me and now he's glad to be rid of me."

"Says who?" she asks.

"Phillip shouted that in so many words when I dumped him. He also confessed he's been *borrowing* vehicles again."

"What? That is terrible!" Mum says in astonishment, "Personally, I think he's crying out for help. From what you told me, his parents don't show him love and he's in conflict about his loyalty towards his culture."

I am furious, angered by the bull that just left mum's lips. "Don't condone his behaviour on any level, mother. Don't defend him. He is totally in the wrong."

"On no level am I condoning his behaviour, just

explaining why he is reacting in this way. A lack of love in one's life and split loyalties, can do crazy things to people, Alena."

Wryly, I laugh unable to feel sorry for Phillip. "Mother, Phillip Gregson behaves like that, because he is a sexually frustrated, thieving liar, who doesn't know which side of the fence he should be rearing his sheep." Pondering on my outspokenness I continue. "Perhaps I should have tried to give him what he wanted long ago, then he wouldn't have chased after some cheap ghetto bitch!"

Silence slices through the air, I can sense the burning fire that is mum's ire.

"Where did you learn this kind of talk from, Alena? I never brought you up to think or speak in this way."

Leisurely, my shoulders shrug. "I don't know. I'm just overtly urban now, I guess. And perhaps, Becca has influenced me too."

"What Becca, your brash Californian housemate?"

"She was right all along, mum... Guys get bored and walk, if you don't sleep with them within the first three months."

"That's crap! Don't listen to what she said!"

"Why is that crap?"

"She doesn't understand love, Alena. A lot of people don't. Phillip is different. He knows what love is."

"He knows, as well as I do, that love and sex are inseparable, mum. You can't have love without sex!"

"That's where you're wrong, Alena."

"How am I wrong?" I say, challenging her.

Mum clears her throat. "Love comes before sex, Alena."

"No, not these days, mum."

Her tone is resolute. "That's why many young people's relationships don't last long."

"What?" I shout, losing my cool. I jump up, pacing the room, plunging a couple of angry hands through my messy hair. "What are you trying to say?"

"Intimate relations alone cannot solve your problems. You need to love yourself before you can completely love Phillip. Love is the foundation of the self and of any relationship. Without love, there is nothing. It is the key to happiness."

"How do I love myself truly, mum?"

"Accept that you are worthy of love, of being loved, and that you have value and purpose."

"Okay, I can try." I say confidently. "All what you're saying makes sense. Thank you, mummy, for listening."

"Any time, pumpkin."

"I *really* needed to talk. I've stopped going to therapy sessions."

Mum is disappointed. "Why, Alena?"

"I felt like a naughty child receiving a lecture. Therapy doesn't work for everyone. Sometimes you just need your mum."

"That's true. I'm always here if you need to talk. Just call." Her voice is gentle and soft. "Do consider returning to therapy at some point though, honey. It is for your benefit."

"Okay, I will." I agree. "Thanks, mummy."

Her voice sings. "You're welcome, baby."

I light up. "How are you, mum?"

"I'm good, honey, just busy at the restaurant, and getting on with laundry, cooking, etcetera."

"Got any new hobbies now?" I enquire.

"I'm in a cinema club, a gardening club. You know? Making new friends."

"Anyone on the scene?" I ask, being nosey.

"Well," she says coyly, "as you ask, there is this one guy in my gardening club."

"Oh? Tell me about him." I smile, very interested to hear about this guy.

"His name is Trevor. He's forty-three, same age as me. He is tall, blond, brown-eyed, with a deep, husky voice. Just my type. We've been on a couple of dates. They went well."

I smirk. "Do you like him?"

"He's nice. We'll see how it goes."

"How's Renny?"

He is the cute little mutt she bought to replace me when I swanned off to college.

"Renny is good. Can't replace you, of course, but he'll do for now."

I laugh.

"If you get back together with Phillip, darling, can I meet him?" asks mum candidly.

"Erm…"

"Well?"

"Let me at least have done the deed with him before you eat him for dinner."

Mum is flabbergasted. "Alena! I'm surprised at you!"

"What for?"

"*I* wouldn't eat him. I'm sure *you* would however. The time you finish with the poor boy, he wouldn't know what his name was!" I can almost see her smirking.

"Mother!" I yell. "That was *so* not appropriate!"

Naughtily, she chortles. "This is your first relationship, Alena. Yes, things will be bumpy along the way. But the love you will share with Phillip will be passionate and true."

I am embarrassed. "Mother, please!"

"I've seen his picture! He's a hottie! A keeper."

"Hmm… On that note, I'm gonna turn in. Goodnight, mummy." I blow her a kiss through the phone.

"Night, baby. Sleep well." She blows a kiss from her end of the phone, too.

"I love you, ma."

"I love you too, Alena."

We both hang up at exactly the same time.

Drying my eyes, I leave the kitchen, making my way down to my room. I feel a whole lot better after speaking to mum. She is good at calming down my wild anxiety.

"Phillip!" I shout, seeing him stagger across the corridor as I vacate the kitchen. His jacket has been tossed over his left shoulder, and he's singing a cheesy 80s track, very poorly. I can tell he is drunk as a skunk.

I go to him.

"What did you have to drink?"

"You're all blurry, baby." His eyes are out of focus. "So blu-r-r-y!"

"How much did you have to drink?" I enquire, holding him up as best as I can by his waist.

"Loads! I had one vodka, two chardonnays, five beers, four shots, and I'm wasted. I like my liquor thicker and quicker!"

Oh, gosh! He's talking crap! He is *so* smashed!

"How was the club?" I ask, partly interested, partly prying, whilst trying to stop him from collapsing on the floor.

"Bull," he slurs. "Music sucked and so did the people there. That's why the boys and I headed back early. Only good thing was the booze."

"Oh, dear," I reply, though secretly happy that his only romance tonight was with alcohol.

His dizzy eyes try to focus on me.

"I owe you an apology, Alena, for my bad behaviour earlier. I was way out of order." He turns away suddenly and pukes an orange, stinky liquid all over the carpet. "Give me a makeup kiss, babe."

That's disgusting. There's no way I'm kissing him!

"I'll pass," I say, my face crinkling with revulsion. "You're damn lucky that I'm even talking to you right now, let alone helping you to stand."

I hold him up. It proves difficult, as he is so muscular and heavy.

"Why don't you want to kiss me?" He persists, his eyes spinning into mine, lips dripping thick, ugly saliva.

"I don't kiss drunks, thieves, or liars!" I state, guiding his limp body towards his door.

Awkwardly, he pulls a funny smile. "Okay then, honey, sugar, baby!"

I try not to laugh at his drunken rambling. "I'll help you inside. But you're still not forgiven for anything."

Disapprovingly he sighs. "I never knew how good a girl I had, until I saw the slutty girls at that club, trying to get off with me. Decent girls are hard to find."

"Yes, they are," I reply coldly, "and you just lost one, due to your own stupidity."

"Please forgive me baby. I'm sorry for what I said," he slurs. "And I returned the car and the bike to their rightful places. I am not perfect. But I'm trying real hard to change."

Dolefully, I roll my eyes. What is this boy expecting from me, a kiss and make up session? He better get real. Phillip Gregson has got to do more than be cute and drunk to win me back. If he wants me back, he better work for it and earn my respect, 'cos I am neither cheap nor desperate. I can cope without him, irrespective of how weak and in need of love he thinks I am.

"Go inside and concentrate on sobering up, Phil. You're making a damn fool of yourself."

As he's fumbling with his keys, eyes still unfocused, legs shaking, and looking like he's going to be sick again, I tease the keys out of his hands, unlock the door and help him into his room. I see him stumbling to the bathroom, where he obviously throws up once more. When he is done, he comes out, better. He's still looking a bit disorientated though.

Blowing me a wonky sideward kiss, he walks forward, almost falling over his own feet.

"Night night, my princess. I love you."

"That's nice," I reply, my voice drenched with sarcasm.

Turning around, I strut down the corridor, full of energy and vigour. Flickering my eyes to his door one last time, I see a girl appear outside. Dark hair, tall, elegant.

North London accent. It's Joanne Jackman. That bitch! Our relationship has been over for less than twenty four hours, and already she's wangling her way into his pants! Dirty lowdown slut! No, Alena. Don't be jealous. He's a deadbeat boyfriend anyway. Let the ghetto bitch claim her booby prize!

Running across the floor to escape the horrid scene unfolding behind me, I hear seventeen-year-old Alena cackling. She is shadowing me, raucously dragging her slow, lamenting feet on the ground. I am not completely rid of her, as I had thought. Sharply, I twist around, growling at the ghost of her presence, and, when I reach my bedroom, I open and slam my door, forcing the quivering child to spend the night in the hallway.

In the morning, she is gone. Nonetheless, I still feel her spirit loitering close by.

CAT FIGHT

Making my way to the laundry room, the small, concealed building behind Ridley House, I feel dishevelled, lost and empty. Approaching this hidden place in my bright blue slippers and pyjamas, I am carrying my dirty clothes, which have been flung any which way into the wash basket. Walking laboriously into the sweet smelling room, I locate a free machine. With an incredibly long face, and a heavy chocolate chip ice-cream tummy, I tip out the contents of my basket into the washing machine. Slamming the machine door shut, I open the draw and pour in the biological powder. Afterwards, I slot the three coins into the money compartment and move the metal coin holder inwards, and then outwards. The Queen's golden heads register in the machine. Then, I press the green 'on' button, starting off my washing. Gradually, my eyes grow tired, my knees weak. A single teardrop sits on my flushed cheek. Forcefully, I slam my back against the nearest wall, as the strong foundations absorb the shock from the earthquake, that tremors inside of me.

Wearily, I watch my pink H&M knickers whirl around with the rest of the attires, and I ponder on the adventures I could have had in these undies, had Phillip Gregson and I got to that stage in our relationship. After eight months of us going steady, I really thought he was the one. I believed that he would wait for me, for as long as it took for me to shed the serpent of the past. All I ever wanted was someone special, a real man, who would support me unfailingly, no matter what. Phillip never was that guy, despite the pretences. He only wanted one thing. That one thing wasn't love. Underneath that endearing smirk and pretty boy swagger, he is just a liar, a cheat, and a fraud. There's nothing authentic about him, nothing at all. He fooled me, and he fooled me good. Now I'm free of him, I just have to learn how to live on my own again. I can do it, I know I can.

Taking charge of my thoughts and emotions, I start to hum a tune, and as the tiredness descends on me, I lie down on a nearby bench. While I recline on the long, wooden seat, murmuring the made-up melody, I begin to drift off, with the sound of the machine droning in the background.

Unexpectedly, a delicate hand taps me, and rests on my hipbone.

Startled, I jump up. To my amazement, Joanne Jackman is standing before me in a tight black mini dress and grey tights. Her dark eyes float over my body like a fallen angel.

"Alena," she says starkly, "you fell asleep." My rival's voice is reasonably civil, except there is a hint of condescension underpinning her words.

My vision is quite hazy. I can just about make out her face. "Did you need something, Joanne? Washing powder? Detergent? A clothes basket?"

Shrewdly, she raises her brow, and carefully responds. "I didn't come here to wash clothes. I followed you here."

Fully alert now, eyes in focus, I sit up. Joanne's tall frame towers over me.

"Why would you follow me here?" I ask diligently.

Leaning in closer, she whispers. "I wouldn't want Phillip to hear us talking in the dorm house. It's quieter down here. No one to intervene in this *girl talk*."

"Phillip?" I ask, trying to downplay my upset. Joanne knows we were an item. She knows mentioning his name has cut me deep. This girl is no fool. She's a vixen in disguise.

"Yes," she asserts brazenly. "Phillip and I are seeing one another now. It's only polite that I tell you in private, and not in front of him. You'd be humiliated if I announced the news on our floor."

Unable to hold in my tempest, I lose my cool. "How quickly he has moved on."

A smirk of triumph appears on her visage. "Yes, he has moved on. He's come back home."

Alarmed by her comment, I challenge her. "What is that supposed to mean – *come back home?*"

Spitefully, she laughs. Her lips pout London street style. A firm pair of hands are resting on her hips. "You see, Alena, black boys like to play with their white toys in the land of fantasy. Eventually, they wake up and come to their senses, and find their way back to the motherland."

Realising Joanne has turned this conversation into a cultural war, I arm myself with weapons of equal measure.

"You know he's still in love with me. That's what is *really* bothering you, isn't it, Joanne? He may be with you now, but deep down, he still wants to be with me!"

She is taken aback by my frankness, yet there is something in her eyes that tells me my assertion is right.

"We have spent every night together since you two broke up. He's amazing, if you catch my drift. How could ya get my meaning though? It's not like you let him touch you. That's probably why he came to me for some sweet loving."

"Please, Joanne," I retort coldly. "Don't flatter yourself. Phillip Gregson doesn't care two straws for you. You're just an available hole that he wishes to fill. Soon enough, he'll run off with another street whore. One that is even sluttier than you!"

Joanne screams, and lunges for me. Pushing me off the bench, I tumble onto the hard marble floor.

"You snooty, English bitch!"

"I am not English. I'm Greek, you ho!" I bellow, sinking my claws into her back.

"Makes no bloody difference," she yells.

Rolling about on the floor, tussling for England; we are both pulling each other's hair, biting, kicking, spitting. Then, when we've had enough, she flops on top of me, completely spent. Sweating and repulsed, I shove her off me.

Blood is seeping from my chin where the vampire bit me. I seal it off with the tip of my index finger. As we both struggle to return to a standing position, Joanne's fists are ready for action, so are mine.

"You want to fight me for him?" she hollers. "Well, let's do this, bitch! Bring it on!"

Bored of this game, I tut loudly, belittling my opponent. "You can have him! I wouldn't want him now. He's a lying, cheating bastard."

Joanne is smirking too much. It's not normal. She is up to something. She's got something up her sleeve.

"Yea, he is a liar. The daddy is bad."

"Daddy?" I ask, dumbfounded.

"Yes! Didn't he tell you that he was a dad?"

"No, he did not!" I scream. "Who's the mother of his child – you?"

She cackles like a crow. "No, I'm not the baby mother. Before he went into the slammer three years ago, he got some Indian chick called Zoya pregnant. Social Services took the child away and put it up for adoption, when he went to juvie. Didn't he tell you this?"

"No," I cry. "He didn't."

Well, Alena," she says with an air of superiority. "He wouldn't tell you. You and him were never on the same *level*. Not like him and me. We are Bajons. Both our parents are from Christ Church, Barbados, so we got a lot in common. All you two ever had were differences. I don't quite understand why he got with you in the first place. It makes no sense."

Inside, I am a burning fireball. I feel angry, used, and betrayed by the man I once loved. Somehow, I hide the choler and disillusion, and I hold it together.

"Race and love – those are the two things people cannot control. God is the one who decides. Didn't ya mother ever teach you that, Joanne Jackman?"

She howls with laughter, as a way of mocking me. "Alena Pavlis, didn't *your* mother ever tell you that a fish and a bird who fall in love, can never find a nest?"

Spontaneously, I feel the need to grab my washing powder to educate Joanne. Shaking out a few grains of powder, I sprinkle it in her hands. "Here, look," I say, watching her squirm as it touches her skin. "A bit of white on your skin won't harm you. That attitude will. Lose that bitterness, Joanne. It only destroys people. Hatred never did anyone no good."

Wildly, she shrills like a banshee and dusts off the powder. "Those sanctimonious words have no effect to me, girl. My black is deep-rooted. It don't mix with nothin'. And that's why he loves me."

Shaking my head in disgust, I turn to leave. Intent on getting the upper hand over my adversary at the eleventh hour, I decide to play my trump card.

"If Phillip's love has eyes that can see you, then you ought to be worried, Joanne Jackman. *Real love* is blind. It has no sight at all. Neither does it recognise colour or nationality. But it sure does have substance, a soul, and a heartbeat."

On that note I disappear, leaving my words to burn Joanne's stone heart.

KNOWING YOUR HEART

Singing the ballad I wrote in the garden, I prepare for the Coolette Singing Audition, which is only fourteen days away. Sitting on my favourite yellow bench, belting out the song I composed in the fresh open air, I feel myself healing, mending from the inside. Singing is my passion, my medicine, the cure to all my woes. It makes me feel so much better. Singing makes me come alive. As I warble, fully opening my lungs, my mind and consciousness are a pair of white doves soaring parallel in the sky. For the first time in a long time, I have found the one thing that makes my heart beat. The one thing that surpasses everything, including the relationship I once had with Phillip. Now he is gone, and out of my life, I can concentrate on myself and being the person that I need to become.

While I skyrocket to another realm, another place, the ambience in the garden changes and the mood is a fierce shade of red. Slowly, I turn around and descry the face of a fervid lion. Flames of determination encircle his essence. His eyes are fixed, rooted, a dark nose broadening, with deep, rich heritage. This is a man who now understands his heart. An indomitable man unwilling to compromise. He knows what he wants. His eyes tell me that he's willing to fight for it.

Floating down to the ground, my angel voice fades, trailing away, my halo's glow weakening around my head. I sense the velocity of this man's strong presence verging towards me, accelerating from a distance. Sprinting, his paces increasing, my anger and pain amalgamate, peaking into a ball of wrath in the atmosphere. Then, gradually, it begins to dissipate, as he ebbs ever closer. I battle hard to keep hold of the anguish. But his eyes are driving back my fury, and a higher power is acting as his assistant, washing clear the spleen and venom from my system.

With all my might, I attempt to cling onto my bottomless rage. It is no good. The Lord won't let me keep it.

Coming closer still, the man lowers his frame, and panting, trying to recover from his pelt, he rests beside me on the bench. Breathing heavily, he demands my attention, calling my pupils into focus. A torch held by his ancestors is illuminating his features, radiating the true purpose and importance of his mission.

"We need to talk, Alena," he insists. "I cannot go on like this. I need us to get back to where we were at the beginning."

"Get back to where we were," I say with a bitter intonation. "I doubt that will ever happen, Phillip."

"Just let me talk, Alena. That is the least you can do."

"I owe you absolutely nothing," I spit out thornily. "Nothing at all. Now go away!"

"Let me speak, for goodness sake! Hear what I have to say."

"Okay, let's talk. What did ya want to talk about, Phil?" I retort.

"Everything!" he exclaims breathlessly.

"So, where shall we start? Shall we converse about that bike you took on the day we met? Or you *borrowing* a car on the day we broke up? Or maybe, we could discuss that secret love child of yours who got removed by social

services and put up for adoption, when you went to juvie. Why not throw in a discussion about Zoya, your ex-girlfriend? Take your pick, Phillip."

My crimson resentment deepens, melting my halo.

He shrinks. His hurt and my ire are crushing his spirit. "I couldn't completely reveal myself to you. I couldn't take that chance."

"Yet, you could tell her the whole truth?" I shriek.

Like a dangerous pneumatic drill, his body shudders, his pupils piercing into me. "Would you have loved me if I confessed all? Would you have?"

"Yes," I scream. "I would have, Phillip. It's the truth that I wanted. I trusted you with my secrets, my past. You should have trusted me with yours."

"I'm sorry," he cries, attempting to touch me.

I pull away.

"You've betrayed me, Phillip, in so many ways."

"I said I was sorry, Alena," he shouts. "Forgive me, please. Take me back."

"No way," I scream near his ear. "It's far too late for sorry. There's no way I'm gonna take you back."

The tears are welling up. I can see he is on the verge of breaking down. "I chose lies over truth, loyalty over love, her over you, and I was wrong. I regret all my mistakes."

Seething with jealousy, my eyes shrivel into an ovoid shape. "Have you been sleeping with Joanne? Did you bed her, Phil? I want to know."

He hesitates. "That doesn't matter. All that matters is that I love you and I am truly sorry."

"I need more than empty words, Phillip. That isn't nearly enough."

"Then what do you want, Alena?" he bellows. "Tell me."

"I don't know!" I snap, throwing my arms in the air.

"I'm gonna need more than *I don't know*," he bellows, banging his fist into the wobbly bench. "I need to know what you want from me, so I can fix this."

"Nothing!" I yell, slicing his face with the sharpness of my stare. "I want nothing from you! You've done enough damage already. My cuts are too deep. I just want you gone, out of my life. So get lost, Phillip, walk. Go back to your ghetto bitch!"

"No," he howls, his jaded eyes commanding my unlimited attention. "I will not go. She is not the one for me. You are. So I'm staying right here, where I belong."

"Well," I confirm, filling with rage, rising from the seat, "I will leave."

Deafeningly, he roars. "I won't watch you leave me. Not for a second time."

"Close your eyes then," I bark, moving five paces from the bench.

"No, close yours," he whirrs, "cos I'm about to take your breath away."

While I am storming away, heading towards the pathway leading to home, Phil runs as fast as the wind, and sweeps my body up, pulling me back into his territory, his world.

"I can't lose you forever, Alena. I love you too much to let go."

"Our love has expired. I've already let go," I mumble, not convinced by the words I am speaking.

His eyes are stark. I look at the ground, avoiding his magnifying stare. With one passionate finger, he lifts my head up to meet his. "No, this love is eternal. It will never expire."

Phil's lips embed into mine. The emotion is so much that I convulse. His love runs through my arteries. Our bodies are close, touching. We are fully magnetised again.

Denying my beautifully crippling feelings, I slap him hard around the face, hell-bent on fighting his affections. "We are finished. Done. Over."

Grabbing me nearer, his masculine frame girds me, placating me. I can feel his loving pulse pumping through my veins.

Phil's resonant voice vibrates in my mouth. "Can you really walk away from me now, knowing that you'll lose the love of your life forever? A true love that makes your heart beat, your lips quiver, and your soul become alive?"

Virulently I laugh, sucking the life out of his enthusiasm. "You've been reading far too many classic novels, Phillip Gregson. This is not Jane Eyre. It is real life."

"Yes, Alena Pavlis," he whimpers, "I am well aware of that."

"Oh, really?" I say, dripping with sarcasm.

"Yes, really," he asserts boldly. "Today, I am bringing Classic Literature and real life into the same realm. The two worlds have collided."

Although I despise him, I cannot refute our connection anymore, or these feelings. The absence of love is breaking me down. I know I don't need this man. I am strong enough to stand on my own two feet. But I want him. He is so special to me, and he is still in my heart. As his bottom lip droops in hopeless exasperation, and he's thinking this love is dead, I nip the rim of his warm red sentiments with the assiduity of my adoration. Every part of me aches while we kiss, reviving this dying partnership.

Together, we rise like phoenixes, our love and faith restoring.

"We need each other," he implores. "If we're gonna make this work, and beat our pasts, we need to support one another. Apart, we don't stand a chance."

"Promise me you'll move towards change," I beg. "Leave that old life behind, or I'm gonna have to report your behaviour to the college principal."

"I promise that I'll change," he vows.

Buoyantly, I nod. "Good. You better keep that promise."

"Yes, Alena," he thrums. "I will."

Our gazes join and dance in synchronisation in the

flaming amber horizon. Without saying a single word, we take each other's hands, and together, we meander about the garden. Admiring the glorious orchard: the green beds brimming with flowers; the array of intriguing bronze statues; the attractive lake and the romantic walkways tucked away in a secret part of the grove, we sigh gently and smile contentedly into one another's eyes.

All of a sudden, there are heavy footfalls behind us, accompanied by a loud scurrying sound that thrashes the air. My heart hammers in my chest as my head swirls into the past. Stanley is chasing after me, trying to grab my arm as I am running towards the exit, desperate to escape. I scream…

A dark, forbidding shadow eclipses us. Two small yet ominous hands descend on my shoulders. Oh, it's him! It's *him*…

"Gotcha!"

I scream again, and rush into Phil's arms. Holding me close, he comforts me. He is concerned by my reaction. His face crinkles with confusion. Why? Quickly, I swivel round. Oh, it's not Stanley! Thank the Lord. It is Becca.

"Gees, B," I gulp, catching my breath. "Please don't ever do that again!"

"I'm sorry, honey," she says, looking musingly at my hot, sweaty face.

Phillip holds me closer, rewarding my head with his calming kisses. He glares at Becca.

"Yes, Becca. Not clever."

She is deflated. "I already said I'm sorry, Phillip. Wasn't it loud enough for you?"

Becca has a glum expression on her visage. I see she is upset, so I leave Phil and give her a heartening hug. She grins, knowing I appreciate her humour most of the time.

Blissfully, Becca and I link arms and walk ahead. Phillip ambles behind us. I look back. I nod at him, non-verbally seeking his consent to go off with Becca. Winking at me, he indicates that it is okay for me to do so.

"So, Miss B," I begin. "How did you enjoy Professor Sanford's lecture today?"

"As much as I enjoy eating lemons," she says contemptuously.

Phillip's laugh is hearty and strong, and soon, I hear his burbled laughter travel north and get louder as the wind takes his voice. The powerful tremor of his deep guffaw ripples through my and Bec's long, stylish tresses.

We turn around for a moment, feeling the sensation of his robust chortle bouncing in the air around us. Bec and I look at one another. We are surprised he found this funny. It wasn't meant to be humorous.

"I *hate* that git! He's as acrid as a barrel of lemons!" My bestie grunts, pulling an ugly scowl. Rolling her eyes, she affirms her hatred for Professor Sanford and the pungent citrus fruit. "That man is always picking on me, expecting me to answer questions! Why does he single me out all the time?"

Murmuring in the background, Phil's manly voice lingers in midair. "Professor Sanford probably thinks blonde girls are total airheads. So he might be testing out that theory with you!" he states bluntly, hitting the nail on the head in the most painful of ways.

"Phillip Gregson!" I exclaim, rather annoyed at him.

How stupid could he be, saying this openly in front of Becca?

I turn back, throwing him an angry stare. Why do men have to be so damn insensitive sometimes? Generalisation, I know. But in my experience, men can be really blasé at times.

His square shoulders jerk, and a blank expression pervades his countenance. He has a carelessly cavalier manner. "What, babe? What did I say that was so terrible?"

Becca's lioness face is capricious. She decides to attack Phil. Spinning round to face him, walking backwards, she throws her meanest growl at the new object of her hatred.

"Is this your opinion of me too then, Phillip Gregson?"

Abruptly, she stops dead in her tracks. Phil and I stop, too. There is a slow, awkward silence, and then her shiny red heels stomp on the hard, unforgiving gravel, her lurid sapphire eyes filling with tears. She places her hands on a thin model waist, which is covered by nothing more than a skimpy black body-hugging dress, possibly designer, and purchased from a prestigious store in Beverly Hills, California.

"No!" Phil yells defending himself. "I do not think this about you, Becca. This is what *some people* think about blonde girls. Narrow-minded people."

Chewing my lip, I stand beside my best friend, knowing she is going to retaliate and kick Phil's arse.

As expected, her eyes blaze. I take a sideward step as she confronts him head-on. He'll have to get himself out of this hot sticky mess. I can't help him with this. I don't get involved with disputes concerning societal issues. They tend to bring on my episodes.

"What if," Becca hollers, encroaching on his personal space, pointing a finger of reproach into his abashed face. "What if I said *some people* believe that young Caribbean men under the age of twenty-five are, more often than not, in trouble with the law? Would that not be a generalisation?"

Phillip begins to snarl. He is mad, really mad, and rightly so.

I gasp. I have no choice but to interject. If I get an anxiety attack, so be it. I have to protect my man from this altercation. I can see Phillip wants to smash her face in, yet another reason for me to intervene!

"No, Becca!" I shout, edging forward and pulling her away from Phillip's flaming rage. "You *can't* go there, not ever."

Forcefully, she shoves me aside. "Why not, Alena? Why can't I go there? Is it because this is a vicious stereotype bordering on racist? And because it is your BF

I am referring to?"

"Yes!" I scream in her face. "Yes, Becca!"

Grumbling, she bounds round the garden like a wild goat. "It's *okay* for Phillip Gregson to diss blondes, but when I twist the tables on him and change the discussion to race, then suddenly I'm a racist?"

Phillip remains silent. His nose twitches. Somehow, he keeps his anger within.

"No, Becca," I correct her. "Nobody is saying that. You're taking things way out of context. Just calm down, honey, chill."

"Is that so, Miss Silky-Haired–Brunette-Never-Been-Blonde?" she shouts in my face priggishly.

"Uh-huh," I assert. "That's exactly how it is. Phil does not deserve to be stereotyped."

Phil's lips curl upwards slightly; his sight is glazed. I can tell he is touched by my heartfelt declaration.

Becca sobs and sits herself down on the ground, dejected. "Why is there injustice for blondes? There seems to be no respect for us!"

Joining her on the gritty path, I set myself next to my bawling bestie. Thank God I'm wearing my classic black Levi jeans today. Getting my arse covered in grit and dirt has never been an option for me. I sink my behind in the gravel, and deftly, I pat her soft sandy hair, smoothing down her apprehension.

"There is always justice, Becca. I've seen it first-hand in the courtroom surrounded by a stupefied audience, a stunned judge, a jury, my traumatised family, my steadfast lawyer, and a fiend, who wanted nothing more than to shatter my confidence and stop me from testifying against him. I had to be strong, tell the painful truth, to get him put away for years for his heinous crimes. Where there is courage and belief, justice will always be a candle in the darkness, a good and faithful friend, a kiss of hope bellowing in the wind."

Both Becca and Phil are astounded. So am I. Boy, I did

not know I could talk this profoundly.

"Just say sorry, the pair of you," I say, reasoning with them both. "And thank God that you have never faced true injustice, not the type of injustice that some people experience in their lifetime."

Phillip's arms, which were previously crossed, gently unfold. Becca rises from the ground, rejuvenated. The two headstrong individuals well up suddenly, and embrace, the extremely emotional moment. I add myself to their embrace.

Naturally, the three-way embrace ends and I stare kindly into the eyes of my comrades. I would be a lost and lonely soul, battling the elements and dangerous surprises in the dark and deadly wilderness, without love, purpose, or motivation. And these two give me that, in generous supply. I am so blessed to have them in my life. Instinctively, our arms link; I am in the middle of the chain. All three of us smile at each other, hearts wide open, spirits as one, breath intermingling. We sit down as one unit on a faithful, yellow, weather-beaten bench. There are several more benches on this part of the green, but this is *our* bench. This seat is special. It has age, insight, and knowledge, a history. It is the most elegant piece of furniture on this campus, and is the oldest, most beautifully crafted object in this whole garden. I see this article as sacred, the hallowed grandfather shrine that should be cherished forever.

"I'm sorry," Becca says to Phillip, her voice quivering with sincerity. "I was way out of line."

"Me, too, and I apologise," Phil says, remorsefully.

Brusquely, we all get up and walk about the garden, inhaling the sweet smell of spring. Then, after an hour's tour of nature's orchard, we come full circle, returning to our beloved bench, which allows us to recline our tired bones on its loving lap. I feel the sunshine smile of the bench seep into my legs. It loves us; we are its family. And for years to come, the bench will bolster his earthly relations, as nature and God intended. Let's hope that, in fifteen years, our great-grandfather bench will still be here in this charming sphere, and Phillip, Becca, and I can return, with our children, to show them off to our proud forefather.

Just as we are revelling in our special three-way friendship, and I am thinking about the future, we espy two burly policemen running along the pathway, speedily approaching us. I squint, seeing them hurtle towards us at an alarming rate.

"Alena," one police officer says in a deep concerning voice. "We must warn you to be on your guard. We have been monitoring the College Secretary's calls all morning. Mr. Hawthorne, the man who… has been harassing her since she started work today. He demanded to speak to you every time he called. Of course she declined his request and notified us immediately. But it's important now that you come with us to the Principal's Office, so we can discuss our new security measures to protect students. We know what happened to you two years ago, and we want to ensure that you are completely safe."

The officer puts out his hand, ready to help me up from the seat. But I can't move. I'm terrified, and frozen to the spot.

"I – I don't think I can…" Suddenly, I can't breathe. My airways clog up, and the world starts to spin around me.

Phillip holds me, rubbing my back to console me.

"I will go," he says imperiously, standing straighter. His chest is puffed out like a peacock, his eyes strong and powerful. "I will *not* put my girlfriend through this anymore. She's going through enough." He points to Becca. "Look after Alena, okay?"

Obediently, Becca nods.

Marching onto the pathway, he steps confidently and stridently, next to the two policemen. Progressively, Phillip disappears into the horizon. As I watch the man I love sail into the distance, I can sense Becca's hurt rising and burning in the atmosphere. She knows that she's not the most important person in my life, and it is slowly breaking her heart.

BESTIE, DON'T IGNORE ME

It's not cool when your best friend in the whole wide world is ignoring you. In fact, it sucks. Becca and I have been friends for only four months now, and already she thinks she owns me. She has no claim over me. I do not need to answer to her. Phillip is my man, and I met him a whole semester before she and I met. As we're boyfriend and girlfriend, and an exclusive item, I have a right to spend a lot of my free time with him. I agree, that when I first met Becca, we were sharing knickers and having heaps of fun chasing each other down the corridor, just being young and free, and being ourselves. That was then. We don't have this closeness anymore. Phillip and I have moved up a gear, and our relationship is getting more intense and more meaningful. We are magnetic, powerful; our relationship is strong, and getting stronger every day. Nothing compares to his love, not even my friendship with Becca. She really doesn't have a right to be mad at me for putting Phillip first.

Of course, Bec and I were, like, so tight. We did everything together, up to a point. Every night we enjoyed talking, laughing, joking, and taking turns to cook dinner for one another. We often chilled together in each other's rooms and in the botanical garden. In class, I can't count how many times we got told off for chatting and messing about when we should have been paying attention. You see, Becca used to transport me to another world. Her crazy-spirited, outlandish personality eased me out of my shell. However, she cannot fill that void that Phillip can, not anymore. She can't love me in *that way*, because neither of us are lesbians last time I checked. My bestie knows all this, so why the hell is this crazy bitch-arsed girl jealous?

I think ignoring me for twelve hours is so cruel. Is she trying to diminish our friendship? If so, she is doing a bloody good job of it.

With a forlorn face, I head to the lounge with my big bowl of chocolate ice cream and plunk myself next to her on the two-seater couch. She is deliberately turning her face away from me. Nevertheless, our legs are touching and I can see her lips twitching. She obviously wants to say something. I don't wait for her to speak. I dive in, headfirst.

"What the hell is wrong with you? Why the hell are ya being so stupid, ignoring me for twelve hours straight? What have I done to deserve this?"

Becca bangs her back into the soft cushions as if to create some kind of dramatic effect prior to speaking. I throw a severe stare, alerting her to her infantile behaviour. Responsively, she slumps in the chair. An honest expression then emerges on her miserable visage. Tears can be seen glistening in her blue eyes.

"I don't want to share you, Alena." She flings the weight of her angst onto my shoulders. Boy, she's heavy when she is burdened with issues. "That's why I'm so unhappy and pouty."

"That's puerile!" I shout angrily. "Why are you acting like a five-year-old? For Pete's sake! Grow up, B!"

Pouting childishly, she pushes her pathetic expression in my face. "I'm jealous, Alena. I want more time with you. We haven't had dinner together for weeks. I need you, too. You're my bestie."

I decide to be bold. I'm not letting her define the parameters of our friendship. No one is going to make me choose between two special people in my life. Dad made me choose between him and mum after the marriage broke up, and I refuse to go down that road again.

"Don't make me choose, B. He is my boyfriend, you are my best friend. These are two different relationships entirely, but equally as important to me."

"But–" she begins.

"There is no 'but.'"

"I'm pissed off, Alena. Don't you get it?" She shrinks in the chair.

Loudly I sigh, realising I have to hear her out. I need to understand my bestie's feelings. "Why are you so pissed, B?"

"Friends like you do not grow on trees, babe. Friends like you are rare. Very rare."

"Bec!" I exclaim. "You have loads of best friends in California. I'm sure they are really good friends, too."

She exhales. Her eyes burn with sincerity. "Those friends aren't real, Alena. They only like me 'cos my daddy is rich now. He lives in Georgia with his entrepreneur girlfriend. He's given me plastic since he and my mom separated last year and he met his million-dollar piece of arse. I have three credit cards with crazy limits. Money seems to excite people. It's easy gaining pals when you can buy their affection. Babe, I didn't have to buy you anything, and you wanted to be my friend, my best friend forever. You're the only thing I have in this world that I haven't bought, or lured in, using the power of the 'ching-ching.'"

I blow out a heavy breath. "Becca, that's deep. I never knew that."

"I'm not as superficial as I look, Alena. There is a real person with real feelings that lies beneath this exterior."

She rubs my knee. It feels nice, yet kinda weird. If I was a lesbian, I'd *really* like this. As a straight girl, this is a little strange. I understand that Becca is comfortable touching other girls in this way, so I let her continue. Obviously, she finds it soothing, calming. This is how she thinks, tactilely. We are all different.

"I must admit, Alena, that I was kinda happy about you and Phillip having relationship issues when we first met, 'cos that meant we could spend heaps more time together, especially in the evenings when I get real homesick."

I scowl. I am disappointed in Becca, although pleased she is finally being honest with me. "That was very selfish."

"I know," she huffs.

"From day one, you knew my history. How could you begrudge me of happiness with Phil?"

"I wasn't thinking."

"Clearly, you weren't."

She lets out a little pungent laugh. "You and Phil are now the perfect couple. So how I felt back then doesn't matter anymore."

"Phil and I are the perfect couple? Nuh-uh," I say, correcting her. "We broke up a few weeks ago, B, and then Phil shacked up with Joanne Jackman. Didn't you know?"

She is tearful and cross at the same time. "What? He slept with Joanne, the lazy slob who doesn't know how to clean a hob?"

"Yes," I answer furiously. "He did."

"Ew," she shouts, screwing up her face. "That's so gross!"

"Totally," I concur. "And worst still, Phil has *borrowed* a couple of vehicles since we have been together. All of them he returned. The biggest shock of all is that Phillip had a kid with some girl four years ago. The child got removed by social services when he went to juvie!"

"What?" Becca is flabbergasted. "You didn't tell me any of this stuff, Alena."

"No, I didn't," I confess, biting my bottom lip. "I shouldn't have kept that stuff from you. At least now you see, that we are far from perfect. We are a serious work in progress. That's why I've been backing off from you lately, hun. It doesn't mean I don't love you."

Becca hugs me so tightly my bones chatter. "I've been an insensitive bi-atch and a bad friend." Her lips quiver. "I'm sorry, Alena."

"That makes two of us."

Leaning in, she smiles, twiddling with my long umber tresses. "*I* need to learn how to zip my mouth sometimes and be less possessive. At the same time, *you* need to stop pushing me away. I have feelings and I am still your bestie."

"This sounds like a sisterhood promise."

"Yea, girl, it is." She simpers. "You in agreement? Are we on the same page?"

I wag my head. "Uh-ha."

"Good." She grins.

Becca grabs the controls and turns on the TV.

Resting a silky blonde mane on my lap, she looks up, her smile shining into my mien. I stroke her warm, golden locks until she falls asleep. Retrieving my now runny ice cream from the coffee table, I eat it all the same. It doesn't actually taste that bad. An old classic movie comes on the TV. I begin to watch it. I don't know the name of the film. It's escaped my memory. I continue watching it since I am fascinated by black and white images. Vintage films are amazing, I love watching them. Eventually, my eyes begin to droop, and I, too, drift off into a deep sleep.

WARZONE

It is a blazing Sunday afternoon. The corridor feels like it is on fire and under attack. I duck and dive, trying not to get burned and scarred by Phillip and Becca's hateful scorn. They are shouting at one another, arguing, battling, over me. Their doors are shields deflecting the other's noxious words. This is highly disturbing to see. I am troubled by their rage and their jealousy. I haven't seen either of them like this before.

"No, Becca, I won't let Alena be trapped in your dungeon tonight. I might never see her again!" Phillip roars, his voice unsparing and bitter.

"You're a bastard! How dare you say that! My room is not a dungeon, and I do not lock her away. She is my bestie, and I deserve some time with her. But Mister 'I Need to Smother My Girlfriend 'Til She Looks Like Cotton-Wool' is keeping my BFF all to himself! You're such a jerk, Phillip Gregson!"

"Oh, be quiet, Miss Far Too Old for Child's Shorts. Has anyone ever told you that skirts on the knee and trousers that reach the ground have actually been invented?"

"Piss off, Phillip. Action-man reject! You better not

shout too much, or your ballooned chest might just burst. Boom, boom, splat!"

Knowing he has got her back up, he smirks. "Now, now, Miss California Dream Barbie! Don't stretch that face too much, the shiny plastic might crack!"

"Oh, you little...!" She hollers, her closed fist pommelling the air.

"Time out!" I yell.

They pay no attention to what I am saying. The pair of them simply carry on.

"Phillip Gregson," she continues, gaining more energy and momentum from the sunlight, which is travelling through the open roof window and beaming into the nucleus of the hallway. "Stop pumping iron in the gym. It ain't doing your tiny brain cells any good!"

Throwing his head back, Phil cackles. "Is that the best you can do, Miss Blondey?"

"Shut it, Mr. 'I'm Really Made Up of Puffed Air and No Intellect!'"

"La, la, la! I can't hear you, plastic girl!"

"Don't pretend you didn't hear what I just said, Rambo reject!" She screeches at the top of her lungs. Venomously, her evil glare shoots into his face from across enemy lines.

Phillip, bold and brazen, is standing like a statue with arms folded and lips pursed, just outside his safe house. He is maintaining his winning position, his stronghold.

Desperately, Becca is fighting Phillip for 'friend time', since he's been hogging me all week and my bestie has only see me in class, and for an hour a day outside of lectures and seminars. Positioned right in the middle of the corridor, I am trying to reason with them both on this issue. It's so ridiculous they are squabbling over 'girlfriend time' and 'friend time.' I hate this riotous bickering. It's childish, moronic, and rather ludicrous! In a strange way, I actually appreciate the pair of them grappling for my attention. It elucidates how much they love and treasure me.

"Calm down, Bec," I say, tossing ice on her hot Californian temper.

"No, I won't calm down. He is stealing you from me, Alena. Can't you see?"

"Look," I begin, my glance darting up and down the corridor to address them both. "You have to stop fighting over me. It's stupid!"

"He started this crap!" Becca thunders, pointing at Phillip.

"No, she did!" Phillip shouts, directing an angry digit towards Becca's vengeful face.

"Oh, for goodness sake!" I screech, pitching my arms in the air and lifting my eyes to heaven like an incensed rocket. "You two are impossible, worse than grumbling infants!"

The two of them come out of their rooms and join me in the centre of the long hallway. Is this a truce?

"Sorry for the bitch fit, Phillip. It's just that you're pissing me off with your selfish behaviour," she says looking him straight in the eye, almost apologising.

Scrunching up his face, and then releasing it, Phil liberates his tight pent up anger. "You've been a total cow since you came to Capendale University. This argument is just another example of how bad your attitude is."

They grunt simultaneously, puffing their flaming balls of anxiety over my head. Soon, their shoulders drop, strained smiles emerge, and the negotiation begins.

"Let's just be civil and respect each other's relationship with Alena. You don't hog her, I don't hog her. Agreed, Phillip?"

Gingerly, he nods in agreement. "Alright then."

Linking arms with my crew, I beam. Proudly, I look at them both. "Awesome! A resolution, at last."

Reluctantly, they smile.

"Shall we have lunch together, all three of us?" I ask mirthfully.

"Yeah, okay," Phil replies.

"Yeah, I guess we could," Bec concurs.

Finally, things are returning to normal. I hate the feeling of trouble in the air. For some reason, my female intuition is still on high alert and I can sense new trouble brewing. Surely, I must be wrong.

THE POISONED LETTER

Trotting down the stairs of Ridley House, I am eager to see who has sent me mail. My feminine intuition radar is still on high alert. It's sending out a distress signal, for some bizarre reason. Going to the postal area on the ground floor of my building is always so refreshing. The air is freer down here, the atmosphere lighter. I love this quaint, little place of escapism. Being at the University of Capendale and away from home is difficult and presents its own challenges. My isolated and bubbled world consists of lectures, seminars, assignments, relationship issues, friendship worries, phobias, and stress of the past whirling in my mind, and that's just the half of it. But here, in the calm circumference of the beige, circular post-collection area on the ground floor of my residency, my problems and stresses float away like magic.

I am at peace here. The atmosphere is bright and fluffy. I converse with strangers in this realm, smile at other Ridley House residents, and enter into frivolous conversations about anything and everything, and it is perfectly normal. If I accidentally bump into an unrecognisable individual, I am not unnerved and I don't have a panic attack. Unlike in the real world, where talking to strangers is kind of weird and detrimental to my mental well-being, here, in this domain, where I collect my post from my mail slot, the regular rules do not apply. I am liberated here, at my happiest. This world shields me from the pain and anxiety that I experience upstairs on my floor. I am free from everything, especially the ghosts of the past.

Jovially, I jump off the final step. I'm now officially on the ground floor.

Excitedly, my knees lift up high, as I sprint to my postal slot for Room 185. I feel like a small kid in a candy store!

Taking a deep breath, I fill up my lungs with fresh rich air. Slowly, I ease the key in the lock of my mail slot and hear the beautiful sound of the brass twisting and clicking in the metal. It sounds like heaven. Peering inside the box, I fling the door wide open, nearly breaking it at the hinges. There is one letter, A5 size, just sitting there. The bulky cumbersome weight stares at me pugnaciously.

I get a strange, chattering feeling rushing through my core. This sensation I recognise from the past, but can't recall when I felt it and for what reason. Picking up the letter, hesitantly, with a floppy forefinger and thumb, I bring it closer into the centre of my peaceful world. It weighs a ton, as if it comes with a history, a dark, heavy story. I scrutinise the envelope. It is rather peculiarly addressed – *Alena, ex-student of Wentworthy High*. Why is the letter addressed like this? The sender must be someone I knew back in high school.

Flipping the white rectangular object, and laying it on a table, on its stomach, I run my middle finger across the top rim of the envelope. It states the following words in thick capital letters: *Delivered by hand by Sergeant Peterson from the Metropolitan Police Department*, and it has the official police stamp. Why are the police delivering a letter to me? It must be important. I am thoroughly intrigued. My heart pounds, beating energetically in my ribcage, my breathing is low, cavernous, resounding. Gently, I remove the correspondence from the table top, and, resting my back against the sea of red student post boxes, I unseal the adhesive to reveal the contents of the letter. As I open the missive, I slide down the slots, my bottom bumping and jolting to the floor. Stretching my arm up, I slam shut my box. The key is jangling an enchanting tune as it sways in the lock.

Focusing my full concentration on the foreign body in my hands, I unfold the formal note, like a fan. My eyes begin to scan it and I read it, line by line:

Miss Alena Pavlis
Third Floor Ridley House
The University of Capendale
Corefield Road
Leicester
LE4

Dear Alena,

I hope this letter finds you well. I would not wish to think that after all this effort it might go astray. Well, the fact I asked the Police Department to deliver it to you personally, by hand, is an indication that you will get it safely.

Alena, I have been meaning to write to you for the past two and a half years. You have been running on my mind for all this time. Cliché, I know. But it is true. You have been on my mind quite a lot. I must apologise, before I go any further. Please believe when I say that I didn't mean to scare you, or the office staff at the university, by calling persistently a few weeks ago, to the point where I almost gave one of the female staff angina. I only wanted to hear your voice, my angel. I've missed that soft intonation, the sweet and demure manner in which you speak. Well, I think I excited the police a little too much and got a ticking off for wanting to get my wish. Naughty me.

Oh, yes, you must be wondering how I knew you were at Capendale University, and living on Third Floor Ridley House. You're thinking that, right? Alf Bernard told me. He is very good at finding things out. Moreover, he informed me that you had a lovely chat on the train during Easter. How nice!

I am very impressed that you're doing an English degree, Alena. How smart and beautiful you are. I'm hardly surprised. I've always known about, and admired, your intellect, from day one. There is something about you, Miss Pavlis, which fascinates me, excites me, sending me into a wild frenzy. From the moment we first acquainted outside the school gates on that chilly day in November three years ago, an imprint was made on my heart, on my soul. I became mesmerised by your stunning beauty, obsessed, even. There is something about you, which is so special, my love. It's in those remarkable and bewitching green eyes to start with, and that face, so endearingly sweet, and those lips, so incredibly rosy and kissable…

I never planned to kiss you in the classroom that day, or invite you back to my house. My animal instincts took over and I got a bit carried away. These impulses were out of character, and moments of complete madness. I didn't think you'd call the police on me that night. And I was stunned when the police arrested me later that evening, and when you testified against me in court. It was shocking for me to get five years, for what can only be described as a 'big misunderstanding' between a teacher and his attractive female student.

Putting aside the past, I can give you some great news: I am being let out early. My sentence has been decreased for 'good behaviour.' See, my sweet, I am a good boy. I always have been. It's just that the law did not see it that way at first. But my lawyer convinced them that I have now changed my ways, turned over a new leaf. I am being released this Friday. Great, huh?

It's Monday today, and since I have a few days left behind bars, I would like an opportunity to meet you. Firstly, I am curious to see how you've grown. Also, I want to talk, get a few things cleared up. This is your opportunity to tell me how you feel about everything, and for us to clear the air. I want to resolve our differences, Alena. I need closure and so do you.

You can come and see me in my cell any time between the visiting hours of 12 o'clock to 3 o'clock on Tuesdays, Wednesdays and Thursdays.

I hope to see you, Alena. In fact, I am waiting for you. Do not bring anyone. Come alone. We have lots of private things to discuss that I do not wish anybody else to hear. Staring at these four walls for two and a half years has turned me a little insane. I need to see you, and only you, to make sense of everything – my past, present, and my future. At least I have had time to think for the last couple of years. Every man needs thinking time.

See you soon.
Stanley Hawthorne

There is also an article, stuck to the back of the letter, which I read, whilst trembling. After reading the poisonous letter and article, I collapse, my head crashing on the floor. I convulse. Everything goes grey. The world is black.

HARD HIT!

Ouch. My head hurts and it's throbbing wildly. I am lying down on a bed, and a cold compress is on my forehead. Long, elegant bronze legs amble towards me. I can just about make them out. Lying back, nursing my head, the room starts to wobble slightly. A soft hand caresses my hair, generating that safe feeling inside of me. I catch a scent of an Elizabeth Arden perfume. It's a beautiful flowery aroma.

"It's okay," the voice says calmly, luscious red lips coming closer in my fuzzy peripheral vision.

I recognise those lips, that smell. It's Becca, my best friend, my saviour.

"What happened?" I ask, totally bemused and lightheaded.

Kissing me sweetly on the cheek, she perches next to me on the bed, not taking her eyes off me for a single second.

"I found you passed out on the ground floor, Alena, in the postal area." Her tone is shaky, nervous, concerned. "And I discovered a letter and article in your hand." She points to her dresser.

Becca shakes her head, and her expression is very

serious. I've never seen her like this before.

"I read it, Alena!" She says tearfully.

"You did? What did it say?" I ask curiously. I seem to have suffered some sort of amnesia. I can't remember the last hour. My memory is hazy.

"Didn't you read it?" She enquires, an acute look of alarm on her mien.

A blank look washes over my ashen face. "I don't remember!"

"What?" She throws her hands behind her head, forming two perfect wings. Her arms flap back, filled with frustration. Then, she sits on the end of the bed, ready to fly into orbit.

Quickly, she turns to me, slapping her right palm to my forehead. "You are hot. That must be it!"

"That must be what?"

"The cause of your memory loss," she says, her eyes laced with panic. Small beads of sweat are trickling haphazardly down her visage.

Screwing up my face in distress, I am very worried about my loss of memory. "I can't remember! This is *serious!*"

She breathes heavily, her eyes darting over my body. "Do you know who I am, Alena?"

I look over at her, letting out a little laugh. "Funny, Becca. Ha. Ha. It's unlikely I could forget you!"

Becca doesn't see the funny side of the joke. She's distressed. Jumping off the bed, she paces up and down the room. Anxiously, she bites her bottom and top lip alternately, and starts to mumble to herself.

"What is it, Becca? Is the letter important?" I point to the dresser. "Pass me the letter, B."

Her vision homes in on my dark emerald eyes, illuminating them. "This letter is why you passed out. I can't let you read it."

"I want to read it, Becca."

"No!" she shouts, a fiery expression burning in her

eyes. "Go to sleep."

"Please let me read it," I plead.

"Shh!" She runs to her bed, pushing a commanding finger to my lips. "Go back to sleep, Alena."

"But I'm not tired."

"Sleep, Alena."

I yawn, and my eyes start to close. Gently, I fall back asleep.

***

Banging. Banging. Someone is pounding a hammer in my mind. I spring awake... I remember! Oh, God, I remember who wrote the letter and what the news article is about. Hysterically, I scream down the walls of Becca's room, and violently, they reverberate. The room is spinning round and round in rings.

"Stanley!" I screech. "He wrote the letter! The newspaper clipping is about his early release from prison!"

Leaping up from the floor, from a deep sleep, Becca comes to my aid. Her face is almost touching mine.

"That man's got audacity writing that shit to you. Who the hell does he think he is? He's an evil man. They should have kept him locked up for life and thrown away the key. He shouldn't be let out prematurely. He's a monster! But I'm here, Alena. I will protect you. And no one can make you go to see him in prison. He can't hurt you anymore, even after his release. It's over, Alena. It's done and dusted! Forever, forever, we are strong, forever, forever, he will be gone..."

Seventeen-year-old Alena does not agree with Becca, and in fact, she's sitting smugly by the window, swinging childish legs back and forth, back and forth from the window ledge. She throws her head up, laughing wickedly. Slowly she penetrates my gaze, knowing she has won. Then I hear that malignant cackle, the elevated tone of Mr. Stanley Hawthorne.

I shake and cry in Becca's sturdy embrace. "It's not over! The past is killing me, Becca. I'm choking. Suffocating."

"I won't let you fall," she says determinedly. "I have your back, always." Repeatedly, she kisses me on the forehead, showing her amiable friendship.

I stroke her neck, desperately wanting to feel her pulse. I need it to survive.

"Phil mustn't know about his attempt to return into my life. He will kill him!"

As I raise my head, turning it to the side, our pretty noses caress. I can feel her heart beating in my soul. Chaotically, I breathe, my cold saliva spraying on the base of her chin.

"No!" she exclaims. "He mustn't find out. This is our secret. Phillip must *never* know about this!"

Tightening her embrace, she rocks me to sleep, rubbing my cheeks to soothe my obvious pain and anxiety. I feel somewhat secure in her arms. Though a part of me knows I am in grave danger.

INTRUDERS!

The blaring lights of the paparazzi are blinding my eyes, burning my vision as they draw nearer, and nearer. A trio of hungry, voracious reporters looking for meat, for a juicy story, have their sweaty, cold palms abutting the window of the Third Floor of Ridley House. The glass in the window is encased neatly within the heavy entrance door. They can peer through the looking glass, other than that, they have no rights in this dominion. The reporters are uninvited guests, with no access to my safe and secure world. It's awfully strange, though, that they are here, now, following my encounter with Mr. Bernard in April and the poisoned letter from Mr. Hawthorne, which I received only days ago. I don't know how they pierced through the robust campus security or how they gained access to the Hall of Residence so easily. Someone must have mistakenly let them into the building, thinking they were professors or visitors coming for a tour of the college.

"We want your story," one of the reporters yells. "Let us in so we can talk about how Mr. Hawthorne's release from prison is affecting you."

"No," I answer, yawning. "I won't talk to you. Now get lost, scum!"

While I hide from the press, sinking into the floor, leaning against the sturdy main entrance, I feel my lids closing. Today's lecture was really heavy. I think I need a nap...

Suddenly, I hear a tap, tap, tapping at the door. My breath is laboured. I sense trouble.

There is a riotous thud. I hear the glass window breaking, and the internal lock of the door is being turned hastily.

Running. I am running down the corridor as fast as I can, my satchel flapping awkwardly across my chest and hipbone. A tall, hefty-footed man is chasing me.

"We want this story, Alena. Stanley is coming out of jail on Friday. You must be terrified, angry, bitter, thoroughly disgusted by his reduced sentence."

Sprinting. I am sprinting now at full speed, and not looking back.

In the horizon I see Phillip. His hand is reaching out, and he is running to me, but he is too far to reach me.

"Come here, Alena," he screams, his voice hard and manly. "Run to me, baby, meet me halfway!"

"I can't make it, Phil!" I holler. "I cannot get to you!"

I'm racing fast, at turbo speed. The man accelerates. He is hot on my heels. Oh no, he's got my wrist, and he's pulling me...

All of a sudden, I spring awake, jumping out of my sleep, realising that this horrible chasing episode was just a dream. I get up and peer through the window. Thankfully, the press has gone.

Ambling to Becca's room in a cold sweat, my bag flapping across my chest, I bang her door repetitively. As Becca opens the door, I rush inside.

"Alena, are you okay?"

"No," I scream, pushing past her.

The force of my movements causes our feet to tangle. My bag hooks around her arm. Our legs intertwine. We both tumble to the ground, and I fall awkwardly on top of her. My big bouncing bosoms are pressing on her small meek ones. Our lips are caressing, our lady parts grazing against each other's. Hair entwined, feet, meshed, eyes conjoined.

"Gees!" she bellows. "Eww."

Expeditiously, she shoves me off of her. At the same time I am trying to peel myself away from her body.

"I love you," she says jumping up on her feet, wiping her lips. "But not in *that* way." She exhales sharply, a stunned look plastered on her face. "Eww. That was a bloody weird lessy moment! Don't ya think?"

"Yes, totes!" I scream, scampering to my feet.

We both burst into a fit of laughter, running on the spot in the usual way we do when we're agreeing and totally in tune with one another.

"What's got you all wound up?" she asks astounded, as she's guiding me to her bed. We sit face to face, legs folded, hands touching, interlocking playfully.

"The press – they want my story, Becca."

"Oh, gees!" She exhales fretfully. "This is certainly unprecedented, reporters hounding old high school students for a scandalous headline!"

I raise a critical eyebrow. "Some journalists are like that, B!"

"That's terrible!" She pulls me in for a girlie cuddle. "That's, like, totally below the belt. So not acceptable."

Holding me close, she encompasses me with her sisterly love. This is the warmth of true friendship. I like the feeling of this. I haven't felt this sort of companionship since I left high school. Oh shoot, Emma, my other best friend from Wentworthy High, is coming to visit tomorrow! Crap! I haven't told Becca about her. She might get jealous!

"Bec, I need to tell you that –"

The door bangs.

"Hold that thought, Alena."

Becca jumps up, though cautiously, she stands behind

the door. "Who is it?" Her voice is dark, menacing, deep. "This better not be the press coming after my bestie!"

"No, it's Phillip! The press has been escorted off the premises! I saw campus police forcing them out of the building as I walked up the stairs."

Quickly, I dry my eyes. I have a face full of tears and laughter. Becca peels open the door.

Phillip moseys in. He immediately walks to Becca's bed and kisses me senseless.

"Are you okay, baby?" he whispers in between kisses.

"Yes, I'm okay," I reply. "Becca's been looking after me."

Phillip's face changes suddenly. I can tell the cogs in his mind are working overtime. "Why was the press here in the first place, Alena? What exactly did they want from you?"

Instantaneously, Becca and I snatch a quick glance. I can almost feel her heart beating as ferociously as mine.

My mouth goes dry, my throat is hoarse. I cannot bring myself to give Phil an answer. Becca looks over at me, her eyes full of worry and panic. In that moment she realises that she is the one who will have to give Phil the response he is asking for. She knows I am on the edge.

Soon enough, her cute rosy lips quaver, a half smile appearing on her face. I can tell she now has a convincing answer for Phil.

"The Leicester Gazette got lost – they were looking for someone else," she says affirmatively, bailing me out.

Thankful, I smile at Becca. She beams, giving me an endearing wink. I can see the depths of her friendship shining in her ocean blue eyes.

Phil drifts into Becca's gaze and nods. Then pensively, he looks at me. "The local press was probably after Joanne. She got expelled from the college this morning, for pouring white paint all over Professor Raynold's swanky new car!"

"What?" I scream in shock. "Joanne Jackman has been

kicked out?"

"Yes," Phillip confirms. "She has."

My eyes shoot to Becca. We share a smug grin.

"This is good news for us, Alena. Don't ya think?"

"Yes, Phillip." I smile. "It is."

Hastily, Phil grabs me closer, holding me in a strong embrace. He pecks me on the lips, and then his kisses get deeper and deeper. Forgetting this is not my room, he begins to French kiss me. I like this level of closeness with my man in unauthorised territory. It's strangely thrilling! I fall into my man's body, allowing him to devour my edible lips and tongue.

"My bedroom, my rules," Becca blasts, scolding us. "No funny business in here!"

Phil and I stop kissing and stare at her in unison.

"So you mean to say," Phillip says, grinning wildly, "that you haven't been enjoying any *funny business* in this room?"

I laugh, and Phil giggles.

Becca laughs with us. "Well, a little bit of action with some Italian exchange student a few nights ago, but nothing more."

I gasp. "You never told me about this, B."

"It's on a need-to-know basis, and you didn't need to know."

Phil smirks, observing the playful banter that Becca and I relish. "Glad you aren't mad at my missus, Becca. I'm thankful for that!"

Screwing up her face, she is confused. Confident American hands find their way onto her perfect pair of killer hips. "Why would I be mad at Alena, Phillip?"

I raise a curious brow. I'm perplexed too. "Yes, why, Phil?"

Taking a deep breath, Phil elaborates. "In January, I discussed with you, Becca, about my and Alena's non-existent love life. You secretly went and told Alena that I had confided in you about this personal matter. Alena, however, was not supposed to relay it back to me that she was aware of this conversation that took place between us. And I'm guessing, Becca, that you told Alena to keep quiet and not inform me that she knew about it."

Oh Shit! Now I'm in trouble. Why couldn't Phillip have just kept his big mouth shut?

"You bitch!" Becca screams, turning to face me. "I trusted you not to tell him that, Alena! We spoke about that in confidence!"

"No, you spoke about it confidently," I say, my pitiful attempt to get myself out of this hot sticky mess.

"*You little —*" she shrieks, jumping up and down on the spot like a bouncy ball. "I could beat you over the head with a baseball bat right now, Alena!"

Remorsefully, Phillip bites his lip. "Oh gees, I didn't realise you didn't know, Becca! Sorry!"

"No, I didn't know, Phillip!" She wails. Revenge is in her eyes. I can see it welling up. "If we are confessing things, I have something to tell *you*, Phillip."

Vengefully, she is heading to the dresser. She's picking up the letter from Stanley. HOLY SHIT! NO BECCA! NO!

Leaping up, I head for the dresser. Wickedly, she stands on tiptoe, waving the letter like a red flag over my head. Then, she starts to read it.

"What is that?" Phillip asks curiously, looking at me. Turning to scrutinise Becca, he shrugs his shoulders.

I shake my head, begging her not to say. Phillip must never find out about this. He'll go nuts if he knows who wrote it and what it says! Becca's a bitch for doing this! What I did to her was minor. This is major stuff. This could destroy my relationship with Phillip. It could destroy our life together.

I beg Becca with my eyes, pleading with her to release me from this hell.

"Nothing!" she finally says, realising what she is about to do.

I sigh quietly. I am saved!

Phillip's eyes glaze. "I'm confused. What is going on?"

Becca tosses the letter into the trash. "It was a letter from one of her other friends, it's filled with terrible jokes. I won't embarrass her."

"Okay," Phillip says hesitantly, buying the lie.

"Thank you," I mouth to Becca, happy and relieved that I appealed to her better nature.

Sinisterly, she scowls at me, and then lifts her head up towards the ceiling like an aristocrat.

"Whilst we're on the subject of friends," I say, moving away from the time bomb that is Stanley Hawthorne's letter. "I want to tell you something, Becca."

In a short while, I reclaim her attention. She re-joins me on the bed. The look of revenge is still a glint in her left eye. "Oh?"

"Emma, my high school friend is coming to see me tomorrow."

"Emma?" Becca and Phil say simultaneously.

"You've never mentioned an Emma prior to today," Becca snaps.

"No," Phil agrees. "Never heard of her."

I spot a quiver of sadness wobbling Becca's lips. "Is she a *best friend* from high school?"

"Yes," I confirm, looking her straight in the eye.

She stamps a pair of childish feet in her pink shoes. I can tell she is seething with jealousy. "Well, I don't wish to meet this *Emma*. Keep her away from me!"

"Becca," I say, concerned by the extent of her envy.

"I'm not sharing you, Alena! End of discussion!"

"That's childish," Phil blurts out, shaking his head. "Even for you!"

"Too bad. This is the way I am! So deal with it!" She pokes out her tongue and storms towards the door. "I'm going to the bathroom. No hanky panky in here while I'm gone, okay?"

Stone-faced and in a huff, she vacates her room.

Phillip cuddles up to me on the bed. We flash a grin at one another and laugh. Becca's so funny. As if anything like that is going to happen between us!

"I think I have a problem here," I say, my head resting on his robust shoulder.

"Yes, another one to add to the list."

"Please, don't remind me," I assert as I stroke his muscly back, the sensation of his soft cotton t-shirt exciting my tender skin.

OUT!

"He's out on Friday, Alena. It's in the papers. Aren't ya the least bit nervous?"

Emma reads the lengthy article aloud, word for word.

I'm sitting on the swivel chair by my dresser, carefully applying my lipstick and eyeliner. I am absolutely disinterested by this article. There are bigger things I have to worry about right now. I need to look pretty tonight. Emma and I are going out to dinner to a new Indian restaurant called *Ranatoo Lama,* which recently opened across the road from the college. This is a big moment for me. I am venturing out to a food joint for the first time in two years, and I am going with my best friend, who I haven't seen face-to-face for ages – for about a year, to be precise. This is a very special day indeed.

I look over at my best friend, who's perched uncomfortably on the edge of my bed as if ready to rocket into the sky. She is chewing her pink, glossy lip, playing with her curly blonde hair. She's a little breathless and ashen in appearance. Slipping a smile her way, I attempt to ease her obvious anxieties. Languidly, she half smiles back, but she is still totally anxious, I can tell.

"I'm not scared that he is being released, Emma, if

that's what you're thinking. I am sorry if it's affecting you, honey. If I'm over that, you certainly don't need to worry about it. Chill."

That is not at all true. I am virtually shitting my pants about Mr. Stanley Hawthorne coming out of prison earlier than anticipated. This is a dark nightmare fast becoming a frightening reality. I might actually pass out on the day he is released out of the fear that the evil man will come to the university and attack me. He now knows exactly where I am thanks to Mr. Bernard.

I'm also frightened that Phillip and I will never be able to progress our relationship with the fear of Stanley constantly in the back of my mind. I won't discuss my deeper feelings with Emma. She is my second best friend. She's only entitled to see the 'superficial Alena' who has moved on significantly with her life. Only Becca, my primary best friend, is allowed to know all. She has earned that right to be my superior best friend. Although I've only known Becca since January, I feel she knows and understands me far more than Emma ever did. Emma and I have drifted apart, since her studying English Literature at the University of Roehampton and me studying English here, has distanced us. This one hundred miles between us have partially severed our close friendship.

Peering at myself in the mirror, I nip my russet hair back in a neat little ponytail, lifting my locks into a feathered arch. Subtly, I blow a kiss at my reflection, admiring how beautiful I look in this appealing light and with my make-up painted skillfully on my face. Having my hair scrapped back also enhances my glorious features: round visage, sparkling verdant eyes, pretty nose and my cute kissable lips. I know I'm gorgeous. I recognise how pretty I am now. These days, I have confidence and self-assurance, to a certain degree.

After putting on the ruby necklace dad bought me as a birthday present ten years ago, I twist around on the brown chair to meet Emma's exasperated face. Her crystal blue gaze is boring into me. Frantically, she's running a pair of jittery hands through her sleek mane. I issue her a jovial smile in an attempt to smooth over her anxiety. I hate seeing her like this. Yet I perfectly understand why she is feeling this way. She is afraid that I might have a nervous breakdown or simply crumble under all this pressure. I'm definitely not that weak. And I will not be crumbling anytime soon.

"Let's concentrate on going out, Emma. I've missed you. This is *our* night."

She smiles at me mildly, yet there is a slight quiver on her lips, as though a worm has penetrated her delicate skin. She's clearly worried about me. Her concern is honourable, and speaks volumes about how much she cares for me.

Her uneasiness is misplaced. Becca is the only one who needs to be concerned about me. She's the one I see every day, the one who I laugh and joke and eat and study with. Emma need not trouble herself with that aspect of our friendship. My bestie has that covered.

I have a black and pink butterfly clip hanging precariously from my mouth. Intently, I focus on her expression. She is sitting on the bed sweating, and appears to be swaying repeatedly. Chewing her bottom lip harder, she dives despairingly into my grass-coloured eyes. Her red lipstick is partially faded, and a small piece of rouge makeup has smudged on her teeth. I slice the sharp clip in my hair, almost grazing my scalp. I enjoy the sensation.

Emma winces.

I give her a slow and controlled smile.

"Stop worrying," I reassure her. "Everything is going to be fine."

"If only I could believe that, Alena," she says, lines of worry crinkling her forehead. "There is a gut feeling which tells me that Mr. Hawthorne is not completely gone."

Flinging my head back, I laugh nervously. "Honey, this

is not Hollywood. This is real life. He's moved on, I've moved on, and he's probably become a better man after spending two and a half years in prison. Being behind bars has a way of changing people."

Reducing the distance between us, she leans in. Quickly, she reaches for me and grabs my wrists. "Why are you talking such bull, Alena? Please don't hide your true feelings from me. I can see straight through you. So why pretend everything is fine, when we both know that's not true?"

I laugh again, except this time it sounds more like an unnerving burble. Shaking her off my wrists, hastily, I change the subject.

"How is college, Em? You enjoying English Lit at Roehampton University?"

"It's really good, but really tough," she asserts coldly, tapping her feet, still mad at me for hiding my feelings from her.

"What about boys?" I ask directly. "In a relationship, Emma? You have anyone?"

She averts her gaze to the floor. "An on-and-off boyfriend. Nothing special."

Secretly I smile, glad I am ahead of her in the relationship department. However, a part of me is sad that she hasn't yet found that special someone.

"He will come, Emma," I say, bolstering her. "Trust me. It will happen."

We share a mutually agreeable smile.

"Thank you, Alena," she grins. "I take it that you and Phillip are serious."

"Well," I say hesitantly. "We are together. That is the main thing."

Sedately, I get up from my seat. Emma looks me up and down. I'm in a tight-fitted, black shiny dress. I know I look hot. My figure and curves are really accentuated in this womanly garb.

"You look gorgeous, babe. Simply beautiful."

"Thanks, hun," I say, admiring her flowing red dress that makes her appear as elegant as a movie star. "You're hot to trot yourself."

"Thank you, babe." She beams.

We struggle to walk to the door in our high heels. Teetering, ready to fall over, we stop at the dressing table mirror. One last-minute check on our make-up and attire. Both of us approve. We look breathtaking! Dazzling! I grab our small clutch bags. We are by the door, ready to leave.

Out of the blue, Emma groans. "This reminds me of old times."

I flop onto her shoulder, smelling the Elizabeth Arden perfume on her neck. Uncannily, she wears the same fragrance as Becca. This is Emma's favourite spray. She always wore this, even back in high school. "The smell of nostalgia is glorious, isn't it, babe?"

Tears start to trickle down Emma's face. She runs and tosses herself on my bed. Dramatically, lying flat on top of my soft purple duvet, and flinging her bag on my bed, she gabbles, "Alena! I can't bear it!" Her voice is frighteningly distressed. "If anything ever happened to you, I don't know what I would do. I love you. You're my BFF."

Sauntering to the bed, I plonk myself next to her purse. I call her with one coaxing finger. She crawls like a toddler towards me, and I pat the bed as she approaches. Wrapping my arms around her, letting the warmth of my skin seep into her chilly body, I plant a warm kiss on her cheek. Gently, I stroke her wild, straw-coloured hair, and she begins to calm down. I pat one of her reddened cheeks to pacify her.

"Nothing will happen to me. I'll be fine, Em. Honestly."

"I'm not so sure," she whispers, overwhelmed by the tears gushing from her eyes. "I am not the only one who is worried, Alena."

"Who else is worried about me?" I enquire.

"Phillip!"

Baffled by her words, I screw up my face. "You haven't even met Phillip yet, so how do you know he is worried?"

Chewing off the left side of her bottom lip, she stares at me. "As I approached your room this morning, Phillip interrogated me. And then he formally introduced himself."

I double blink. "He did what?"

Now she is the one calming me down, patting me on the arm. "He told me he knows everybody who goes in and out of your room. Like a hawk, he watches from down the hall constantly. Since Mr. Hawthorne tried to harass you with his unacceptable calls and the Leicester Gazette paid a visit, he wants to ensure you are safe. Why didn't you tell me about all this stuff that's been happening, Alena?"

"I didn't think you needed to know!"

She gives me a look that tells me she's insulted.

"Do you now see why I am concerned about you?" she confirms.

"No!" I say defiantly, folding my arms tightly to my chest and peering up at the plain white ceiling.

Persistently, she beckons my rebellious pupils. "Does your mother know what's being going on here?"

I gasp, glaring at Emma. "I don't need my mother having a heart attack! I've already lost my father."

Comfortingly, she rubs my back, her eyes paying attention to my forlorn face. "How are you coping with your dad's death on top of everything else?"

"Okay," I say, taking a deep breath, lying my arse off.

"You do know that I just want the best for you, Alena, and so does Phillip."

A wave of amity surges from me, and I see Emma's love through the glass clouding my sight. I misjudged our relationship. She is special to me, just as special to me as Becca, so what was I thinking discarding her affection, downgrading our level of friendship to 'somewhat insignificant'?

"I know," I whimper throwing my head onto her warm, inviting torso. "Your friendship means a lot to me, Em. And I'm happy you're here with me right now. I need you. But what I don't need is a stalker for a boyfriend. I already had a crazed psycho, and look how that turned out."

She pats me on the leg to appease me. This doesn't reduce my anxiety.

"Phillip really loves you, which is so incredibly sweet."

Raising a critical brow, I look up at her. "You would think so!"

Emma grins, squeezing my thigh in an attempt to lighten up my blue mood. "Yes, that is adorable. I want a man like Phillip Gregson. Wanna hand him over?"

That gets me grinning. Emma is right; he is a keeper.

I smile so broadly that it is like a ray of incandescent light beaming on Emma's face. "Are we ready?" I am determined that nothing is going to spoil our night out.

Ardently, she pecks me on the base of the chin. "Come on then, bestie, let's hit the town."

I giggle. "*Ranatoo Lama* is across the road, hun."

"Maybe it's down the road to you, babe. I travelled one hundred and seven miles for this."

"One hundred and seven miles is a stone's throw away." I tease. "Try going to California. That's 5,233 miles from here!"

She chortles. "True, true. Now that I cannot disagree with."

MADNESS!

Our warm bodies are intertwined on my bed. You would have thought I was lying with Phillip, but I'm not. It is Emma and I who are meshed together on the warm mattress, talking, reminiscing about the past. Suddenly *his* name is mentioned and I start to lose my sense of rationality, almost going insane.

"Emma, I was thinking... I need to go and visit Stanley Hawthorne," I assert daringly, staring into her ocean blue-coloured orbs. "I need closure."

Swiftly, Emma untangles herself from the mess that is my complicated consciousness and distances herself from me. She perches at the edge of my bed, chewing the inside of her mouth, vigorously scratching her porcelain-like face like a distressed and wounded cat that needs to visit a vet. Then, she jumps up from the bed as fast as a cheetah, hurling a thin pink weapon in my face – her French tipped fingers, which are ready to launch an attack. Rolling back on the bed, I am a little frightened by these bizarre, ungainly movements.

"What the hell is wrong with you?" She screams, flinging wild limbs into the air akin to a crazy monkey. Shaking her head, she flies towards me, pinning a pair of desperate hands around my shoulders. Emma pulls at the hem of my frilly cream blouse. I am secretly praying she doesn't tear it, as it is a ninety pound designer shirt Phillip bought me as a Christmas present. He'd go mad if it tore! Indefatigably, her palms slide down my silky top. She grips my arm and won't let go.

"No!" she screams, scratching her face again, and then seizing my arms. There are long white marks on the sides of her cheeks. It must hurt. Clearly, she doesn't care about the pain. She's virtually gone nutso. "No, Alena! I won't let this happen. Not for a second time. No way!"

I twist my apt limbs to outmanoeuvre her. Laxly, she gives in, releasing her hold on me. Taking control, I loosely grab her two strong hands. They start to tremble. Letting go of her hands, I grip her wrists, hard.

"I am going to see him, no matter what you or anyone else has to say about it. I *need* to finally move on. For some things in life, you have to go back in order to then go forward."

"Don't go back to the past. Leave it alone, Alena, for God's sake!"

"I want him out of my life, forever!" I say resolutely.

Plunking herself on the floor, thudding into the ground, the weight of Emma's problems land like a heavy bag of ice cubes on the carpet. Her eyes squeeze closed in pain. She is close to tears. Two watery eyes look up at me desolately.

"He is out of your life, Alena! Let it stay that way. Look at what you've achieved in the past two years. You're at university now, studying English, doing something with your life. You have a lovely mother who's so proud of you, and you have Phillip Gregson, a wonderful and caring boyfriend, and Becca, and me. There's no room for the past, so let it be free. Move on, without going back into the depths of despair! I've seen you there, Alena, when we were seventeen. He almost destroyed you. I'm not letting it happen again! Never!"

Slapping a pair of heated palms over my ears, I block out her voice of reason. "No. I'm still not clear of him. He's in my blood system. I need him *out*!"

Repeatedly, I feel the horror of the past reverberating in my mind, hear his sick voice vibrating in my eardrums, eating away at my brain and my sanity. Doctor Hannah did say I may feel this way upon Stanley's release. I didn't think it would happen. These feelings are so unnatural, involuntary. I can't control them. Suddenly I am broken again. I see him in my mind's eye, laughing wickedly.

Now, I'm unfixable. I cannot be mended. I'm completely torn, and I think I always will be. And the worst part is I may have to live with this for the rest of my life. These thoughts that are haunting me, like a spectre roaming about in my consciousness. Somehow, I need to escape *them*. I need *them* to go away, and the only way out is to confront my attacker, to get him out of my system forever.

"No, I'm still not clear of him!" I scream, frantically pacing up and down my room.

Emma rises from the ground, and gently guides me onto the bed, coaxing me to sit next to her. I allow her to summon my attention and lead me into the light. As the sunlight burns my eyes, I squint, reducing the irritation.

"Alena." Her voice is calm, soothing, yet holds a degree of anxiety in its tone. "What do you think will happen if you visit him in prison? Don't you think you will be provoking him, giving him justification for what he did in the past?"

"No," I answer plainly. "By seeing me, he will know it's time to move on. He will know that it is the last time he will ever see me."

A soft hand rests on my knee and strokes it, placidly, endeavouring to put sense back in my veins. Emma's soothing hands cannot assuage my agony. I am a damaged woman beyond all normal rationality. I've lost sense of reality, all sense of time and space.

"If you go to him, then he still has a firm hold over you! He wins!"

Rigidly, I slap Emma on the leg. My eyes are glassy, like marbles, ready to fall and crack and break into a thousand screaming memories from the past. "If I don't go, then I remain trapped, and a prisoner in my own head!"

"If you go to him, then psychologically, you still are his prisoner. He will own you!"

"Bullshit!" I glare into Emma's concerned face.

She springs up from the bed. "Phillip won't allow this. He loves you. He'll stop this if I can't!"

Imprudently, I smirk. "No, he can't! He cannot control me!"

Emma sobs. "How do you think he will feel, Alena? He's stood by you for almost a year, helping you battle those demons. Now you're going to face those demons, head-on, in one of the most unsafe places where he cannot protect you!"

Tears well in my eyes, and I lower my head. "He'll understand."

She is bemused, and her face wrinkles in despair. "Understand! He will understand that you want to visit this teacher in prison who interfered with you back in high school. Hmm. I'm not sure he'll quite get that. Do you?"

Pausing for a moment, I think rationally about what I am about to do. Pondering on my decision, I know I have to follow my mind. It's been over two years since it all happened. I am nineteen now, and I still haven't got over the past. This could be my last chance to close the black, swirling portal of yesterday and move forward with my life. Phil might disagree with my decision, yes. Nonetheless, I feel going to see Stanley will allow me to destroy the barriers that are holding our relationship back, the thick walls that are coming between us and stopping us from going further with our romance.

There is a knock at the door. Becca bursts in.

"Alena, I borrowed some milk." She looks at me on the bed and then turns to Emma, who is sitting next to me. "Hello, and you are?" There is a flash of jealousy in her eyes.

"Let me introduce you both," I say hurriedly, breaking the ice. "Becca, this is Emma, my high school best friend. Emma, this is Becca, my best friend and housemate."

Becca's eyes turn cold, and she scrunches her nose like she caught a whiff of a nasty smell.

"I don't remember you telling me about *her*," she snaps, pulling her attention away from Emma to face me head-on.

Gees, what a temper. Clearly, Becca thinks she owns me.

I did tell her about Emma. She knew that. Though I think seeing Emma and how beautiful she is in the flesh is making Becca envious. They both look quite similar, now that Emma's blonde hair has grown to her waist and she's lost a stone in weight. The two girls are the same build, the same complexion. The only difference is their height. Becca is an inch taller. Apart from that, they could pass as sisters.

"Pleased to meet you, too!" barks Emma, extremely offended.

"Becca, be nice to Emma," I grunt, addressing her behaviour. "She is *also* my best friend."

"No, *I am* your bestie, not her," she says tersely, plonking herself on the bed and squeezing her tight bottom between Emma and I.

Infuriatingly, Emma rolls her eyes. "I see. The possessive type. Where did you get Malibu Barbie from, Alena?"

Frenetically, my heart begins to pound. I feel an anxiety episode coming on.

Pointing rudely at Emma, Becca retorts. "I am from San Francisco, not Malibu, you English bimbo!"

"Who you calling an English bimbo?" shouts Emma, completely insulted.

"Deaf as well as dumb, are you?" yells Becca, raising a hand, looking like she is going to slap Emma in the face.

Persistently, I stamp my feet into the carpet, and press my sweaty, perspiring palms over my ears. "Please stop, children! Now!"

Reluctantly, they stop the bickering. Two pairs of avid eyes then relax and suddenly shoot to the wall at the far end of my room.

"He's gorgeous. Isn't he?" Becca says, summoning Emma's concentration.

They are gazing at someone. I think they're looking at one of the three posters Becca plastered in a messy line on my wall to make my room appear 'more homey.' One poster is of Jason Derulo, a second one of Orlando Bloom, and the last one of Taylor Lautner. I am not sure which one of them they are referring to. Already they are speaking a 'twin language.' Should *I* be jealous now?

"Who's gorgeous?" I ask, a perplexed expression sweeping across my face.

"Taylor Lautner, duh!" I receive a joint response.

Evidently, he has two massive fans right here in this room.

Sitting crossways, the two turn to face one another, and Becca continues. "Those vampire movies he starred in, oh, gees, how fine did he look?"

"Simply sublime," says Emma, drooling.

"Keep that shirt off for the whole movie, Taylor. Please, script writer and director, make it happen in his next cinematic venture! I *need to* see his manly chest, like, in every shot!"

"I know!" Emma squeals, leaning happily on Becca's shoulder. "His shirt should be permanently off. I think he's our age, right? So it's so okay to dig him. Right?"

"Uh-huh! I think he's around our age!" Becca replies breathlessly.

The two girls exchange a solid stare, which illumines the room, generating a fire of envy in my heart. I scowl and pout my lips as the duo gets closer and closer. Should I have introduced them? Maybe this was a huge mistake!

They continue to chat as I simply twiddle my thumbs, staring up at the ceiling. Now I'm totally jealous and bored. What a great combination!

"Even if he was older, I would still *so* want to tap that!" Becca giggles, knocking into Emma coltishly in the same way she used to bump into me when she was *my* exclusive best friend.

I'm now the one who is having issues with sharing. I don't mind Becca becoming friends with Emma, as long as they don't shut me out of their 'blonde world!'

Strategically, I decide to insert myself into the conversation. I think I'm going to lose the will to live if I don't.

"Tapping," I say quietly, my eyes bouncing between the two girls who are enchanted by the hot guy's picture. "Can we leave that out of the conversation?" I shiver with repulsion at the thought of people 'tapping.'

The duo roll their eyes at exactly the same time. It's rather scary how quickly they are becoming a unit.

Becca turns to Emma. "Alena doesn't *like* that kinda talk. She's a real prude."

Emma nods in agreement. "Hmm. Seems that way."

I have a strong desire to defend myself. "No! I am not a prude. I just have issues."

Shrugging her shoulders, Emma says. "Well, Bec, unfortunately, that isn't the same as prudish. I'm with Alena on this one."

Becca huffs loudly, scowling at us both. "Okay, then! You win!"

Ungraciously, Emma raises a stern brow. "This is not about winning or losing, Becca. It seems you have an obsession with winning everything! Clearly, Alena isn't the only one with problems."

A vicious grunt cuts through the air. Oh, dear. Becca is upset and *really* angry. But she doesn't defend herself; she can't. She knows that Emma is right.

The atmosphere begins to get extremely intense. I need to quell this tension.

"Becca," I say changing the subject. "Before you came in, Emma and I were talking *serious talk*."

Attentively, she nods. "I can do serious. What was the convo about?"

"Mr. Stanley Hawthorne!" Emma's piercing blue eyes are honed in on Becca's astonished countenance.

Becca gasps. "What about him?"

"Alena wants to visit him in prison to tear the shit out of him," Emma replies pungently. "Bad idea, right, Bec?"

Instantaneously, her thumb plummets to the ground. "Uh-huh. Very bogus move."

"No, it makes sense," I say peevishly. I come up against a hard impenetrable wall, the pair of them giving me a really harsh stare.

Emma gets up and perches next to me, and her and Becca slope into my body like Siamese twins, with their lips, eyes, and noses close to the sides of my face. I feel like I am being ganged up on, big time!

"No, Alena!" They yell in unison. "Not happening!"

Recalcitrantly, I fold my arms. "I need to tell him what a shithole he is, so that I can feel better and move on with my life." My body propels forward, back arching, and a look of distress emerges on my phiz. "He needs to know how he's affected me. Then, and only then, can I be rid of him and banish the ghosts of the past."

"Alena, no!" Emma shouts, pulling me back on the bed, forcing me to face the fiery eyes of two furious yet concerned best friends. "This is not the answer!"

Our legs are touching, all three of us. It feels kinda nice, yet really peculiar and weird at the same time. I shake that thought out of my head.

"I need to go, and I'm going tomorrow. It's Thursday,

the last visiting day before he's let out."

"It's dangerous, don't go," warns Becca, grabbing my arms. "He could be leading you into a trap! You can't trust this man after all he's done. He's beyond devious."

"Yeah, she's right," confirms Emma. "Don't attempt to go near the bastard!"

Unpleasantly, I suck in air, and soon, I find myself grumbling quietly. "He's in prison. What can he possibly do to me? He's locked up. There are prison guards all around him. I'll be safe."

Unpredictably, Emma bounds, flying back next to Becca on the far side of the bed. Becca mouths something to Emma, and they share a strange concentrated gaze. They nod at each other fervently. I am unable to fathom what their agenda is. I think they are talking about me, speaking their own telepathic language again – the language of the blondes! Together, as a unit, they spring up from the bed and travel to the door.

"Where are you going?" I demand to know.

"Phillip needs to know about this," wails Becca.

"Yes, absolutely," Emma concurs.

Fleetly, Becca guides her newfound friend by the arm, leading the way. I try to yank both of them back, however, Becca is strong, and she drives me into retreat with one inflexible and resolute palm.

"No," I shout. "Don't tell him! He'll go mad!"

"Yes, that's exactly what we want," hollers Becca, speeding up, her long, graceful legs taking bigger and mightier steps. Emma moves quickly, keeping up.

"Perhaps he can put some sense into you," Emma adds, looking back at me displeasingly.

Briskly, the blonde duo walks into the corridor. I trail behind them as swiftly as I can manage.

THE RACE

This is a race to the finish line...

Becca is sprinting.

Emma is running fast.

I am jogging quickly.

Becca reaches Phillip's door first, and bangs at it frantically. My heart races. I can't believe she's going to tell him about the explosive letter and article from Mr. Hawthorne.

Hesitantly, Phillip eases the door ajar.

She is right in his space, right in his face. He is half naked, only clothed by a soft, skimpy towel.

"He sent her a letter, and a newspaper clipping," puffs Becca, completely out of breath. "She's going to meet him. Stop her, please, Phil!"

"What letter?" He asks, opening the door wider. "What clipping? I'm to stop her from seeing who?" His fiery globes race halfway down the corridor to meet mine. "What is going on, baby?"

I bite my lip, wishing to melt into the ground. Astutely, I decide to remain dead silent.

"Becca? Emma?" he hollers. "What the hell is going on?"

As he has just a flimsy towel on, he doesn't come fully out of his room. Nonetheless, a deep look of concern is prevalent on his face.

Becca babbles, "She's going to see him. *Him.*"

Phillip's eyes swivel to me. "Are you cheating on me, Alena?" he barks. "Is that what this is about?"

Everyone goes quiet. I cower in the corner. Becca takes a step back. Emma steps forward and explains.

"Stanley Hawthorne sent Alena a letter on Monday, and an accompanying newspaper clipping. His sentence has been shortened. He's on parole. He'll be out of prison this Friday. Before he is released, he has expressed a wish to meet with Alena, alone, in his cell. She wants to go. Becca and I have tried, but failed, to talk her out of it. That's why we are all here, to see you, Phillip!"

A deep anger pollutes his face. He points at his large, bare feet. "Get over here, Alena. We need to talk! Now!"

"I have to see him," I cry. "I need closure, Phillip!" I begin to whimper, my body trembling. I pray the ground will eat me up before Phil gets his hands on me. Who knows what he'll do in anger!

"We're not talking here," he yells, his dark eyes penetrating straight through me. "Get up and come into my room."

"No," I whine. "I've decided. I'm going!"

"Right!" he bellows, his countenance menacing and his eyes burning with rage.

Pounding his hefty feet into the ground, Phillip marches down the corridor, his deep, heavy footsteps beating the rough carpet. With one sturdy hand, he hauls me up and drags me into his bedroom, grabbing me by the wrists. The letter and newspaper clipping, which are in my hands, flap in the air. His grip is strong, determined. He ain't messing around. The door slams shut. I'm concealed with his fury and his fear about my decision. His manliness is covered only by a small white towel, his chest bulging in my face. Waving a potent finger in the air, he admonishes me like a child.

"What the hell is this shit all about, Alena?"

I shake insuppressibly. My body's involuntary actions are wild, incapable of being constrained. But Phillip is powerful enough to handle me. He clutches me tight to stabilise this nervous anxiety. Looking into my restless eyes, he knows I am on the edge, on the verge of a breakdown. I feel my nervousness rising from my ankles all the way up to my head. Quickly, I grow faint, weak, powerless. Phillip holds me securely by the waist, his strength saving me from collapsing onto the floor.

"I need to end this, to tell him how he has messed me up!" My breathing is irrational, heart beating crazily in my shell of a body. "I'm falling, Phillip. I am falling. And *he* is the only one who can end this nightmare."

"No. *I* am!" He bridles me, grinding his teeth irately. "I am your man, and I won't let you go! *This* is where the madness ends!"

My tears begin to burn. I am wilting into the ground. "You have to let me go!"

"No, I don't!" he screams, puncturing my emerald eyes with his perfunctory stare.

Dolefully, I look up at him. My visage is beginning to crumble with sorrow. "If I don't go, I will be screwed up, unable to move on."

He points a heavy finger at me. His thick index finger seems to be pulling me towards him, as if he is a magnetic force drawing me to his authoritative centre. "You're already screwed up, and it's because of that arsehole!"

"If I don't go, I'll be screwed up forever. I need to finish this, once and for all!" I screech, peering at him from between the gaps of the thick wavy hair covering my face and obscuring my vision.

His eyes are aflame. "He's the reason why we don't have a proper relationship. You think I'm stupid enough to let you confront such a man? A man who wants to destroy you, destroy us, and possibly wants you dead?"

"He would never kill me," I explain exasperatedly. "He only wants to level with me. And when his defences are down, that's when I'll tear him to shreds, make him regret what he did to me!"

"An evil man like that will kill you in a heartbeat, prison guards or not. He is resourceful, cunning. Visiting him won't help you. Only I can. He will obliterate you, Alena. Finish you off for good." Phillip's eyes are intense, controlling; his glare is like a hammer hitting me repeatedly in the head. I feel as though I might pass out from the intensity of his resolute focus.

Tree trunk arms encompass my shuddering shell, providing thick, dark protection that soaks up my tears. Phil is holding me close, yet he doesn't break me. He's making me feel stronger. I don't understand. Right now I should be repelling his embrace, because he is killing me with his solid grasp. But I feel safe. How is this possible? I start to feel secure, like I can depend and rely on this protection forever, rely on this special man, who I have partially let into my life.

"Don't go, Alena," he begs, keeping me tight to his body, kissing my lips softly. "Don't end us!"

Hastily, Phillip lifts me up, so I meet him at eye level. His love lets me levitate, like a halo on an angel's head. His affection, scorching and powerful, is rubbing against me. Carefully, he helps plant my feet firmly on the floor, and yet I don't feel like I'm affected by the pull of gravity. I get the sensation I am floating. He contemplates me, and then his towel drops, and the beauty of his masculinity, dark and refined like Muscovado sugar, is fully exposed and realised. Travelling two steps back, Phil allows me to see him in his natural state, as God intended.

Naked, fully bare, his muscles rippling, manhood growing inch by inch, he whispers, "Tonight, we need to start a new chapter in our relationship."

His breath is hungry, his eyes eagerly searching mine. Phillip transforms into a tiger, an animal desperate for meat. Except, I am not his victim. I am his woman, his equal, his mate.

Slowly, our eyes fully connect, and we both tremble, knowing what is about to happen. Oh shit, I want him. I am scared to let him inside me. But I actually want this to happen. I'm ready.

Whimpering gently, I run forward, climbing about his dense body, wrapping my slim frame around his hard, shiny stature. His muscles are glorious, and his love, mighty. I press my lips passionately to his mouth, my figure gyrating against him. Strong hands hold me up, and I devour Phil's delicious chocolate body. We smash into his dresser as we fondle each other, standing up, his small stack of sports magazines tumbling on the floor. We don't give a damn! We're feral, rampant, ravenous.

"Oh, Phillip, oh Phillip," I murmur, thoroughly invigorated with the feeling of his lips on mine.

"Are you sure you want to do this?" he says, tears streaming down his cheeks.

"Yes!" I groan. My breathing is jagged, nervous. My mouth presses firmly onto his. "I am ready now, and I love you, Phil."

Sensuously, Phillip puffs a gust of air into my mouth as he speaks. His eyes burst with passion. "Alena, I can't tell you how happy I am to hear all this."

Scooping me up in his arms, he carries me to the bed like Tarzan. Powerfully, he throws me down, his body inclining, his hands frantically undressing me. Off come the shoes, the socks, the skirt. He flings off my top, whips off my knickers and unhooks my bra in record speed. Earnestly, he mounts me. I start to pant, partly nervous, partly excited.

"I can't believe this is actually happening, Phillip, we are going to…"

He over-blinks and closes his eyes for a second, savouring my sweet words. "Yes. Thank you, Jesus!"

I laugh, biting my lip, reaching my hand up to touch

him.

Whipping my bra clean off, he begins to caress my breasts, swirling his finger in the centre of my receptive nipples.

"Oh Phillip, oh darling."

Affectionately, he kisses me all over, and then his mouth descends on my breasts. "These are gorgeous, Alena," he whispers. "So blooming gorgeous."

"And tonight, they are all yours."

"Yes, all mine..." He puffs.

I giggle, allowing him to knead my body, leaving his warm, sexy mark on every crevice, dent and line of my skin.

"I think you've forgotten something," I wheeze, prompting him.

"Shit," he screams, rushing a pair of flummoxed hands through his hair. "I don't have a condom!"

"I have one," I say massaging his glowing muscly back.

"You do?" He is surprised.

"Yea. It's in my skirt pocket." I point at the floor, where my skirt is happily soaking up the sun, which is shining directly on its top hemline.

"Skirts have pockets?"

"Mine does."

"But I thought…"

"You thought what?"

"That you didn't want to have sex before now."

"Doesn't mean I didn't think about it, Phil."

Lasciviously he smiles, and dives across the silky covers, reaching for my skirt. His back is pressed against the bed. "I've got it, Alena."

"Sweet!" I smile.

I watch Phillip roll on the rubber as speedily as he can. I'm fascinated. I've never studied a man intently whilst he puts on a condom. He begins to struggle. It proves to be rather time-consuming for him to put it on. Eventually, he gets it on well.

I beam. My eyes burst into flames of passion, and his eyes sparkle. Voraciously, his body comes for mine. He touches me everywhere, tenderly, softly, and then he eases my legs apart. Closing my eyes for a second, I take a deep breath. Nervously, clutching onto Phillip, I find that my palms are sweating.

As I open my eyes, Phil is gazing at me. Intently, his eyes embed into mine, and slowly, carefully, he enters me…

I gasp. "Oh! Ouch!"

It hurts quite a bit the first time. Plunging into me again, we work out a rhythm and I begin to enjoy it. In fact, it starts to feel really good.

Strongly, Phillip kisses me and then whispers in my ear, "Baby, are you okay?"

Looking up at him, I nod. I'm unable to speak, the sensations I'm experiencing are so intense. God, I never knew sex could be this great.

When the passion surges within me and the fireworks begin to explode inside me, Phil holds me closer, and we join, moving together as one.

"Phil," I plead. "Oh Phil, oh baby, I love you."

We both unleash a cheetah pant that colours the walls red.

"I love you too, Alena… Oh, gees. This was so worth the wait."

"I know." I cry. "This is freaking awesome!"

Summoning my hands and gaze, Phillip manipulates my fleshly female form, and gets me to roll over on my front. He runs his open, salivating mouth across the breadth of my bare torso, and parts my legs. I am still saturated, and I want him. He takes me again. I grip onto the satin covers, and soon, I gasp loudly several times as the deep vibrations send me to the moon. Enjoying every single second, I shut my lids. As I reopen them, I find my eyes spinning into orbit, and I holler profoundly. I am happily dizzy, joyously disorientated, in a divine state of heavenly bliss. My breathing is erratic. I wail passionately, and then I convulse, my head meeting the pillow, my slender frame on fire and sopping with sweat.

Zealously, I twist my head to face him. We kiss deeply, arduously. I feel his tender love rushing through my veins. His hands slip underneath my body to fondle my breasts and their juicy centres, and after, his burning palms descend, caressing my lady lips.

I murmur. "This is wonderful, out of this world. I know it's only gonna get better from here."

Using his robust upper strength, Phillip flips me around. I lie flat on my back. My body is all his and for the taking. His eyes go glassy. Unable to hold it in any longer, Phillip cries like a baby, and lays back on top of me, his tears now joining mine, since I am crying hard, too. Lovingly, he clutches onto my hot, naked figure for dear life. I don't ever want him to let me go.

"That was so bloody amazing, Alena," he says his voice rough, hard, his hunky drenched body completely happy and satisfied. "If it gets any better than that, then I might need to call an ambulance!"

We burst into a jovial titter as we snuggle, laying cosily in each other's embrace.

"No paramedic needed. I can be your nurse, doctor," I say kinkily.

He laughs.

"When we are married, you can play nurse every night, Alena." Naughtily, his lips curve into a smirk.

I adopt a serious countenance. "Married? Us?"

"Yes, Alena."

"When? This year?"

"No silly," he chuckles. "In a couple of years, when I'm a successful Sports Therapist and you're a sensational elementary school teacher."

My warm green eyes pierce his sexy dark-brown ones. "You really wish to marry *me*, in this lifetime?"

Meticulously, he explores my mouth with his hot,

throbbing tongue. "Yes, of course I do."

Completely overwhelmed by this moment, I start to cry again. I can't believe we have got to this stage in our relationship. Oh, God, this is tremendous.

Phil pulls my body nearer. I recognise that twinkle and glint in his eye. My breath grows laboured. He has an insatiable look; he is hungry again, and wants his dessert. I want dessert too. We start to devour each other. Our sensual forms are melding, pulsating, our hearts racing…

Bang! Bang! Bang! It's the door!

"Oh, crap!" I shout. "Bad timing."

"I know!" he exclaims.

"Don't answer it," I advise.

"It might be very important."

"Okay," I say. "Attend to it then."

Phillip leaps up, running around the room, not knowing what to do.

"We are naked." I remind him. "Get some clothes for us, Phil."

"Right!"

Flying to his wardrobe, he throws on a dressing gown. Hastily, he goes to the door. Forgetting I am naked, too, he sprints back to the closet, grabs a t-shirt off the hanger and lobs it to me.

"Put it on, quick!" He says.

I struggle to put it on. I have no stamina left.

"Quick!" he urges. "Get it on!"

"I could have said the same to you earlier, when you couldn't get the rubber on fast," I jibe.

Cocking his head to one side, he offers me a sarcastic, 'not funny, Alena' expression.

I get the t-shirt on. "It's on, babe. Open the door."

He nods. Unlatching the door, he whips it open.

Responsively, my ears prick up. I lean forward, raising a curious body two inches from the bed. Despite my efforts, I still can't see who's at the door. I'm at the wrong angle to see the ingress fully.

"Hello, Phillip," a very posh, quintessentially English voice says.

"Can we come in?" a high-pitched American voice adds.

Oh shit! It's Emma and Becca. What the hell do they want to come in for? They are going to know we had sex. Don't make it obvious, Phil, please. Discretion is the word of the day. What am I thinking? Phillip never has been discreet about anything. He told Becca we hadn't had sex practically the moment he met her!

Phillip flusters. "What do you want, ladies? We are… a little busy."

I slap an irate hand on my forehead, falling back on the bed. What an idiot! Why did he have to say those exact words? I sigh gently, knowing my boyfriend is beginning to crash and burn out there. Those blondes are tough – they won't stop until he makes a confession as to what we've been doing. Going on all fours, crawling forward on the bed, I become very inquisitive, eager to see exactly what is happening at the door. I manage to catch a glimpse of Becca and Emma, who are sniggering hard, and I can tell Phillip is growing more and more flustered as the girls probe him further. He's babbling; he is about to crack under the pressure. Stay strong, Phil, don't admit to anything. This is our first time. It's supposed to be kept totally private. Get rid of them now, for goodness sake!

"Getting busy, more like!" Becca shouts, poking her finger naughtily in her mouth. "You randy kids! Just be honest, and admit to it!"

Playfully, she pushes Phillip out the way with Emma's help. They see me on the bed with his t-shirt on. And, oh crap, all our clothes are on the floor. Now I'm the idiot, not reminding him to move them. Great pair we are, perfect for each other.

"Damn! This is mega awkward!" I burst beetroot red in embarrassment. My head drops on the bed. Phillip sits beside me. There's no point us denying it. They know. The secret is out.

Becca's hand flies across her mouth, and then she and Emma share a gleeful look. Emma stands next to her, hands on her hips, staring at us in amazement.

"Finally!" Becca exclaims, doing a little dance on the spot. "It's about bloody time you two went to the land of humpy-hump-bump!"

Everyone in this room knows that Becca Richardson-Smith, the fun, lively American girl, is the only person who'd have the guts to blurt out those exact words. Emma is too British to be so forthright.

"Yes," Emma concurs. "It took nearly a year!"

Phillip draws me to his body, sharing my embarrassment.

"Was it a mind-blowing experience, like you've always dreamed of, Alena? Remember you told me you wanted that?"

"Bec," I assert. "I told you that in confidence."

"Nuh uh," she says, smirking. "You told me confidently."

"No," I say, flummoxed. "Never mind."

An intriguing expression clouds Phillip's dreamy eyes. "Did you really tell Becca that, honey?" He whispers near my ears, but loud enough for our audience to hear.

I blush.

"The rubber?" Becca asks, picking up my denim clothes, which are scattered on the floor amongst our other clothes. "Was it in this skirt?"

"Yes, B, in *that one*." I am short with her, this whole 'we know you had sex thing' is getting a bit too invasive and weird.

"I'm glad you took my rubber, hun." She winks. "Paid off, didn't it?"

I roll my eyes to heaven and don't dignify her comment with a response.

Emma laughs, pointing at Becca. "You told her to

keep the condom with her?"

Leaning into Emma, Becca's nose caresses her luscious blonde hair. "Yes, and she kept it in her skirt pocket this whole time. It obviously worked like a charm, just like I told her it would. I knew she'd get super horny one day and Phillip would totally do her. They are, like, the perfect couple, after all. So cute."

"I know," Emma agrees. "So adorable."

"Hello!" I shout, banging my fist into the springy bed. "We are still here and we can hear you!"

"Sorry," Emma says apologetically.

"Oh dear," retorts Becca sarcastically, running her hand from her knee all the way up to where the frayed part on her tiny, butt-hugging shorts begin. "Getting cranky, are we? Best leave you lovebirds alone, so you can hump the night away."

"Bec!" Emma exclaims.

"What? It's true!" she replies brazenly.

I raise an irritated eyebrow. My arms fold, and so do Phillip's.

"Please leave us. We would like to be alone. Okay?" I say firmly.

"Okay!" Becca squalls. "I'm just *so* happy for you guys."

I force a smile. "That's great. Be a doll and be happy for us on the other side of the door, all right?"

"I take it that you're not visiting Stanley now, then?" She adds.

"No, Bec. Now, please, for God's sake, we want to be alone." I point an irate finger towards the door. "Go! Please!"

Finally, Emma gets the hint, and makes for the exit.

"Can I be a bridesmaid at your wedding?" Becca asks, still squealing and clapping zealous palms together.

"Yes, Becca. Both you and Emma can be."

"Swell!" she hollers.

"Cool!" shouts Emma.

"Can I smash big white ceramic plates at your wedding, Greek style?"

"Yes, Becca! That will be fine." My voice is tired and exasperated.

"Awesome!" she chirps.

They both leave.

"Now, where were we?" Phil jokes.

"Like you need reminding."

He kisses me. I ease him off for a moment.

"What is it, baby?"

I look at him pensively. "The letter from Stanley and the article."

His lips purse. "What about them?"

"Let me rip them up."

"Now?"

I nod. "Yes, now!"

He is confused, his forehead crinkles. "Why right now?"

"It's symbolism, for how far I've come. I want to remember this day for the rest of my life."

He smiles and encourages me. "Tear it up then, baby, and toss it." Methodically, he points to the bin.

Sliding off the bed, I grab the letter and article, which are underneath our clothing on the carpet, and I rip them up vigorously into a thousand tiny pieces. I walk to the bin near the window and chuck away the past. Aah, I feel so much better, like a heavy weight has been lifted from my shoulders. As I breathe a sigh of relief, seventeen-year-old Alena soars out of me and flies into the bin as well. Her vacant eyes stare vacuously into my soul. Then, gradually, she disappears, going back to her realm, her world.

"Bye, forever," I say, my voice deep and emotional.

Phillip reaches out a hand for me. I go to him. The rich yellow light from the sun is setting beautifully as we touch. He coaxes me into bed. His muscular form immediately surrounds me. I feel safe, calm, free.

"Can I put on the stereo, low?" I ask him.

Nodding avidly, he gives me his consent. I reach over his head, where the dresser is situated, just by the far right of his headstand. I turn on the radio.

It's fate that one of Christina Aguilera's songs is playing, the same one that played when Mr. Hawthorne kissed me. Tears violently fall down my cheeks, and I wail into Phillip's sturdy chocolate body.

"Are you okay, baby?" He is concerned. His anxious voice tells me this.

"Yes," I whisper, allowing the past to exit the corners of my eyes, leaving room for happy tears and happy memories to enter my life.

Little by little, I close my eyes, singing along. I know the words, all of them. Rocking me gently, Phillip hums along, too. Then, there is that glint in his eyes. As Christina warbles the final note, he smothers my lips with his soft beatific love, taking me to a new world, a place where only he and I exist, a place where love is safe and meaningful. Tonight, I am overawed with passion. All I see is my man.

THE CONFESSION

"Becca, I would like to make a confession," I confirm, nibbling the corner of my lip.

"What confession is this?" Becca is bemused.

We are in my room, listening to Capital FM Radio, heads banged together, hips touching, legs thoroughly intertwined.

"I don't feel a shed of guilt that Phillip and I have been together, for two days and two nights, and missed today's lecturers and seminars. Should I be feeling bad right now?"

Cheekily she smirks at me and bumps into my left hip. "For the average student, that is bad-arse behaviour. For you and Phillip, that is the biggest victory of all time!"

"Bec," I say, with stars in my eyes. "The last couple of nights have been *so* freaking amazing!"

She radiates a smile, which warms my glowing visage. "Of course they were amazing." Becca tweets. "How could ya not have enjoyed a few nights in paradise?"

Raucously, I laugh. "I promised Phil I wouldn't talk about it, but –"

"But what?" she blurts out eagerly, wanting me to spill at least a small portion of the beans.

"Oh gees, Becca," I exclaim, my nose touching her nose, our eyes wedged together into a solid block of concentration. "He is a good mover between the sheets... and he is also a gentleman, in and out of the bedroom."

Becca exhales. "You are a very lucky girl."

We stare at each other and burst into a joyous laughter.

"You were right about *almost* everything, B." My gaze remains soft on her face.

"I know," she boasts, a big grin raising her cheeks. "Generally, I am almost always right about relationship stuff," she beams, stroking my long, dark tresses. "Thank God you were wearing 'the condom skirt' the night you and Phillip finally got it together. Can you imagine if you were wearing your ra-ra skirt?"

I look over at her, blowing out a huge sigh. "Oh, gees, B. It doesn't bear thinking about, does it?"

The pair of us give birth to a heavy puff of air, as we express our relief, pondering on the enormity of this 'what if' scenario.

"I haven't told you about my audition yet," I tell her confidently.

She is surprised. "What audition is this?"

"I'm auditioning for the Coolette Singers Group next Tuesday."

Becca is elated. "This is a huge step for you, Alena. I am so proud." She gives me a big hug.

I grin. "Thank you, honey. I'm nervous, yet excited."

"I'm so pumped about this," she grins. "You're gonna kill it, babe. I know you will. I'm gonna come watch you!"

"Awesome!" I chirp. "Thanks for the support, hun."

"No problem." Gradually, her cheery expression changes. "Is Emma going too?" asks Becca candidly. "Or will she be back at her college by next week?"

"Emma will be busy then. But I know she supports me too. You really like Emma, don't you?"

"Yeah, I do," she states, smiling broadly. "She is a pretty cool chick."

"She really likes you too, Becca," I say, smiling back at her.

"Emma and I are good friends now," Becca asserts. "She will never be my BFF though. I only have one of those."

Mildly, I stroke her sunshine tresses. They shine lovingly into my eyes. I am completely filled with love for this gorgeous, special, and totally faithful friend who has been beside me since day one. She is a rare find. There's no one on this planet quite like the fantabulous Becca Richardson-Smith.

"I take it that the BFF you are referring to is me?"

"Duh!" she snorts. "Of course, babe."

A single tear twinkles in my eyes. "I don't think I have ever met anyone quite like you before, B. You're so *so* special to me. *So very* close to my heart."

"And you're so close to mine," she whispers beckoning my gaze. Tenderly, she caresses my fawn locks. I purr with contentment. "We've been through so much. But it has only made us stronger, tighter."

"Yes." My voice is hoarse, as the emotion takes me. "Our bond is super strong, like bread and jam."

Becca chortles. "Yea, like bread and jelly."

"Jam, jelly – wobbly belly," I say mirthfully.

We burst into a fit of hysterics and a pair of girlie heads bang together with glee.

Quickly, Becca's expression changes; her temperament is mercurial.

"Alena," she whines staring profoundly into my mien. "I'm so glad you and Phillip are okay now. I always knew you'd be fine and never end up like me."

"What d'ya mean?" I ask frankly, my pensive eyes upon her face.

"I was sixteen, Alena. He was seventeen," she begins tentatively. "We'd been going out, on and off, for five months. Then one evening, there was a glimmer of passion in his eyes, and he told me he loved me. I lost my senses. I was foolish. That night, I gave my virginity to him."

"Who?" I ask astonished, my sight imbedding deeper into her lamenting blue blurs.

"Kevin Jones. My first proper boyfriend," she confesses, biting her lip. Her hand reaches for my leg, and circles on my skin in an attempt to reduce her anxiety. "He got me pregnant, Alena!"

"What?" I shout moving sideward, my nose caressing her streaming nostrils. "Didn't you use protection?"

"I told you, I was foolish!"

Smoothing my hands around the contours of Becca's wounded and sorrowful visage, I close my lids. "Is that why you carry condoms now, wherever you go?"

She bawls. "Yes, that's the reason why." Tears are streaming down her ashen cheeks. "I am the self-professed black swan in room 178, Ridley House. The girl with the dark maculate past which squirms in her mind. Yes, this is me. I confess!"

"Oh, Becca, hunnie." I cry, blanketing her body with the softness of my regard. "Oh, I'm so, *so* sorry."

"I shouldn't have let her go, Alena," she says distressfully, repeating these words in a dangerous loop. "She was mine. I should have kept her."

"Babe," I say calmly cocooning her shaking shell. "Where is she now? Where is the baby?"

"She was given up for adoption. My daughter lives with Aunt Tilley, in Ohio. I get to visit her three times a year, four, if I'm lucky."

Her voice is cracking, her eyes gushing with tears. "Alena, she doesn't even know I gave birth to her. She thinks I'm her cousin. Aunt Tilley said telling her this fable made sense, to protect her from the truth and to free me from my clangers." She cries inconsolably. I hold her close, my body absorbing a proportion of her sadness.

"So why did you give the child up for adoption in the first place? Who convinced you?"

"Mom and Aunty Tilley," she wails. "Tilley couldn't have children, and her and Uncle Iain wanted kids *so* badly. So, mom *told me* a month before I gave birth that she would be adopted by my aunt and uncle."

"That was selfish of them," I reply my voice shaking with rage. "They should have let you keep the baby."

Becca squints, her eyes wonder about the room, bouncing off the walls. She is sweating, her face reddening as she speaks. "I was preparing for my debut in the Miss Teenage California Pageant, when I discovered I was pregnant. Mom's a respectable Headmistress of a prestigious Californian middle school. She didn't want bad press. She didn't want the City of Sunnyvale, CA, pointing a finger at her perfect, blonde haired, blue eyed, commercially viable daughter, so she sold me down the river. Mom was the driving force behind my decision. She *made me* give her up. Coupled with this was the fact that Aunt Tilley was on the edge. She needed a baby to save her and Iain's marriage. And I had exactly what she wanted. So it made sense for them to manipulate me, persuade me, that giving her up was the best option, the only option. Six months after I won the pageant, I gave birth to a beautiful and healthy baby girl. A few hours later, she was virtually ripped from my arms and placed into the clasp of her new parents, my aunt and uncle. Then, the official adoption process sanctified them as her parents. Now I'm older, and looking back on those dramatic events, I realise that my family coerced me into giving her up, when I didn't want to do that. If they had supported me, I wouldn't have let her go. I would have kept her. She was mine, Alena, and they stole her from me."

Suddenly Becca eases me off, and goes to cower at the left corner of the bed, scrunching her knees and feet and spine into a foetal position. She hides her waterfall of tears from me. Not letting her bury the pain anymore, I crawl over to the edge of the bed, and pull her hands away from her face. An ocean's tears flow openly. Soon, her body opens up and she allows me to embrace her again. Rocking her gently, to and fro, to and fro, I even let out the high level of anxiety pummelling through her veins.

"Oh, gees," I say, feeling the terrifying waves of Becca's torment. "I am so sorry, baby."

"It's okay," she whimpers. "It's not your fault."

I grab her close. She falls flaccidly into my frame and flops in my arms.

"What's her name?" I ask. My strong hands support the trembling sensation that can be felt in the core of her pale, lifeless body.

"Jaicee," she maffles. "Her name is Jaicee Jones-Smith. She's two years old now. In fact, it was her birthday yesterday." As she slams her eyes shut, the uncontrollable tears start to quiver her lips and crinkle a beautiful forehead.

"Why didn't you tell me about Jaicee, about all of this?" I cry, rubbing my index finger softly across the breadth of her nose.

"Your problems were bigger than mine, Alena. I needed to be there for *you*."

All of a sudden, her eyes open wide. I see the reflection of the deep love and devotion she has for me, pooling in the rimmed ledge of her weeping orifice.

"You needed me, Alena. You needed me *more*. I'm strong. I am capable of destroying my own demons."

Doggedly, determinedly, I lift her head up. "No!" I shout. "I won't allow you to fight these demons on your own. You helped me, now I will help you. I will be your pillar of strength, for as long as you need me to be."

"Thank you," she wails as our eyes lock together, and our hearts beat as one.

Turning my head clockwise to meet hers, Becca pecks me softly on the lips. I know this is not a lesbian kiss, as both of us are straight. It is a kiss of comfort, a kiss of safety and security. Our friendship has gone beyond the stage where anything feels uncomfortable. This special companionship is extraordinary. It surpasses the boundaries of a normal and regular friendship. I am blessed to have this kind of friendship that some people only dream of.

The music plays sweetly in the background, waving around us. Becca holds onto me tightly. I don't want her to ever let me go.

MOVING ON

"Stanley is coming out of prison today. How are you feeling, baby?"

Phil and I are lying next to each other on top of his bed. He's caressing my neck, rubbing his nose against my nape in the most sensual fashion. Eagerly, he is waiting for a response. I pause for a minute before answering Phillip, trying to consider my feelings. Surprisingly, I feel nothing, indifferent. I hope that is a good thing.

"I'm feeling okay, actually, thanks to my great support network. In fact, I feel so good, I wanna burst into song."

In haste, Phil's eyes dart and crash into mine. He is puzzled. "What? You want to burst into song? That's an interesting reaction."

Heartily I laugh, looking at his bewildered face. "I've recently rediscovered my passion for singing. And I'm working on this song I wrote for the Coolette Singing Audition on Tuesday night. You wanna hear it later?"

In astonishment, Phil's mouth opens and he blinks, double-time. "You've certainly been keeping things under wraps... Yea, I'd love to hear your song. What is it called?"

"It's called *The Dove's Wings.*" Joyfully, I smile.

234

"I love the spiritual name. It rocks!"

I beam. "Will you come to the audition to support me?"

"Yes, absolutely," he says quickly. "I will support you in everything that you do, Alena."

"Thank you hunnie." I kiss him sloppily on the cheek. "I've decided to go back to therapy next semester, too. I could do with Doctor Hannah's help to work through some of my unresolved issues."

"Glad to hear that," he says softly. "And I support your decision to go back to therapy. I, myself, have signed up for stuff. In September, I'll be going to a rehabilitation support group and drama therapy. Both groups are running in the local area. Wanna come with me to drama therapy?"

"Yeah, it sounds incredible. I'm *so* coming with you," I say, my eyes rolling into his gaze.

"And I think we should meet your mother now. Are you in agreement?" He licks my shoulder, planting his lips into this tasty part of my body.

"Yeah, we should. How about we visit her tomorrow?" I puff, tilting his head sideways so that I can masticate his delicious coffee neck. "Let's surprise her."

"Yea," Phil trills. "Let's."

We both chortle, our love burning into each other's eyes like a pair of sparkling fireworks.

Soon his gaze deepens. So does mine.

My legs straddle his solid frame. I play with his ears, laughing in his eardrums. He is wriggling wildly beneath me and murmuring, enjoying the pleasure of his woman being in control.

I kiss him on the lips, sucking his mouth like a gobstopper. "It's your parents next," I hum as we are clutching each other in a tight embrace.

"Okay," he says sheepishly, stroking my face and hair. "But I warn you now, my family is nutty professor crazy!"

Vivaciously, I titter. "I know all about crazy people,

remember? I am fully prepared for whatever madness your family throws at me. And besides, I am so looking forward to seeing Jermaine. You will invite him when I come over, right? I got so much to say to him."

"I will invite him, promise," he whispers, kissing my ear. "He is enthusiastic about meeting you too."

"Is he?" I am astounded.

"He is, yes," Phil confirms. "He told me last week that he can't believe your life has come full circle. It's no coincidence that us Gregson's came into your life like we did. You know that? God never works with serendipity. It's not in his master plan."

I swim into my man's hardy, puissant gaze. "If I didn't believe that before, I sure know it now." I murmur, smooching him until he almost catches fire. "Can we go to *Ranatoo Lama* tonight, baby? I want to raise a toast, to us. I know this is a totally spontaneous idea."

Lightly, he grazes my forehead with his soft, spongy mouth. "I love spontaneous Alena. She is new and exciting. Yes, let's go there tonight and raise a glass to us."

"And next year," I say passionately. "Let's think about planning a holiday, to Barbados. A romantic trip, just the two of us."

Phil's eyes ignite with euphoria. "Yes, I adore that idea, a blissful vacation in the sunshine with my sweetheart."

Deeply, he kisses me.

"Can I sing my song now?" I ask him, my green irises glimmering in the darkness.

"Yea, let me hear it."

While I sing enchantingly, my lungs working to full capacity, Phil holds me really close. The sun is setting in the sky. It is a beautiful scene to watch with my man's arms wrapped securely around me. I feel safe knowing I am with the man I love, and sharing my one true passion with him. Taking this one huge step closer to healing my soul, I am an angel who has found her wings.

GONE

I have a sassy smirk on my face as I walk towards Becca's room, preparing myself for another cheesy joke or playful comment, about how Phil and I finally got it together in true dramatic Hollywood style. At a local lunch bar this afternoon, when Becca and I relished our first ever lunch date off campus, she couldn't stop giggling about mine and Phil's big cinematic moment, which resembled the epic scene in a film where the lead girl gets it on with the lead guy, and the magic happens. I laugh to myself for a second, thinking about her amusing remarks at the lunch table and the jokes she's been cracking about Phil and I for the past few days.

Unhurriedly, I approach her door. It is ajar. That's strange. Inch by inch, I push the door open. To my surprise, her dark purple suitcase is standing mulishly in the integral part of the room. Glaring up at me, its big bulging body bursts at the seams with clothes. What? This is crazy! What is going on?

"Becca?" I cry out, begging for an explanation.

Suddenly Becca crashes into my view. She was peering vacantly through the window before, but now wishes for me to see her eyes, shrouded with dark circles and violent tears. A stark yet empty look washes over her pallid face. Her arms are crossed, nose is flushed, and fragments of glassy despair are clinging from the sides of her cheeks.

"What the hell is going on, Bec? Why is your case packed?" I run to her, grabbing a couple of tense shoulders. My long hair tickles the base of Becca's neck.

In slow motion, she pivots on one foot, spinning around to face me. She is like a ballerina with her flawless alabaster skin and beautiful poise and grace. Except, she is performing to an audience that can see through the veil, an audience that is thoroughly unconvinced by this tentative display of confidence. Inside, she is falling apart, crumbling, praying she will not lose her balance and crack into pieces under the immense pressure. Becca's feet plant firmly into the ground, reaffirming their roots. The stunning young woman with the azure gemstone eyes squeezes my long, sallow face. Her grip is strong, resolute, yet an air of timidity undermines her show of strength.

"Alena," she whispers, sobbing, and shaking like a leaf in the wind. "I have to go. I have to leave you, leave this splendid place..." Becca's voice trails off as she turns her attention back to the window and peers into the clear, yet clouded pane. The picturesque view she sees outside is no longer enough to sustain her thirst for a better life. Neither is being here, in England, with me, enough anymore. Her vacant expression says it all. It speaks a thousand words.

"No," I reply exasperatedly, gasping for air. "I can't let you go! You can't leave me! Where will you go?"

Clutching on to my thin arms, Becca guides me to the bed. She forces me to sit down. Sluggishly, she plonks her hollow husk of a body next to me.

"I visited a lawyer this morning," she begins. "That's why I'm leaving."

I crunch my face in confusion. "A lawyer? For what? Why would you visit a lawyer, Becca?" Pensively, I stare into her darting blue eyes, trying to steady them.

"Jaicee," she cries, her gaze now piercing mine. "I want to get her back, Alena. I miss her *so much*."

A perplexed expression darkens my countenance. I sort of understand Becca's pain, but I can't see how a lawyer can help her with this matter. "It's too late. Jaicee is gone. She's been adopted by your Aunt Tilley, babe." I remind her. "She is not legally yours anymore."

My gaze is compassionate. It strokes her torment with one calm, sweeping motion. Languidly, she looks up at me. A small degree of calmness wells in her eyes. I can tell she is grateful that I am trying to soothe her angst. An enigmatic determination alters her deportment. Her sight is focused, dogged, untiring. She holds me steadfastly by the waist.

"That's what I thought, too," she explains. "But Mr. Anderson, my lawyer, told me I could fight for her. He flew all the way from Santa Clara to break this hopeful news. I met him for breakfast in a Leicester City Café in the centre of town. Zack Anderson believes I have a good chance of winning the case."

I am astonished. My green eyes dive into the unfathomable depths of her ocean blue orbs. "How can you win Jaicee back? She's been adopted. Once a child has been adopted, it is final. The decision cannot be overturned. Sorry, Bec."

Obstinately, she shakes her head, and then pins down my rebellious gaze. "No, Alena, that's where you're wrong. Zack informed me that if the child's parents were coerced into giving up their infant, and then an adoption took place as a direct result of this coercion, then legally, the biological parents can challenge the ruling in court."

"What?" I say, clutching her loosely by the wrists. "Is this even possible?"

Frantically, her eyes swim into mine, paddling into my green waves of frustration. "Yes. It is not foolproof, but possible. Aunt Tilley duped me, and forced me to give Jaicee up. If I can prove this to a judge, I can-"

"Get her back! Officially be her mother again," I holler.

She nods. "Exactly!"

Our noses touch in perfect sync. We are totally in tune with one another. However, this is a blessing as well as a curse.

"What does this mean for you and me, Bec?" I say, wailing sorrowfully. "Will I ever see you again?"

We lock eyes; our sight is chained together. Our hair intertwines as we get closer. We are breathing into each other's mouths, painfully, mournfully, like two Siamese cats having to deal with the prospect of separation.

"I don't know," she puffs distressfully, almost grazing my lips. "But I will never forget you, Alena. Never. You're the greatest person I have ever known."

My tears blur my peripheral vision; my eyesight grows hazy. I start to shake and tremble in Becca's arms. Her body is trembling too. I can feel the earthquake that is her torso vibrating against mine.

"Next September, I'll try and come back to finish my final semester of the first year at the University of Capendale. Even if I have Jaicee, I can hire a nanny and complete my term here, and then finish my degree at UC Berkeley."

"I can't live without you for that long," I cry, holding on to the tiny straps of her black designer tank top.

She covers her face to stop me from seeing her unbridled tears. "You have Phillip," she muffles. "And you got Emma, too, and your mom."

"But they are not you, Becca," I shout, throwing my distraught body on her, falling into her embrace. "No one is like you, babe. *No one!*"

Firmly, she grips me. I continue to shake, and so does she. "Don't get all pop star fanatical about this, Alena," she says, trying to lighten the conversation. "You know I can't handle you getting obsessed with me."

My expression is dejected. "So this is it, then?"

Her head bobs. "I guess so."

"Promise me you'll be back in September, Becca."

Becca's voice is low, melancholy. "I can't promise, babe. But I'll try."

"And bring back Jaicee. I want to meet her."

"Okay, babe. I'll do my best."

A notch of concern forms on my brow. "Who's gonna help you fight for her? I doubt your mother will help."

Nervously, she bites her lip. "Jaicee's father, Kev. He's gonna help me."

I am dumbfounded. "What?"

Scratching her head, she acknowledges her scattiness. "Oh, yes, I forgot to mention, Kev and I have been communicating on Facebook for the past two weeks. We got talking, got chatting – remembering old times. Then, we started reminiscing about the past… He wants us to start over, Alena. And he wants Jai back, too. We can be together again, a real family, as I planned from the start. He is doing well now. He can look after us all."

I clutch onto Becca tightly, tighter than I have ever held her before. I sense this is the last time I will see her face to face for a long time. Inside, I ache with sorrow.

"Promise you'll send me a postcard. Skype me, Facebook me, text me, email me and send me tweets, every day."

She kisses me on the cheek. "I'll do all of those things, Alena. Promise."

"You better."

The atmosphere is still, inert. We remain quiet for a few minutes.

"It's time," she finally says, rubbing my face. "My flight is in four hours."

"Where are you going? California?" I ask.

Her face is straight, composed. "Ohio. Aunt Tilley's house."

"Will you be okay, B?"

"Yes," she reassures me. "Kev is meeting me at

Cleveland Hopkins International airport. I'll be staying with him in Avon Lake. We'll rest for a night or so, and then we will be making the difficult and emotional three and a half hour journey to Aunt Tilley and Uncle Iain's house in Oakwood."

"I'll be praying for you," I say in a hushed tone.

"Thanks, babe." Becca's eyes begin to take flight and they dart around the room once again. "Kevin is respectable and doing so well for himself. He's got a flashy car and a top executive job in advertising. He's twenty, and looking to connect old ties, make amends, and possibly tie the…"

"Does he want to marry you, Becca?" I ask, astounded.

Her eyes light up. "I think so, Alena, yes! Could this be my happy ending? Me, Kev, and Jaicee?"

I hug her. "I pray it is."

"Me, too," she blubbers. "Me too." Becca's voice trails off as she weeps joyously.

Steadily, she ends our sisterly embrace and gets up, walking towards her heavy luggage. Gingerly, she picks it up. "Walk me to the train station, bestie. I want to enjoy your company for at least another 30 minutes." She begins to bawl.

"Yes, I will, of course," I say, grabbing her hand.

I get up and throw myself on her again.

"Go kick some butt at the Coolette Singing Audition tomorrow," she whispers. "Be the shining star you were born to be."

I smile. "I will try."

"That's my girl." Her voice cracks with the emotion.

Clinging onto my best friend's diminishing verve, we leave her room together for the very last time.

Miss Teenage California is about to vacate the building, and a part of me will never be the same again.

THE RETURN

Sunlight of the purest kind enraptures my soul as I leave my dorm house, taking the long half a mile journey to the Coolette Singing Audition. Thinking fondly of all the special people – mum, Phil, Becca, Emma, and Doctor Hannah, who have helped me defeat my fears, I shut my eyes, breathing deeply. Drumming up mighty courage from deep within my core, I invite The Lord into my heart, and let the light of His love warm me up. I continue walking towards my future. Each step I take, seems like progress. And with every light tap of hope, the shadows beneath my feet dance, driving away the devil.

As I reach the weathered ingress leading towards the corridor of the Elderflower Building, something, a sensation so minute, so small, is niggling in the pit of my stomach. A strange devilish pull dragging me back to the past grows powerfully, as it swirls dangerously in the atmosphere.

Crawling from the ground up, a puff of darkness spreads across the horizon, blackening the happy impression, which is resting joyously in my heart.

A repellent scent blows on my cheek. Swivelling round, feeling the sharpness of the wind scratching my face, a dark shadow rises, propelling into my focus. Instantly, I recognise who this fiendish figure is, an evil man with the sheer impertinence to stand before me.

Before his noxious hand is able to press into my petite shoulder blades, I catch the villain's arm, in mid-flow.

Instantly, my eyes fill with rage. "Mr. Hawthorne – what the hell are you doing here? You have the nerve to come to my college, knowing the police surround this place?"

His eyes are devious, a tempestuous storm rushing in his hazel globes. "Why didn't you visit me in prison? I was waiting for you."

I grind my teeth, restraining my hands from strangling him. Suppressing the urge to kill him is not easy. "I wasn't gonna let you ruin my life. Not for a second time."

Skittishly, he pulls a fake frown. "Oh, such a shame you didn't come. I thought we were friends, Alena."
Edging closer, he undresses me with his sickening gaze. Shaking slightly, lips quivering, I move back.

I shudder with repulsion. "Twisted! I realise how bloody twisted you are, how twisted you've always been." Instinctively, a pink finger erects, a sharp weapon prepared to wound its attacker. "I understand now, that the assault, was never my fault. It was yours. All yours. People like you, Mr. Hawthorne, are truly sick, abusing authority and power, to get kicks."

"With you," he whispers distastefully, "I forgot who I was. Everything about you excited me, Alena, still does. So, yes, you're probably right. I am twisted. But it is pleasing for me to be this way. It makes me feel alive!"

"The baby," I mumble distressfully, looking into his dark, frozen eyes. "So glad I lost it. I thank God for taking it from me. Every day I prayed for The Lord to lessen my suffering, my agony. Thankfully, he answered my prayers in the very early stages of pregnancy. I could *never* have *your* baby. Never bring an innocent child into this world under such terrible circumstances!" I scream at the top of my lungs.

Red flames of repugnant affection shoot from his pupils. He grows nearer, and nearer still, aiming to grab me. There is a knife that appears in his hands.

"You killed our child. So now, I am going to kill you…"

Running across the corridor as fast as I can, I let out a yelp. Mr. Hawthorne grunts, hard on my heels. His heavy feet are desperate to catch me his hands eager to annihilate me. The man is crazy, unhinged. This ferocious beast needs to be put back in his cage.

Heart yammering in my chest, breath uneasy and frenetic, I scramble for my mobile phone, which is in the pocket of my Levi jeans. With not a second to lose, I quickly tap in the number, dialling for the campus police.

"Security!" I cry, bellowing down the receiver. "Mr. Hawthorne – he's here, on campus. He is chasing me along the corridor. I'm in the Elderflower Building, Ground Floor. There's a knife in his hands. Come quick. I'm in real danger!"

Abruptly, I hang up. My phone falls to the floor as I speed up, running for my life.

The lunatic disappears. I hear nothing but my fearful heartbeat. Panning around the building, I cannot see him. I know he is there somewhere, hiding, playing a cat and mouse game with me.

I stand still, my eyes scanning dizzily across the area. There is quiet, a deadly silence. Then… from nowhere…

"Gotcha!"

Mr. Hawthorne springs out from under a row of green scrubs, in which I am standing in front of, and he grabs me from behind. Instantly, the kitchen knife is pressed against my back.

Harrowingly, I holler, contemplating my fate.

"Now, I can't have you, no one else will. This is the end, Alena Pavlis," He hisses, his malignant voice fizzing in my ear.

Struggling, I try hard to break free, to get away, but his strong arms are wrapped around my neck, like a nocuous serpent. Shooting my green blurs into his wicked visage, I see the callousness in his cold, marble eyes. Oh, God, he is actually going to kill me!

Campus police rocket onto the scene. They close him in from every angle, trying to rip me from his devilish clutch. Mr. Hawthorne is not a stupid man. He knows how they think, how they will respond. This man is a mastermind criminal. He knows exactly how to shield my body, to prevent the police from rescuing me.

"Come any nearer boys, and I'll stick this knife right in her," he snares, warning the campus police.

"Let Alena go, Hawthorne!" The lead police officer roars, glaring at him. "Or you're gonna get life! You've already done enough damage! So just surrender, make it easier for yourself."

"Yes, let me go," I screech, squirming, begging him to spare my life. "Please!"

"I'll never let this girl go. She is *mine* to love! *Mine* to kill! Don't care if I get life for this!" Toxically, Mr. Hawthorne laughs, slowly slaughtering my spirit.

A large crowd, made up of horrified students and professors, assemble on the perimeter of the yellow police cordons. Re-tuning my ears, I block out their screams and tears. My focus is solely on the policeman, with determined grey eyes, who is giving me vital instructions. The police officer is working hard to save my life.

"Time to be brave!" the cop mouths. "Kick him and duck, Alena. Now!"

Just as I kick Hawthorne in the nuts and dive forward, landing on the hard surface, the officer runs towards us at full speed with a taser in his hands. As Hawthorne quickly regains his composure and goes to stab me in the leg, the officer leaps onto him, punching him in the face, and strikes Hawthorne in the arm with the weapon. Mr. Hawthorne collapses, when the strong current runs through his forearm. Like a dog, he is cuffed and dragged away by the law enforcers.

A piercing cry hurtles out of my mouth, and the crowd yowls. The realisation of this dangerous and dramatic situation has finally hit us.

Phillip scurries onto the scene. Breathlessly, I run to him, into the sunlight, burying myself into his warm embrace.

"You're safe now. It's over, baby," he says softly caressing my hair. "It is all over!"

I simply bawl and quaver, not having the energy to speak.

As I take Phil's arm, and begin to walk towards the audition room, he holds me. A deep level of determination gleams in my eyes.

"Don't you want me to take you home, Alena? You're shaken and have been through a terrible ordeal. Forget about the audition."

"No, Phil," I say, digging my heels in. "I'm going."

I plod on. My legs are shuddering, my hips aching, my arms throbbing, my teeth chattering. Phil supports me, holding me up. I am determined to get to my audition.

Hypnotised by my outstanding tenacity, the horde of people cheer me on, chanting out my name. Regaining a small portion of strength, I advance, moving up the stairs, and I enter Room E30, where the audition is. The throng is scampering behind me, increasing my oomph, and so is Phillip, who's now gripping my hand, and streaming with tears.

Aided by my man, I mount the stage. The assemblage rushes into the room, still hollering my name. Keisha Wilson, who is head judge for the singing auditions, and the most popular girl in college, comes out of the crowd, and climbs up the stairs to the stage. With two shaking hands, she gives me the microphone. Keisha is smiling at me, and joyful tears are rolling down her honey cheeks.

"Give us all ya got, girl!" She says gutsily.

Assuredly, I nod. "Uh-uh."

The crowd roars with excitement. Hundreds of mobile phones are thrust in the air as many students begin to film me. Then encouragingly, they shout and clap to a passionate rhythm. The swarm of electrified people are in eager anticipation, waiting for me to sing.

Letting the light of The Lord enter my heart once again, I open my mouth, ready to sing my soulful song, *The Dove's Wings* to the huge audience.

Closing my lids for a second, I see my beautiful future sparkling like a firework in the night's sky. Nobody is going to stop me from fulfilling my dreams now.

This is my time. This is my chance.

ABOUT THE AUTHOR

Michelle Diana Lowe was born, and grew up, in London, United Kingdom. She has had a deep passion for writing from a very young age. Experiencing domestic violence in her earlier years and being a victim of school bullying, Michelle penned stories to self-heal. After graduating from the University of Roehampton with a Bachelor of Arts Degree in English Literature with a Philosophy, Michelle began working as a Children's Centre Administrator. Appearing on British Chatshow, The Chrissy B Show, in October 2014, gave her an opportunity to speak publicly, for the first time, about the difficulties she faced in childhood and the work she now does to help others. Exploring sensitive issues in her writing, such as violence against women, and finding solutions for those affected, is very important to Michelle. Michelle enjoys being with family, taking walks around town, meeting up with friends and watching popular US shows, movies and period dramas, when she is not writing. UnShatter Me is her debut novel.